# THE *POISONERS*

Also by **Donald Hamilton** and available from Titan Books

DONALD HAMILTON

A **MATT HELM** NOVEL

THE **POISONERS**

**TITAN** BOOKS

The Poisoners
Print edition ISBN: 9781783292967
E-book edition ISBN: 9781783292974

Published by Titan Books
A division of Titan Publishing Group Ltd
144 Southwark Street, London SE1 0UP

First edition: December 2014
1 2 3 4 5 6 7 8 9 10

A CIP catalogue record for this title is available from the British Library.

Printed and bound in the United States.

**Did you enjoy this book?** We love to hear from our readers.
Please email us at readerfeedback@titanemail.com or write to us at
Reader Feedback at the above address.

To receive advance information, news, competitions, and exclusive
offers online, please sign up for the Titan newsletter on our website:
**www.titanbooks.com**

# THE *POISONERS*

# 1

Nobody was supposed to meet me at the Los Angeles Airport, and nobody did. I made sure of this, although I wasn't really expecting to attract attention so soon. It was highly unlikely that anyone in the area, friendly or unfriendly, could have learned that I was arriving, if only because there had been no time. I was running an errand, for which I'd been selected on a moment's notice, chiefly because I was the only agent Mac had had available within easy flying distance of the West Coast—at least the only one without more important things to do.

"Anyway," he'd told me over the phone, calling from Washington, "you know the girl; you recruited her for us. If she does manage to talk—the doctors don't have much hope that she'll regain consciousness—she might tell you something she wouldn't confess to a stranger."

"Confess?" I said. "Is she supposed to have something to confess?"

He hesitated, a couple of thousand miles away. When

he answered, his voice had a kind of baffled shrug in it.

"No, but she wasn't supposed to be in any danger, either. She wasn't even on assignment. And before she came to work for us, she established quite a record for getting into trouble on impulse. If you'll remember, the only way you got her cooperation in the first place was by reminding her that the alternative was a Mexican jail. She's a hot-tempered, redheaded young lady, and I had occasion to reprimand her rather severely just before she went on leave. There's a possibility that she did something foolish, or worse, by way of retaliation."

"In other words," I said, "you think she might have tried to sell us out, only the deal backfired in some way."

"I have to keep the possibility in mind." There was a hint of defensiveness in his voice. "You worked with her below the border on her first assignment with us. Presumably you got to know her fairly well. Do you consider it unthinkable?"

I made a face at the phone. I had got to know the girl in question pretty well. She'd been a competent assistant despite her inexperience, and she'd been a pleasant companion. Personal loyalty, however, does not play a large role in our line of work—it's not supposed to play any role at all.

"It's never unthinkable, is it, sir?" I said, speaking objectively and feeling like a heel. "She's a good kid, but as you point out, she's got one hell of a temper. If something made her mad enough, she'd do just about anything to strike back. As you say, that's how she got into that Mexican trouble we bailed her out of so she could work for us down there. She'd regret it later, but she'd do it."

I heard Mac draw a long breath, like a sigh, far away in the nation's capital. "Sometimes I think I should have been a wild-animal trainer, Eric," he said, using my code name as usual. My real name is Matthew Helm, but it isn't supposed to figure in business conversations except under special circumstances. Mac went on: "I suspect that tigers, for instance, are more predictable, and no more dangerous, than the type of humans we have to employ for this work."

"Gee, thanks," I said. "Is there anything else you'd care to tell this particular tiger?"

"Of course, what I just said about Ruby was pure speculation," he continued calmly, unembarrassed. "We don't know how she got mixed up in whatever got her shot. It could have been a personal matter or a completely accidental involvement. The only facts we have, at present, are that she was found in a vacant lot in Los Angeles early this morning in very bad shape—her assailant probably thought she was dead—and that she wasn't engaged in any official business that could account for her being the recipient of this kind of murderous attention." He stopped, and was silent for a moment. Then he went on crisply, "Well, get out there as fast as you can. I hope you make it in time. In any case, try to discover what happened. I don't like unexplained mishaps to our people. The explained ones are bad enough."

When he'd called, I'd been on leave myself, spending a couple of weeks with some friends in Santa Fe, New Mexico, my former home town. In the business, you have no home, and therefore no home town, but there had been a period, some years ago, when I was out of Mac's clutches and had lived in one place like an ordinary citizen. I still go back there occasionally to do a little fishing and tell a few lies about how I earn my living nowadays.

Although it's the capital of the state, Santa Fe is off the main air routes. A little over an hour of driving had taken me the sixty miles to Albuquerque, and a little under two hours of flying had taken me the eight hundred miles to the coast; just time enough for me to do some research—in a couple of news magazines and a Los Angeles paper I'd picked up—on the area to which I was now assigned.

I learned that a lot of California had been washed out to sea in the heavy rains that had recently plagued the state, and that what was left was expected to slide into the drink whenever the San Andreas Fault decided to stage a repetition of the San Francisco quake on a larger scale. Various psychic and seismic characters seemed to think it would happen fairly soon. Apparently I was taking my life in my hands just crossing the coastal range into this unstable hunk of geography.

But even if the state of California stayed put, I learned I wasn't safe. The water was polluted and the air wasn't fit to breathe, according to various groups struggling desperately to stave off total disaster. One group in particular, boasting a considerable array of scientific talent in the fields of biology and meteorology, was meeting the problem head on by advocating an absolute ban on the internal combustion engine before it irrevocably contaminated the state's atmosphere with its by-products. It was an interesting idea. I found myself reading the column with mixed feelings. I like pure air as well as the next man, but I'm also rather fond of fast automobiles.

Even if I wasn't carried out to sea by a mudslide or an earthquake, or killed by the California air or the California water, I was still, I discovered, jeopardizing my health and morals by entering the state. According to one reporter, the quantity of marihuana and other drugs crossing the border from Mexico was enough to addict a man just standing by the highway sniffing at the vehicles roaring past. The U.S. government had just instituted another major operation—there had been some previous efforts—to cut off this supply of happy, unhealthy dreams. According to the newspaper, the valiant protective work of the Customs and Treasury boys was not appreciated by the tourists delayed by lengthy searches, or by the Mexicans whose businesses were suffering as a result.

All in all, California seemed like a hell of a perilous spot for an innocent lad who'd been hoping for an undisturbed vacation on a peaceful bass lake or trout stream; but undisturbed vacations are hard to come by in our organization. I buckled my seat belt as the plane began to lose altitude. We descended into something that looked like a giant basket of dirty laundry—the smog clouds trapped by the coastal mountains—and discovered, to my considerable relief, that there was an airport under the grimy-looking mess.

I disembarked, retrieved my suitcase after the usual delay at the stainless-steel merry-go-rounds, and grabbed a taxi that looked a little blurred to me, because the impact of the acrid Los Angeles air I'd just been reading about had set me weeping. I wiped my eyes, blew my nose, and told the driver to take me to the Royal Viking Motel on Third Street.

The trip took almost as long as the flight out, and was considerably rougher. The Los Angeles department of streets seems to be boycotting the Los Angeles department of airports. There's no simple and direct way of getting from the terminal into town, or if there is, my driver didn't know about it or had no faith in it. After we'd switched boulevards and streets and freeways a number of times, I was quite certain nobody was interested in me.

Of course, there was no reason anybody should be, yet. So far, I was just another tourist in the big city. Things might change when I made myself conspicuous by visiting a certain patient on the critical list in a certain medical institution. It depended on just what, or whom, our girl in Los Angeles had got herself involved with.

With this in mind, I took time to check in at the motel. It was the only reasonable-looking hostelry around, a logical place to keep under surveillance if you'd shot somebody who hadn't died as she was supposed to, if you had plenty of hired help to spread around, and if you wanted to learn who would come rushing to L.A. to see her. I even made a point of announcing where I was going next, for the benefit of a gent busily reading a newspaper in the nearby lounge.

"Room 37, eh?" I said clearly to the lady behind the desk, as I pocketed the key. "Thanks. I'll just leave my suitcase right here for a little, if you don't mind. I've got to get over to the hospital across the street."

I didn't look at the man with the paper as I went out. Of course, he could be just a guest tired of the four walls of his room, or a man waiting for his wife or someone who wasn't his wife, but I hoped not. If the wounded girl couldn't tell me who'd shot her and why, I'd have to work it out some other way; and a character with a guilty conscience—guilty enough to keep watch on her visitors—was a good starting place, assuming that such a character existed.

At the hospital, I found that the way had been cleared for me. After giving my name at the desk, I was taken straight up to the room. Annette O'Leary lay in the bed surrounded by enough equipment, it seemed, to synthesize a brand-new human female from the basic elements.

I picked the side on which the apparatus jungle seemed slightly less impenetrable, and stood looking down at her, remembering how we'd met. As Mac had indicated, she'd been involved, in an amateurish way, on the wrong side of a job I'd been doing down in Mexico. Afterwards, needing some female help on my next assignment, I'd put her to work for us. Perhaps because I'd known her first by her real name, before there was any question of her joining the outfit, I'd never been able to think of her as Ruby, the corny code name she'd been given later, presumably because of her red hair. Ruby always sounds like a tart name to me, and she was no tart.

She was a bright kid with a lot of guts and a lot of spirit, but you'd never have guessed it now, looking at the pinched little face below the neat white cap of bandages. There seemed to be bandages under the hospital gown as well. Her eyes were closed. I couldn't help remembering that I had, after all, got her into this racket—all the way in, on a permanent, professional basis. Even if her alternative had been prison, it didn't seem, at the moment, like something of which I should be very proud.

I reached down for the nearest hand, first making sure it was connected to no vital wiring or plumbing. It was cold and limp and unresponsive in my grasp. Her eyes remained closed.

"Annette," I said softly, "Netta…"

She didn't move. I glanced at the doctor who'd brought me up here. He moved his shoulders very slightly, as if to say that nothing I could do—nothing anybody could do—would hurt her now.

"Hey, Carrots," I said, "snap out of it! This is Matt."

For a moment, nothing happened. Then the eyelids came up very slowly as if infinitely heavy, and her eyes looked straight at me. I felt a very slight pressure of the cold fingers, just enough to tell me she saw me and knew me and was glad I was there. A moment later the eyelids dropped once more. I stood there holding her hand as long as I figured there was still a chance that she was aware of my presence; then I laid it down gently and went over to the chair in the corner to wait.

Three hours later they declared her officially dead.

# 2

When I came out of the hospital, it was dark. A damp, chemical-smelling mist put haloes around the street lights and motel signs. I picked up my suitcase and a newspaper from the motel office and went up to my unit, located at the end of the second-story balcony.

I set down my burden outside the door and, hands free, checked the knife in my pocket, a folding Buck hunting knife that's a little bigger than I like for casual wear, but I'd had to leave my previous edged weapon behind on a job last fall, and this had been the only replacement available at the time. Having got it nicely sharpened and broken in, I was reluctant to change again.

I also checked the little five-shot, .38 caliber Smith & Wesson revolver reposing inside my belt forward of my left hip, butt to the right. The clean-cut boys of the F.B.I. carry them way over on the other side for a fast draw, and I understand they're real good at it, but I'm seldom in that much of a hurry, and I want my gun where I can reach it with either hand, to use it or ditch it as circumstances require.

Having given anyone waiting for me in the room plenty of time to get nervous, I made my entrance cautiously the way the book recommends in times of uncertainty. There was nobody inside. I retrieved my suitcase and closed and locked the door, frowning thoughtfully. I'd been playing it safe by assuming the worst: that Annette had run into somebody who was part of a dangerous organization, political or criminal, and that this organization was now, since I'd got to see her before she died, very much concerned about who I was, what I'd learned from her, and what I'd do next.

That was the only safe theory for me to act upon, but I had as yet no evidence that it was correct except a man reading a paper who might have been just what he seemed. My histrionics and precautions might be a total waste of time. Annette could have been shot by a jealous lover who subsequently went home and blew out his brains, or by a drunken thief who ran for the Mexican border a hundred-odd miles away. If so, I'd have a hell of a time getting a line on the solitary murderer unless the police turned him up for me.

If an illicit organization was involved, however, and if it could now be goaded into revealing itself by taking action against me, I was in business, if I survived. In any case, I had to make my plans on the basis of the toughest opposition possible: say, some kind of undercover outfit run by a gent with brains, an outfit familiar with firearms and, perhaps, with other gadgets as well.

I glanced around casually but made no search. I had no desire to find the bug if it was there, as I hoped it was. I'd certainly made it easy enough for them to plant one on me. I'd loudly announced the number of my room and given them over three hours to work on it. If they couldn't take advantage of their opportunities, to hell with them.

It was a big, pleasant room with two double beds, which seemed a waste. Under the circumstances, even one double bed would be fifty percent wasted unless something unexpected happened, and I wasn't in a mood to hope for it. She'd been a good kid. We'd once had a pretty good time together, not to mention doing a pretty good job together down in Mexico, never mind the top-secret details. I could spend a night alone by way of mourning.

I threw my suitcase on the nearest big bed, tossed the paper down beside it, picked up the phone, and had the office lady get the long-distance operator to put me through to Washington. It took a while. Waiting, I leafed through the paper on the bed, playing the fine old secret-agent game of trying to guess what item or items in the news might possibly have a bearing on my mission here. You have to guess most of the time; they won't tell you. Security being what it is, you're seldom given the full background even if it's known. In this case, of course, it seemed likely that nobody knew the full background except the person who'd shot Annette, and he wasn't talking, at least not to anybody who'd talk to me.

The afternoon paper on the bed contained practically the same news as the morning paper I'd appropriated on the plane. There was a front-page picture of a hillside giving way due to rain and depositing a movie star's house gently in the middle of the highway below. There was an interview with a seismologist who predicted that a violent earthquake, long overdue, would soon wipe California off the map. There was an editorial on water pollution, a smog warning, and an interview with a Mexican official who considered that the resumption of the U.S. anti-smuggling campaign along the border, with its harmful effect on the Mexican tourist business, was a clumsy and insulting way of putting pressure on his government to crack down on illicit Mexican growers of marihuana and opium poppies.

Still holding the phone, waiting, I flipped the pages one-handed, looking for the continuation of the story, but stopped at a short column headed: SCIENTIST MISSING. Dr. Osbert Sorenson, a meteorologist at the University of California, Los Angeles, had left his office at his usual time, one evening last week, but had never arrived home. Fearing kidnaping, his family had kept the news quiet until now, waiting for a ransom note that hadn't come. The police were reserving judgment, but an associate of Dr. Sorenson's was quoted as hinting darkly that the doctor had received threats from large business interests—very large business interests—opposed to his work for a better environment. It seemed that the doctor was president of the Abolish the Internal Combustion Engine Committee of California, also known as the AICEC, which I'd read something about earlier in the day.

I frowned at the newspaper page, thinking it was the most promising item I'd encountered. Weather, earthquakes, pollution, and drugs were kind of out of my line of work, but I'd had to do with several missing scientists with slight crackpot tendencies during the course of my undercover career.

It seemed unlikely that the theory of the disappearance hinted at by Dr. Sorenson's colleague was correct. To be sure, the big auto companies had run up a record of abysmal stupidity in dealing with real or imagined threats to their profits, but kidnaping or killing a respectable member of the UCLA faculty would be overdoing it, even for them. And if Ford, Chrysler, or General Motors hadn't got him, who had?

Anyway, it seemed like an interesting coincidence: a scientist missing in L.A. at roughly the same time an agent turned up dead. It would be a very long shot, I reflected, but if all other leads to Annette's murderer failed me, I might flip it and take a closer look at the Sorenson case, if only because I was intrigued by the notion of anybody having the nerve to try to abolish the conventional, petrol-powered automobile, particularly here in California where they practically take their beloved cars to bed with them.

A familiar voice on the phone interrupted my meditations. I said, "This is Matt, sir."

The use of my real name instead of my code name was supposed to let him know that we might not have the wire to ourselves.

"Who?" Mac asked, making sure it wasn't just a slip on my part.

"Matt Helm, in L.A. Can you hear me all right?"

"I hear you, Matt," he said, acknowledging the warning. "What's the situation out there?"

"Not good," I said. "Have you got your red pencil handy? Scratch Agent Ruby. Our brick-top just left us."

There was a little pause. "I'm sorry to hear it," Mac said at last. "She was a promising prospect. A little erratic and impulsive, but promising. We don't get too many of them these days."

"No, sir."

"The sincere peace-lovers and humanitarians have my respect, Matt—I'm in favor of peace and humanity myself—but I get weary of interviewing these warlike young candidates who'd just love to kill all communists by remote control, but wouldn't dream of getting real blood on their hands. As far as I'm concerned, they fall into the same category as the people who are happy to eat beef butchered by somebody else, but look with righteous horror at the man who goes out into the woods to shoot his own venison."

That was, I decided, a little homespun philosophy thrown in to make the conversation sound authentic to anyone listening.

"Yes, sir," I said.

"Did you get to the hospital in time to talk with her?" He put the question casually.

"Yes, sir," I said. "It wasn't much of a conversation,

but she did tell me something. I don't know exactly what it means yet."

"What did she say?"

"I'm calling through the motel switchboard, sir."

"I see. Does anybody else know what you've got?"

"There was a doctor in the room. He was too far away to hear, but he was watching. A Dr. Freeberg."

"That's all right. He's good and he's safe."

"I questioned him a bit afterwards," I said. "As you probably know from the medical reports, she was shot twice: a bullet in the chest and what was supposed to be a finish-up shot in the back of the head. Dr. F. says that either bullet should have killed her instantly—they were 240-grain slugs from a .44 Magnum—but you know how it goes. One guy brushes up against a cholla cactus and dies of blood poisoning and the next fellow absorbs a full clip from an M-1 rifle and is back on his feet in a month. She was tough and stubborn and Irish and she made a fight of it. The question is, sir, who do we know who makes a habit of using that much firearm?"

"I'll check it out. I can't think of anybody at the moment."

"Neither can I, sir. I remember just one man who lugged around a cannon that big," I said, "but he was pretty stupid and I know he's dead because I killed him. With a cute little .22 target pistol. But the .44 Maggie is not a common caliber in the profession, sir. It's a bear-hunter's gun—not that any one-hand weapon is adequate for really big game, but this one comes about as close as you can get. The last time I looked through a catalog, the smallest weapon made for the cartridge weighed over three pounds. Even with that much weight to hold it down, the .44's got a brutal recoil. It takes a masochist to shoot one, and he'd better be at least a two-hundred-pound masochist, if only just to lug the thing around."

"We'll feed it into the fancy new computer they insisted on giving us," Mac said. "I'll let you know what comes out. I understand there were signs that she'd been interrogated."

"Yes, sir. They'd worked her over a bit before they shot her. Was she carrying information somebody might be after?"

"Not as far as I know. I told you she was on leave, and she certainly had access to nothing of importance here before she departed—unless they wanted just general information about our latest training and operations procedures."

"Well, it could be," I said. "There's still a lot of curiosity about us in various foreign government bureaus. You said something about a reprimand, sir, but you didn't say what she'd done to earn it. It might be significant."

"I rather doubt it." He hesitated, and went on: "The details don't matter, but essentially she did something her own way instead of the way she'd been instructed to do it. Her way worked, as it happened, but it was much more risky and no more profitable." He waited for me to comment, but I remained silent. I'd never been a great one for following instructions to the letter, myself. He must have guessed what I was thinking, because he said, rather sharply: "When an agent has been with us long enough to develop some professional judgment, Matt, shortcuts are sometimes permitted or at least condoned; but first they have to learn to do what they're told in the way they're told to do it."

"Yes, sir," I said.

"Whatever she did to get herself killed, she must have done it fast. She only left Washington yesterday."

"Did she have any relatives or friends in the Los Angeles area?"

"None that we know about." Mac sighed on the other side of the continent. "Well, I guess you'd better stay with it. We ought to know what she ran into. Oh, and Matt…"

"Yes, sir."

"Retribution is not our business."

"No, sir."

"However, I would say it was bad public relations—bad for our image, as the Madison Avenue gang would put it—to allow our people to be used as targets by any joker with a big revolver. Besides, murder trials tend to involve a lot of publicity that can be avoided by presenting the police with a case nicely closed by the death of the murderer. Under the circumstances, if the matter can be handled inconspicuously, I really see no reason for the person or persons responsible to survive, do you?"

"No, sir," I said, thinking of a small girl in a hospital bed, "no reason at all."

# 3

There seems to be only one taxi company operating in Los Angeles proper. The relationship between this lack of competition and the fact that it took me forty-five minutes to promote a cab may be wholly coincidental, but then again, it may not.

When he finally arrived, I had the driver transport me through the foggy streets to a restaurant recommended by the motel, which turned out to be only half a dozen blocks away. That was a long enough distance, however, for me to determine, with a certain sense of relief and triumph, that I'd aroused some interest somewhere. I was being followed.

It was a rather dilapidated Ford station wagon colored a sort of faded bronze: a repaint job that hadn't weathered well. The driver seemed to be alone in the vehicle. He tailed me as far as the restaurant and continued up the boulevard out of sight while I was paying off my taxi, but I didn't think he'd go far. I had a hunch that my time of loneliness was over and I'd better get used to having company, which suited me fine.

Inside, I found the place decorated in turn-of-the-century bordello style, with red leather upholstery, red wallpaper, and red shades on the lamps, which didn't throw much light. As a result, I couldn't get a good look at the people who entered after me, but it didn't really matter, since I hadn't the slightest intention of eluding my escort, no matter how large it might be. I just settled down to a pleasant dinner. Despite the thick period atmosphere, often used as a substitute for good liquor, food, and service, the martinis were fast and acceptable, and the steak was slow but excellent.

When I came out, none of the elusive Los Angeles taxis were in sight. Having no way of knowing what the chances were of catching one cruising in this part of town, I decided that walking was better anyway. I palmed the snub-nosed revolver, slipped it into my coat pocket and, keeping my hand on it, set off.

The battered bronze station wagon was right on the job. It passed me once as I strode briskly through a little park with a pond full of ducks. Well, some of the birds floating out there could have been refugee seagulls from the nearby ocean—in the dark it was hard to tell—but the quacking ones along the shore were certainly ducks. The automotive relic passed me once more as I reached the big thoroughfare on which the motel was located, turned left, and started up the hill towards the illuminated sign still three blocks away.

Nobody sprayed me with buckshot from a sawed-off shotgun, or .45 caliber slugs from a Thompson submachine-gun, or even .44 slugs from an overgrown Magnum revolver. I was disappointed. I'd hoped for some action before I got back to this well-lighted street. Nevertheless, it was a cool, misty, pleasant night for walking; and after spending the day riding in planes and automobiles, not to mention waiting in a hospital room for death to pay a visit, I was happy to be stretching my leg and lung muscles, even though the local air still wasn't anything I'd want to make a regular habit of breathing.

The station wagon made a final pass right in front of me as I waited for the traffic light at the intersection by the motel. I started to cross when it became legal to do so, noting that the vehicle had pulled to the curb half a block away. Changing my mind, I turned back to the sidewalk I'd just left and walked down there. The driver leaned over and shoved the door open for me.

"Get in," he said. "The Man wants to see you."

I sighed. There are so many of them: The Man, *El Hombre*. Every wide spot in the road has got one, and every damn one of them thinks he's Mr. Big himself. I wondered how the hell this particular bigshot had got involved with one of our people or vice versa. Of course, he didn't have to be a simple gangster or syndicate man just because a messenger boy had referred to him in that particular way.

"Get in," said the driver of the station wagon impatiently. "Hell, what does a guy have to do to attract your attention, Mister? I must have put fifty miles on this crummy heap trying to get you to look at me. Get in. He doesn't like to be kept waiting."

They never like to be kept waiting, none of the little underworld emperors, if that's what he really was. I looked into the wagon. It was empty except for the driver.

I got in and pulled the door closed behind me. As we drove away, I couldn't help laughing.

The driver glanced at me with quick suspicion. "What's so funny, Mister?"

"Never mind," I said.

I was thinking of the elaborate scheming I'd done to attract trouble; and all the time trouble had been waiting impatiently to hand me an engraved invitation. I glanced at the man beside me. He was a large, heavy-set specimen with a big jaw, a lumpy nose, coarse skin, and curly brown hair. He was wearing grubby gray work pants and shirt, and a dark green windbreaker. I classified him, tentatively, as low-priced labor: bright enough for a simple job of open surveillance, but inadequate for anything more demanding, like homicide. Of course, I could be wrong.

He drove badly, never thinking far enough ahead to be in the proper lane when a turn was to be made. When other drivers objected to his sudden last-minute maneuvers, he became childishly indignant. Apparently it had never in his life occurred to him that the whole street wasn't his to do with as he pleased.

I didn't even try to figure out where he was taking me. I just memorized a few landmarks for later reference.

Life's too short to spend any part of it committing to memory the whole sprawling geography of Los Angeles. At last we wound up in front of a big apartment house in a neighborhood of similar buildings.

My chauffeur said: "Just walk straight into the lobby and turn left to the elevators. The punk in the monkey-suit knows how high to take you."

I glanced at him. "No escort?"

"Hell, you want to see him, don't you? They said you did. And he wants to see you. So who needs muscle? I'll be waiting with the wheels to take you back."

"Some wheels," I said.

"It runs. But if you complain, maybe he'll send you home in a Cadillac."

I grinned and walked into the building, past the doorman, who asked me no questions, and across the carpeted lobby to the open elevator. The boy sent it up without speaking, to the seventh floor, where a big, jowly man in a neat dark suit was waiting in front of the doors when they opened.

"Mr. Helm?" he said, backing me into a little hall or foyer. "Turn around, please. Hands against the wall, high. Nothing personal, Mr. Helm. Just routine…"

"Never mind, Jake," said another voice. "We'll dispense with the frisk in Mr. Helm's case."

I looked around. Another big, jowly man stood in an open doorway across the hall. The difference was that he'd had a closer or more recent shave and used more lotions and powders, or had them used on him. He was wearing the West Coast uniform of the day: sports shirt and slacks.

The man called Jake said, "He's rodded and bladed, Mr. Warfel. At least I think that's a knife in his pants, and I know there's firepower in his coat."

He had sharp eyes, but of course that was his job. The man in the sports shirt waved him aside. "Never mind… Come in, Mr. Helm. I have a present for you." As I approached, he held out his hand. "I'm Frank Warfel. You may have heard of me."

They always think you must have heard of them. Shaking his hand, I said, without committing myself to a downright lie: "I may have. But why is Frank Warfel giving me presents months after Christmas?"

"Come on in," he said without answering my question; then he went on earnestly. "Mr. Helm, everybody makes mistakes. And sometimes in my business—like maybe in yours—mistakes are pretty hard to correct, if you know what I mean…"

He stopped, because I wasn't looking at him any longer. I was looking at the blond girl in the ice-blue satin lounging pajamas who'd appeared in the doorway behind him. She was a tall girl, made taller by her piled-up silver-blond hair and the high-heeled pumps she was wearing. The obsolete hairdo and footgear told her story at a glance. She would know that her bird's-nest coiffure was a couple of years out of date, but if that's the way it pleased The Man, that's the way she'd wear it.

She would also know that the high, slim heels of her

blue satin pumps were no longer in fashion. New York and Paris had decreed that women should now stand around on lower and chunkier foundations that were undoubtedly more comfortable, not to mention being easier on the floors and rugs. This woman was undoubtedly aware of it, but she would also be aware that to a lot of men, Frank Warfel presumably included, a woman isn't really sexy unless she's got on narrow heels at least four inches high and to hell with the dictates of fashion. Much as I hated to agree with a guy like Warfel about anything, I had to admit that I felt pretty much the same way on this particular subject.

"Aren't you going to introduce us, darling?" the girl said throatily to Warfel.

The wide satin pajamas rippled and gleamed as she came forward, swaying sinuously. It looked hard on the vertebrae. Her voice, like her movement, was straight Hollywood, just vibrating with artificial sex appeal. It had to be artificial, because in a sense she had no sex. I mean, she had no waist and hardly any hips, and she wasn't even particularly well-endowed up above.

Please understand, I'm not saying this in a spirit of criticism. I never did go for the Jersey-cow ideal of feminine pulchritude. I think it's real nice that nowadays they're allowed to admit it when their udders aren't up to State Fair standards.

But the fact was that this willowy blonde was so slender as to be practically useless for bed warming or child bearing—at least that was the impression she gave. It had to be wrong. Warfel might not be interested in procreation, but it seemed unlikely that he'd keep a female around who was totally unemployable in bed. And rightly or wrongly the girl obviously considered herself the sexiest thing since Jean Harlow, or at least since Marilyn Monroe.

I glanced at Warfel and made a soft little noise of appreciation. "Some Christmas present," I said, deadpan. "Remind me to tell you when my birthday is, Mr. Warfel."

He didn't like that. I'd known he wouldn't; I guess I was just getting a cheap kick out of teasing the animals. Or maybe I was making a scientific test to determine how much his greasy affability would take; in other words, how important it was to him, for reasons yet unknown, to be nice to me. It must have been pretty important. They're all the same, those little hoodlum kings, and what's theirs is theirs and nobody poaches on their territory, not even in a joke—but he took it from me and even managed a hollow laugh.

"Bobbie, this is Mr. Matthew Helm, who works for the U.S. government," he said. "Mr. Helm, Miss Roberta Prince."

"He's cute," Miss Prince said in her throaty voice. "I'm simply mad about tall men, particularly tall government men. Can I keep him for a pet?"

I wondered if she could be doing a little testing, too, because this was also against the house rules. No lady receiving Frank Warfel's favors should be foolish enough to indicate in any way that she might possibly be interested in lesser men, even just for laughs. But he took this, too, with only a faint narrowing of the eyes and sharpening of the voice.

"Run along, Bobbie. We've got business."

"Oh, you and your tiresome old business!" she said petulantly, but she turned away.

I watched her move out of sight in her exaggerated, undulating fashion. It was a good act, or rather, it was a lousy act that would have been laughed off the screen, but what did she care as long as Frank Warfel liked it. If rippling like a snake in high heels and ice-blue satin was what it took to keep the money-tree shedding its crisp green syndicate foliage all over her, and she could do it, more power to her. I just hoped that that was all she was after. I had trouble enough without blonde trouble.

"So I'm a government man," I said sourly to Warfel. It seemed just as well to clarify the situation, since he'd taken the first step. I went on: "I didn't know it showed. Or could you possibly have had my motel room wired for sound when I made a certain call to Washington a little while ago."

He grinned. The idea that he'd put one over on me, electronically, was making him feel better again. He said, "Maybe. Over this way, Mr. Helm. Follow me." He led me through the living room where the blonde, holding a magazine, had draped herself over a big chair in a position that could only have been assumed by a teenager or an acrobatic dancer. "Right through that door ahead of you," Warfel said. "There's your man."

It was a bedroom, but it wasn't being used for the

purpose at the moment. I looked at the man tied to the chair at the foot of the bed. He was black, with bushy black hair standing up and out from his head the way it's worn nowadays—proudly. He wasn't as big as the man beside me, but he looked compact and powerful. His nose had been broken in times past, and one ear had been thickened. There was another man in the room to guard him, a nondescript individual with a wide, flat, pock-marked face.

I said, "I liked the first sample better. This one isn't so cute. Who is he?"

"Arthur Brown, known as Basher Brown, or simply The Basher," Warfel said. "You may take him with you if you like, Mr. Helm, but it might be more convenient if you dealt with him right here. Convenient for you, I mean. I'll be glad to have the boys clean up after you, inconspicuously. That's how your chief said it should be arranged, when you spoke to him on the phone just now, wasn't it? Inconspicuously. We're happy to oblige. It's part of the service."

I looked at the black man, who looked back at me with the careful expressionlessness of a member of another race who's damned if he's going to show fear before a bunch of alien tormentors.

I said, "I see. This is the guy I'm looking for?"

"That's your murderer," Warfel said. "I suggest you use the knife, if you want to take care of him here. I own the building, but I'd rather not have any gunshots, if you don't mind."

He was needling me in some way, deliberately

challenging me to commit a cold-blooded killing in front of witnesses. I couldn't make out if his purpose was to heat me into it or cool me off it. Or maybe he was just sneering because it was his nature. Or maybe he was simply overacting a role, which brought up the interesting question: what role, in what play?

"What did he use?" I asked. "Where's the cannon?"

"The gun?" Warfel made a gesture at the guard. "Give The Basher's gun to Mr. Helm."

The man went around the bed and picked something off a chair that also held a jacket presumably belonging to Arthur Brown, who was in his shirtsleeves. The guard handed me a large Smith and Wesson double-action revolver with a six-and-a-half-inch barrel. Longer tubes are made, and for a powerhouse cartridge like the .44 they have some advantages, but they're even harder to hide.

I studied the weapon thoughtfully, pressed the cylinder latch on the left side of the frame, swung out the cylinder, and looked at the brass heads of the six cartridges. Two of the primers showed firing-pin indentations. Annette had been shot twice. It was very neat. I had no doubt the rifling would match the recovered bullets, if they were in condition to be matched, which doesn't always happen.

I closed the gun once more and walked up to the bound man in the chair. He looked up at me with steady brown eyes.

"This is your gun?" I asked.

"That's my gun." His voice was as expressionless as his face, flat and toneless.

I said, "Tell me what happened."

He said, "What's to tell, man? She looked like somebody else, red hair and all. I got the wrong girl."

"But you got her?"

"Me and nobody else. Like Mr. Warfel told you, everybody makes mistakes. I'm paying for mine, like you see."

"How did it happen?"

Warfel spoke behind me. "That doesn't really matter, does it, Mr. Helm? This is your man. He admits it."

I turned slowly to look at him. "If you overheard my telephone conversation at the motel, you know that my instructions cover the person *or persons* responsible. Somehow, I don't think Mr. Brown went out and killed a girl just for private kicks. Who gave the orders?"

There was a little silence in the room. I was aware that the big man who'd greeted me at the elevator—the official frisker called Jake—had taken up a station in the doorway.

Warfel said softly, "I wouldn't push it, Mr. Helm. We made a mistake, a bad mistake. We admit it. We don't want any trouble with you or your chief in Washington, so we're giving you the man who shot your agent. I suggest you leave it at that, Mr. Helm."

"And if I don't?"

Warfel sighed. "We don't want to buck Washington, not unless we have to. But if you try to push it we'll have to, won't we? I mean, you'll give us no choice. And it's not your line of work, is it, Mr. Helm? I don't know exactly what you are, but you're damn well not F.B.I. You're not pretty enough, for one thing, and for another, nobody ever told a G-man to go out and kill somebody, not in so many words. They've got scruples; they're gentlemen."

"And I'm no gentleman?"

"No offense, Mr. Helm, but you're a professional killer, aren't you? I've seen a lot of them, and I knew you the minute I saw you. An executioner, a rub-out man. The only difference being that you seem to be a government rub-out man. I'm guessing that you belong to some kind of high-powered secret espionage or counterespionage outfit that plays pretty rough. And now you've lost one of your people and you're mad. You're not used to having your agents knocked over by punks like Arthur, here, working for hoodlums like me, are you, Mr. Helm? And you're going to show us that no little private creeps can monkey with a big, bad government agency like yours!"

His voice had turned harsh. I said, "Easy, Mr. Warfel. You're saying it, not me. Don't work yourself into a coronary on my account."

He drew a long breath, and forced a grin. "Ah, hell, there I go, losing my temper. Excuse me, Mr. Helm. I'm just upset about losing Arthur, just for one lousy mistake. He's a good man... Okay, so the mistake was his and you can have him. But don't try taking it any farther. I'm not crazy enough to think I can buck the U.S. government and win, but I can sure as hell give you a lot of publicity while I'm losing. And I don't think you secret-agent hush-hush types would like that. Check with your chief and see if I'm not right. He said inconspicuously, remember? Well, you can settle for Arthur, inconspicuously, or you can have a fight that'll make you conspicuous as hell. Take your choice, Mr. Helm. Check with your boss and see if he really wants to go into the syndicate-busting business just because somebody made a mistake. Okay?"

I looked at Arthur Brown. "You worked her over before you shot her. Why?"

The black man looked up sharply, frowning. "What do you mean, man. I didn't…"

"Never mind, Arthur," Warfel said quickly. "Mr. Helm, it was a simple case of mistaken identity. And who your girl was mistaken for, and why, is none of your damn business."

"I guess not. May I make a phone call, collect, to Washington, D.C.?"

He gestured towards the other room, magnanimously. "Be my guest. Live it up. Charge it to me." He hesitated. "Just one thing, Mr. Helm. On the phone you reported that your girl had told you something before she died. What did she say?"

I laughed. "Hell, she didn't say anything. I figured somebody might be listening. That was just sugar to draw flies, Mr. Warfel."

The blonde looked up from her magazine and winked at me playfully as I went past. It was quite a wink, since her lashes were almost an inch long. I couldn't match it so I didn't try.

**4**

The station wagon was waiting when we came downstairs. I opened the door and let Arthur Brown get in first. He was a little clumsy because of his bound hands. They were tied in front of him, with his jacket draped to hide the ropes.

Warfel had seemed to think it was sissy of me to want him tied, just as it was sentimental of me not to slit his throat on the spot. I wasn't really much of a guy, in Warfel's opinion. I worried about this like I worried about the opinion of the ducks in the pond I passed earlier in the evening, or even a little less. As a hunter of sorts, I have a lot of respect for ducks.

Arthur Brown looked like a professional boxer to me, and I don't play games with those; I know some trick stuff that'll handle the amateurs, but I wouldn't dream of trying it on a real pro fighter. If he came for me, I'd have to stop him with a gun, and I didn't want to, at least not yet.

"All right, Willy," I said, having learned the driver's name from Warfel. "Head back the way we came, slowly.

If somebody pulls alongside and blows a horn, don't get excited. Just take it to the curb and stop it. I'm assuming it does have brakes."

"If they don't work, I'll open the door and drag my foot," said Willy, cutting out into traffic without a glance at the mirror. Three blocks later he said, "We've got company like you said. Do you want me to stop now?"

"They'll let you know when."

"I don't like this."

"Sure you do," I said. "Mr. Warfel said for you to do exactly what I told you. I heard him. Sure you like it, Willy. You're paid to like it."

"Okay, I like it."

We rode along for a while without conversation. I was aware of Arthur Brown, silent beside me. I'm a firm believer in racial equality, but that doesn't mean I kid myself that I'll ever know exactly what thoughts are going through the head of a member of another race. We may all be equal as hell, but that doesn't mean we necessarily think alike.

"What's your real name?" I asked.

"Arthur Brown," he said.

"Go to hell," I said. "There may be Arthur Browns— there undoubtedly are—but you're not one of them. Every time you hear the name, your nostrils flare like they'd caught a bad smell."

He said, "All right, so my name is Lionel McConnell. Can you see a Lionel McConnell in the ring, man? A black Lionel McConnell? Anyway, they told me I was

Arthur Basher Brown, and if you know them, you know that who they tell you you are, that's who you are."

"Sure." After a while, I said, "Lionel McConnell. That's pretty damn fancy. Almost as fancy as Annette O'Leary." The man beside me didn't speak. I went on: "That was a nice kid you shot. We had plans for that girl, McConnell. You ought to be more careful whom you go firing guns at…"

"I told you, it was a mistake. A case of mistaken identity."

"Sure. The streets of L.A. are just lousy with good-looking little redheads, one exactly like the next. You've got to beat them off with a club. What do you think we're going to do with you, McConnell?"

"Hell, man," he said, "it's obvious. You're either going to shoot me or talk me to death…"

He stopped. A car had pulled up on our left as we rolled down a wide boulevard. A horn made a brief, beeping sound. Willy glanced over his shoulder.

"Now?"

"Now," I said.

When we came to a stop, I helped the bound man out onto the sidewalk and escorted him to the big tan sedan that had pulled to the curb ahead. The rear door was open and a young woman in a neat gray suit stood beside it, surprising me a bit. I hadn't really been expecting a woman, although there are plenty in the business.

She wasn't one of ours, and neither was the driver or, for that matter, the car. We don't have enough manpower or money to cover the world in depth, or even the country, like some agencies. But there is a certain amount of interdepartmental cooperation, meaning that Mac had apparently done a favor for somebody in the past and now he was collecting a favor in return.

"Here he is," I said to the girl. "Can you hold him for me, temporarily?"

"It can be arranged. Temporarily."

Her voice was curt. I glanced at her and decided that for some reason she didn't like men very much, particularly not a man named Helm, with errands to be run. She was another tall girl—the climate of California, difficult though it was to breathe, seemed to favor the long-stemmed variety—but in other respects there was little resemblance between this girl and the blonde in the shimmering blue pajamas.

This one was wearing horn-rimmed glasses and had her hair cut shorter than that of a good many men these long-haired days. It was crisp, glossy, and light brown in color with a chestnut tinge—in other words, it was pretty nice hair that deserved a better deal. Her face was handsome rather than pretty or beautiful, with a high nose, strong cheekbones, and a big, contemptuous mouth. What she had to be contemptuous about, besides me, remained to be seen.

The mannish flannel suit she was wearing was no shorter in the skirt than it had to be, considering the current vogue for mini-garments. Even so, it was mostly jacket, displaying a considerable length of fine leg encased in dark stocking. Her figure was also pretty good, if somewhat more substantial than the one to which I'd recently been introduced by Frank Warfel. This wasn't an acrobatic dancer's figure, but I thought it would probably swim pretty well and swing a mean tennis racket if required.

A white silk shirt and low-heeled black shoes completed the picture, along with a black purse of practical size, the flap of which was open, leaving the contents ready to hand. I'd caught a gleam of blue steel as she turned to face us. All in all, she was the image of the efficient lady agent. At least she was right in there trying.

I said, "Okay, he's yours. Temporarily. What about a quiet place to fire a gun? A fairly big gun?"

McConnell glanced at me briefly, his black face impassive. The girl frowned and didn't answer at once, looking from one to the other of us dubiously.

Then she said reluctantly, "I suppose that can be arranged, too, if it's absolutely necessary. I'll check."

"You check," I said. I hauled out the heavy Magnum revolver. "Here's the gun. Keep it safe for me. Him, too."

"How long? We do have other business to attend to besides yours, Mr. Helm." She hesitated, but went on before I could answer: "Incidentally, my name is Charlotte Devlin. In case you have to ask for me, or about me or something."

Her tone was still far from gracious. I realized that she disapproved of me not only because my lousy little errand was beneath her dignity, but also as a matter of principle. Well, our agency isn't the government's pride and joy, exactly. Even the C.I.A. boys, much as they're criticized in some quarters, are popularity kids compared to us. We're only consulted, as a rule, when people find themselves stuck with something they can't handle— or don't want to handle because it stinks too badly. In between the times they need us, they'd like to pretend we don't exist.

"Hello, Charlotte," I said. "Excuse me, I mean Miss Devlin. I won't be long. I've got a kind of hunch I want to check out; I'll be right back to take care of him properly. Just tell me where."

She told me. The driver never turned his head; maybe he disapproved of me, too. The girl got into the rear seat with her prisoner—well, my prisoner—and the sedan moved smoothly away from the curb.

I went back to the old station wagon and told Willy to take me back to the motel. You had to say this for his driving: it was consistent. I was happy to get out of the ancient heap intact. A blare of horns behind me, as I crossed the sidewalk, told me that Willy had taken off in his usual never-look-behind fashion. There was no accompanying crunch of metal. Maybe he was lucky, or somebody was.

I entered the motel grounds. It was a rambling hostelry clinging to a hillside, its different levels served by two intersecting lanes, or drives. The one at which Willy had deposited me was practically a tunnel running up between the buildings, dark and narrow. He could, of course, have dropped me around the corner at the office, under the lights, but I suppose if he had, he wouldn't have been Willy. Or perhaps he had some motive other than pure meanness for sending me up this gloomy passageway.

I slipped my hand into the pocket that still held the .38 Special. As I climbed the slope towards the better-lighted cross-drive above, something moved in the shadows ahead. I could make out three figures struggling. Two were apparently ganging up on the third, much smaller than either of them.

A girl's voice gasped: "Let me go! Oh, don't, you're hurting... Ahhhh!"

Her breathless little whimper of pain was followed by the sound of a blow. I saw the smallest of the shadowy figures fall as I pulled out my revolver and started warily to the rescue, looking around for signs of an ambush. Ladies in distress aren't taken at face value in my business, not by any agent concerned about his mission or his life.

**5**

It was a simple rescue as rescues go. I just stalked up there cautiously, displaying the gun and making some restrained noises indicating that I disapproved of what was going on. The two men, who had grabbed the fallen girl by the arms and were starting to drag her away between them, looked around guiltily. Seeing me, they released her and ran. I waited until they'd disappeared around the corner of the building and a little longer.

Nothing moved. The girl just crouched where she'd been dropped. I could make out that she had rather long hair, which was a point in her favor according to my personal scoring system. On the other hand, she was wearing some kind of a pants outfit, which counted a couple of points against her, unless she could produce a valid excuse like a horse or a pair of skis. I went up to her, holding the gun ready.

"All right," she whispered, without looking up, "all right, you've got me. You've got your gun. You've got your orders from Frankie. What are you waiting for?"

Then she buried her face in her hands and began to sob. I dropped the revolver into my pocket, picked up the good-sized purse lying on the ground a few feet to one side, and slung it over my shoulder by the strap provided. I went, back to the girl, lifted her gently, and led her up the passageway and across the intersecting drive to the building beyond. We climbed the stairs and made our way along the balcony to my room at the end.

I was beginning to feel a little disenchanted with the assignment. Except for Annette, who was no longer a participant, it had shaped up as a simple, rugged, masculine job of work. Now, suddenly, it had turned into a complicated coeducational caper involving not just one, not two, but three attractive females—well, I still hadn't got a good look at the latest addition to the cast of female characters, but she had an intriguing little figure and under the circumstances it seemed unlikely that she'd be here if she were ugly.

Please don't get me wrong. I like girls. I just don't like to have them coming at me, in the middle of a job at least, faster than I can count them.

My damsel in distress offered no resistance or protest. Nobody came out to ask any questions. There hadn't really been much noise to attract attention, just a scuffle, some gasps and whimpers, and a spoken word or two, not loud. I checked the door of my unit. I'd left a few indicators to tell if anybody had opened it in my absence. Apparently nobody had. I unlocked it, reached around to switch on the light, pushed the girl inside, and followed her, closing the door behind me.

She turned slowly to look at me. After a moment she gave a little toss of her head to get the long straggling hair out of her eyes. She wiped her eyes and nose with the back of her hand, childishly. We faced each other in silence, taking stock of each other in the light.

What she saw, I suppose, was a skinny, elongated gent wearing slacks that needed pressing after a hard day, a sports coat with a bulge in the pocket, and a suspicious expression. What I saw was a smallish girl with hazel eyes in an oval, small-featured face that was now rather tearstained and dirty. Her disordered hair reached well down her shoulders and was that reddish shade of coppery gold that's almost always artificial, but it's a pretty color anyway.

As I've indicated, I kind of favor long-haired girls over girls who are so closely clipped or carefully pinned up or tightly curled, as to leave nothing blowing in the wind. On the other hand, given a choice, I'll pick the ones in skirts over the ones in pants any day—or night—in the week.

This one was wearing a ducky little pale green suit of thin wool, with sharply creased flaring trousers. There was also an immaculate white turtle-necked sweater or jersey. The suit itself wasn't quite immaculate, having picked up some smudges from the driveway. The jacket had got pulled awry. Automatically, under my regard, she made as if to straighten it, but checked herself, glancing down distastefully at her hands, which were too grimy from the pavement to be allowed to make contact with her clothing. She looked at me once more.

"I'm sorry," she said. "I didn't mean…"

"What didn't you mean?" I asked when she stopped.

"Back there," she said. "I didn't recognize you in the dark, Mr. Helm. I guess… I guess all I could see was the gun."

"How do you know my name?"

"I was in the hospital waiting room this afternoon when you came in. I heard you tell the nurse who you were and whom you wanted to see. I was… I was waiting outside, here, to talk with you, just now, when those men grabbed me…" She shivered. "If you hadn't come along, they'd have taken me away and killed me."

"Who wants you dead?" I asked. She didn't answer immediately, and I said, "You mentioned somebody named Frankie out there. Would that be Frank Warfel?"

"Y-yes. Do you know him?"

"We've met," I said. "Just barely. What's your name?"

She hesitated. "I'm Beverly Blaine," she said, but after a moment she went on quickly. "Well, for Hollywood purposes I'm Beverly Blaine. Can you see Mary Sokolnicek on a movie marquee, Mr. Helm?"

"What were you waiting to talk with me about, Mary-Beverly?"

"It's about… about the girl you went to see, the redhead, the one who got hurt. I… I wanted to find out… I mean, can you tell me how badly… Oh, hell, I mean how is she?"

"She's dead," I said.

Beverly Blaine stared at me for a moment without moving. Then she stepped back blindly and sank down on the bed, still looking wide-eyed at my face.

"*Dead?*" She licked her lips. "But I thought, since she'd hung on so long, that she had a pretty good chance of..."

"She's dead," I said. "She never had a chance, not really. Not with two .44 slugs in her. What's it to you, Mary-Beverly? How well did you know her?"

"I hardly knew her at all. I just…" The disheveled little girl on the bed licked her lips once more. "I just killed her," she whispered.

There was a long silence in the room—well, as much silence as you ever get in a big city like Los Angeles. The girl was probably so used to it she didn't even hear it, but having just spent a couple of weeks in a relatively small town, I was aware of the unceasing roar of traffic outside.

I said softly, "That's a damn popular murder, sweetheart. Everybody seems to want a piece of it. I was just talking with a man called Arthur Brown who claims he killed Annette O'Leary."

"You know The Basher?"

"Introductions courtesy of Frank Warfel," I said. "It's too complicated to explain, but Brown claims he shot Annette by mistake. How did you shoot her and what was your motive?"

"Oh, I didn't actually shoot her, Mr. Helm!" Beverly sounded shocked by the idea. "Heavens, I don't know anything about guns! I just… just sent her to her death. Instead of me. That's how The Basher came to make his mistake, don't you understand?"

"Not exactly," I said. "Tell me."

She drew a long breath, sitting there. "Well," she said, "well, as you've probably gathered, I'm in trouble in this town, bad trouble. I was trying to get away. I'd done something, something they couldn't let me get away with. Like talking out of turn. Well, I hadn't done it yet, but I'd threatened to do it. Me and my big mouth."

"They?"

"Frank Warfel and the people behind him, who are even worse if it's possible. And you'd better believe it's possible." She paused a moment, and went on: "When things didn't go right for me in Hollywood—that fancy stage name never even made the screen credits, if you know what I mean—when things went bad, I got a job in a certain place... Well, never mind the gory details. Anyway, Frank saw me and liked me and took me out of there. For a while. A couple of years. Until he got tired of little girls and found himself a big girl for a change. He likes variety, Frankie does." Beverly frowned at the nylon carpet between her green suede shoes. "It wasn't... wasn't easy work while it lasted, but it paid well, if you know what I mean, Mr. Helm."

"Sure," I said. "You said you were trying to get out of town."

"That's right." The girl's voice was dull. "When I got near home that day—my God, it was only yesterday!—after putting on my bigmouth act for Mister Frank Warfel and his current sweetie—and what a slinky blonde boa constrictor-type she is!—when I got near home I spotted

The Basher waiting across the street from my apartment building. That's when I realized that I'd, well, talked myself to death, getting mad and jealous like that. The word was out, and little Beverly might just as well cut her throat with a dull knife and save Frankie-boy the trouble. Only I wasn't going to make it that easy for him, so I turned the convertible around and headed it for the airport. I had a little money, enough for a ticket somewhere, and it was better than dying, or having my face smashed into something nobody could look at without puking, like one girl I knew who talked too much..."

She shivered. After a little, she giggled half-hysterically. "You never figure it could happen to you. Do you know what I mean? You've got it made: an apartment, a car, good clothes, furs, jewelry, a bank account, the works, and you think it's going to last forever. And then, suddenly, you're on the run with just the rags on your back and the few bucks in your purse and death right behind you... You've got to understand how it was, Mr. Helm! You've got to understand why I did it!"

"Tell me," I said.

"When I got to the terminal, I caught a glimpse of one of Frankie's other goons waiting there, and I knew they'd be all around the place. I knew I'd never make it, and then along came a kid off a plane and she wasn't too big and she had longish red hair kind of like mine. I remembered that Arthur Brown had never seen me. Frankie-boy doesn't like to mix his pleasure people with his business people any more than he has to. Of course I'd seen a few people in the time I'd been with him, and heard a few things, that's why he had to shut me up. I'd heard of The Basher and seen him perform in the ring, but we'd never actually met. And I had this… this awful, bright idea how to get them all off my trail, and I bumped into this girl and made with the tears and the sob story…"

"She fell for it?"

Beverly drew a long breath. "Sure she fell for it, Mister. I'm a pretty good actress, if I say so myself. If it wasn't for studio politics… Well, never mind that! Anyway, I talked her into driving me home in the car she'd reserved at a rental agency. I got her to go in to pick up some things for me, things I didn't dare get myself because my estranged husband, a real maniac, was watching the place, waiting to make trouble if I showed. Something like that, I don't remember exactly what lies I used. I just made them up as I went along." The girl closed her eyes briefly and opened them again. "And she went in, a red-haired kid about my size, into my apartment building, and I saw The Basher leave his doorway and go in after her. I got behind the wheel of the rental car and drove like hell away from there."

In some respects, I reflected, it wasn't too unlikely a story. Annette O'Leary had been an inch or two taller than the girl sitting on the bed, and her hair had been a different, more natural, more carroty color, but a man waiting for a slim small redhead to enter a certain building wouldn't have been making such fine distinctions…

I said, "Considering the trouble you went to, you don't seem to have got very far."

Beverly was still staring at a spot between her shoes. "How could I?" she breathed. "What do you think I am, a monster? I must have been crazy with fear to do it in the first place, and then I had to know, don't you see? I had to *know* what I'd done to her. So… so I came back."

"How did you learn where Annette had been taken?"

"It wasn't hard. It just took some calling from a pay phone this morning, to find the right hospital, but they wouldn't give out any information. So I went there. I was afraid to call attention to myself by asking questions. I just sat where I could see and hear the people who came to the desk. Finally you came in and asked for her… Was she a good friend of yours?"

"Pretty good," I said.

"I… I'm sorry," Beverly said. "That's pretty feeble, isn't it? But I *am* sorry."

"Sure." I went to my suitcase, on a stand by the wall, and took out a small bottle of spot remover. Returning, I put it into her hands. "Use that," I said. "We don't want people thinking you've been rolling in the alley, even if you have." I examined her purse. It was one of those capacious, elaborately carved, but rather flimsy specimens of Mexican leather work you can buy quite cheaply in any of the border towns, say nearby Tijuana. I opened it. It contained no weapons. I gave it to her. "A little soap and water, and a comb are also indicated," I said.

She was staring at the purse and solvent bottle as if not quite certain what they were for. "What… what are you going to do with me?" she asked.

"We're going to see some people," I said. "As soon as you're presentable, I'll call a cab."

She ran her tongue over her lips and spoke mechanically, "We don't need a cab. I've still got the rental car, *her* rental car. It's parked a couple of blocks the other side of the hospital."

"Your friends could have found it by now," I said. "I hate loud noises when I turn on the ignition. Or steering wheels that don't steer or brakes that don't brake. That door over there should be the bathroom. It was a little while ago. If it isn't now, come back and we'll try again."

I watched her go across the room. The door shut behind her. I waited, making a little bet with myself. Presently the door opened again, and I chalked up one wager won.

Now the red-gold hair was smooth and bright and the face and hands were clean. The current condition of the clothes could not be determined from where I stood since she wasn't wearing them. I mean, all she had on was a white brassiere and a pair of little white nylon pants. The total coverage was about that of a bikini, but the opacity was considerably less.

"I… I'm waiting for that stuff to dry," she said, standing there more or less nude. "It burns if it gets on you."

"Sure," I said. "Burns."

"I don't suppose you want to make love to me," she said. "I don't suppose you even want to touch me. After what I did."

It was a rather neat twist in an otherwise rather predictable gambit. It was supposed to make me take her in my arms and tell her she wasn't so terrible after all, after which—considering her costume or lack of it—nature would undoubtedly take its predictable course. The only trouble was, I wasn't in a receptive mood and I don't like playing games with it unnecessarily. There are times in this racket when you've got to fake a lot of emotions, including passion, but I couldn't see that this was one of them. I just stood there without saying anything. At last Beverly flushed slightly, and shrugged her bare shoulders.

"Well, it's all I have to offer now," she said. "For saving my life. Unless you want fifty-seven dollars and some change."

"Cut it out. When I want to get paid, I'll send you a bill." I regarded her coldly and went on. "That cleaning fluid evaporates pretty fast. I think you can safely get dressed again. I'll call a cab."

She turned away sharply. She didn't exactly slam the bathroom door behind her, but it didn't close as gently as it might have. I grinned and went over to use the phone.

## 6

Charlotte Devlin, complete with car, driver, and prisoner, was waiting outside the address she'd given me—an address I figured didn't mean much to anybody or she wouldn't have disclosed it to an unsavory character like me. It was a run-down business block with a filling station on the corner. The public phone at the station was probably the main reason the place had been picked as a rendezvous. After all, I had asked her to do a little research for me.

I paid off the taxi driver and helped Beverly out of the vehicle. She seemed a bit startled, looking towards the other car, to see a woman awaiting us. My female associate got out and came to meet us. She looked Beverly up and down coldly during the introduction ceremony. It could have been professional wariness, but more likely, I thought, it was just tall Miss Devlin's normal way of regarding all smaller and prettier women.

"What now, Mr. Helm?" she asked.

Beverly had spotted the black man sitting in the car, guarded by the driver. She drew back against me fearfully, forgetting that she was mad at me. I pressed her arm in what I hoped was a reassuring way, holding her there.

"Have you got a place lined up for target practice?" I asked Charlotte Devlin.

She said, rather stiffly and disapprovingly, "Well, there's the pistol range we use, but I didn't think that was exactly what you had in mind, so I called around and learned that there are some deserted oil properties..."

"The pistol range will do fine, if the backstop will handle Magnum loads."

Charlotte raised her eyebrows, looking relieved and at the same time annoyed—relieved that what I was going to do, with her assistance, was innocent enough to be done at a public firing range, and annoyed that I'd let her believe, or at least suspect, otherwise. I was aware that McConnell, listening in the car, had shifted position slightly. I couldn't see him clearly enough to know whether or not he looked relieved, too.

I hoped he did. I'd wanted him more or less anticipating that I was either going to execute him or shoot his ears off to make him talk. As long as he was brooding about the tough time I might be giving him soon, he wouldn't be trying to figure out what other kind of shooting I might have in mind, and why.

Helping Beverly into the front seat, I said to the taller girl: "Incidentally, you'd better tell your wheelman that some evasive action may be indicated. That taxi turned up just a little too conveniently. I have a hunch it was planted on me, and I'd prefer not to have certain people know where we're going. They might start wondering about things I'd rather not have them wondering about, yet..."

It was a fairly long ride. The driver knew his stuff, however, and by the time we reached our destination there wasn't anybody behind us, but there had been. The driver got out to unlock a wire-mesh gate in a forbidding wire-mesh fence topped with barbed wire. Then he drove us past a shadowy building and spoke for the first time.

"We've got up to a hundred yards available here, Mr. Helm," he said. "What range do you want to shoot at?"

"Short," I said. "With silhouette targets if you've got them. I suppose there are lights."

"Sure, it's rigged for night firing." He drove a little farther and stopped the car. "Here you are. The beginners' range. We like to make it easy for them to hit something. It's good for the morale. Just a minute while I unlock the switchbox."

We sat there until the floodlights came on, illuminating the backstop, a high ridge of dirt out there, much too neat and level to have been formed by nature. The lights also picked out the roughly man-like and man-sized silhouettes lined up in front of the bank like two-dimensional soldiers at attention. I figured the range at twenty-five yards from the rearmost firing line, closest to the car; but the ground was also marked for shorter ranges.

I was glad to see that the firing points weren't covered. It wasn't raining, we needed no protection, and the .44

makes quite enough noise without having it bounced back at you from any kind of a roof.

"All right," I said. "Bring him along, Miss Devlin. Where's the cannon?"

She handed it to me over the back of the seat. Checking the loads once more as I got out of the car, I regarded the weapon without fondness. I've never really understood the fascination of these outsized, overpowering weapons; yet it seems you can't sell a gun these days if it hasn't got Magnum in the title. This was the second job I'd had recently involving this kind of hopped-up hardware.

Charlotte had backed out of the car, covering McConnell as he got out clumsily. We walked to the nearest firing point.

"I'm going to untie him in a minute," I said to the tall girl. "Keep him covered. He's a confessed murderer, remember. He's got nothing to lose. Don't hesitate to shoot if he gives you the slightest excuse."

She said stiffly, "I know my business, Mr. Helm. I hope you know yours."

This was her way of saying, I suppose, that she wondered what the hell we were doing here. Well, it was a good question. I hoped the answer would become clear shortly.

Having no spotting scope handy with which to check the targets, I walked down there and made sure there were no bullet holes in the one directly opposite, at least none that hadn't been covered with the patching tape they use—at better than a buck a crack for the target face alone, not to mention the backing, you can't throw away a whole silhouette every time somebody puts a few bullets through it. But these silhouettes must have been about ready for the discard or they wouldn't have been left out in the weather. Some of the patches were peeling off, but for my purpose it didn't matter greatly, and I went back to Lionel McConnell and untied him.

"How's the circulation?" I asked when his hands were free.

"All right," he said.

"That's fine," I said, "because you're going to show us just how you killed Annette O'Leary. She had two bullets in her. Say that's her down there, third target from the left. Your job is to put two slugs from this gun through the vital zone—if you can."

He studied me suspiciously, trying to guess what I had in mind. "Listen, man," he said, "you can't make me re-enact…"

"No," I said, "I can't *make* you. But I can call Mr. Warfel and tell him that I think he's pulling a fast one because I never knew a pug who could shoot for sour apples. I can tell him that you refused to demonstrate your marksmanship, so I've got to figure you don't really know a trigger from a cylinder crane. I can tell him that I'm mad at having such an obvious fall-guy wished off on me, and that I'm going to tear things apart until I find the gent who *really* shot our girl O'Leary…"

McConnell cut me off with a sharp gesture. He glanced towards the illuminated targets scornfully. "You just want me to hit that great big man-sized poster-thing down there with two shots, slow fire?" His voice was contemptuous. "At twenty-five yards, single action, no time limit, using sights and all? Hell, give me the gun!"

"I'll give it to you when you're ready to fire," I said. "And if it swings more than ten degrees out of line, either way, two .38 Specials will make hamburger of you. Okay?"

"Relax, man. I've confessed, haven't I? Why should I make trouble now?"

He rubbed his wrists, flexed his fingers, and stepped up to the line. Back of us, I could see the driver leaning against the car, watching. Beverly Blaine's small face was a white blur behind the windshield. McConnell scuffed his feet in the dirt and settled himself in position with his right shoulder towards the floodlighted target. I glanced at Charlotte, who nodded.

"Ready?" I said to McConnell.

"Ready."

Bringing out my own sawed-off little belly gun to cover him, I handed him the big revolver. He took it with his left hand and, in the manner of the experienced pistol shooter, fitted it carefully into his right hand—if you don't get hold of it exactly the same way every time, it won't shoot in the same place. Obviously, McConnell had used a one-hand gun before.

His thumb, I noticed, rested on the cylinder latch, high on the left side of the frame, braced against the recoil to come. That's fairly common target-shooting practice. I started to speak, but checked myself. McConnell cocked the big revolver, thrust it out level, and began to press the trigger gently as the sights lined up. Presently the Magnum fired.

Even in the open, it made a fearful racket. A long tongue of flame licked out down range. McConnell was shoved backwards by the recoil. His hand and arm kicked high, the big gun twisting violently in his grasp, almost escaping him. I grabbed the weapon from him. He took his right hand in his left and hugged it to him, making no sound but rocking back and forth a bit with pain.

"Let's see it," I said.

He gave me a hating look, and showed me the hand. The side of his thumb was bleeding, cut by the cylinder latch. The thumb joint, sprained by the kick of the .44, was already beginning to swell.

"You bastard," he said. "You honkie bastard!"

"Take it easy," I said. "What are you squawking about? I asked you if it was your gun and you said it was. Why should I tell you how to shoot it?" He glared at me and didn't speak. I said, "But you really ought to know better than to rest your thumb up there on the latch, *amigo*. That's all right with a .22, or maybe even a gentle little target .38, but with the heavy artillery you get your thumb the hell down out of the way of the recoil unless you want to lose it."

"I'll remember that," he said grimly. "I'll sure enough remember that now, man!"

"It's too late now," I said. "What's Warfel got on you, McConnell? What's he got that's strong enough to make you confess to committing murder—with a gun you obviously never fired before in your life?"

# 7

It was an anonymous kind of office in an anonymous kind of building, don't ask me where. I can find my way around Washington and New York, not to mention London, Paris, Stockholm, Oslo, Copenhagen, and East and West Berlin, but Los Angeles is an unexplored and unmapped wilderness as far as I'm concerned. Anybody who can figure out those freeways is wasting his time behind a steering wheel. With that kind of genius, he ought to be doing advanced research on space travel.

Anyway, it was the place to which Charlie Devlin—so help me, Charlie was what they called her around home base—had brought me after the firearms demonstration, when I asked to make a long-distance phone call. I thought it was damn nice of her. She could have taken me back to that filling station pay phone and made me call collect and supply my own dime. I had a hunch that her new, accommodating attitude was due, at least partly, to the fact that she felt she'd misjudged me: I hadn't shot up anybody after all.

"Yes, sir, it was a phony," I said into the telephone. "That's right, sir. Strictly a snow job for our benefit."

I looked across the desk at the black man and the red-haired girl watching me from the doorway. Charlie stood behind them, guarding them. I didn't feel the nickname really fit her—or maybe there was more to her than I'd been allowed to see. An arrogant, inhibited, self-righteous young lady who nevertheless allowed her colleagues to address her as Charlie just couldn't take herself as seriously as she seemed to. But Miss Devlin's character was strictly beside the point, at least for the moment.

"Yes, sir," I said. "Warfel must have got a scriptwriter over from Hollywood to do the screenplay. It was good typecasting, but the sinister pug-type didn't shoot Annette O'Leary and the heartless starlet-type didn't set her up for it, even though they were both eager to claim the glory. No, sir, I have no idea how Warfel got them to cooperate. They aren't saying. But guys like that have ways of applying pressure."

I watched the two faces as I said it. McConnell's features remained impassive, but Beverly's eyes widened and darkened a bit as if at a frightening memory.

"What was the tipoff? Well, no one thing exactly, sir, except that Warfel looked like a man putting on an act and overdoing it, casually inviting me to spill blood all over his bedroom carpet, for God's sake! And McConnell was willing enough to confess to murder—maybe a little too willing—but when he heard that the girl had been roughed up before she was shot, he was jolted just like any black man accused of manhandling a white girl would be. He hadn't expected that, and he wasn't braced for it... Just a minute, sir."

McConnell had taken an angry step forward. "You're just playing Sherlock Holmes, man!" he snapped. "What do you know about black men and white girls?"

I regarded him without affection. The name he had called me, back at the pistol range, didn't bother me greatly, but the attitude it illustrated did. I don't like people who think tolerance is a one-way street. If Mr. McConnell wanted his origins treated with respect by me, he could damn well treat mine the same way, and keep his loaded racial terms to himself.

"I don't know too much," I said, "but you did react, *amigo*, and you didn't know how to handle that big pistol that was supposed to be your pride and joy. You may have shot lots of people with other guns, but not with that one or anything like it, and that's what killed Annette O'Leary. Maybe I got the right answer for the wrong reasons, but I got it, didn't I?"

I waited. He was silent. The girl known locally as Charlie spoke a soft command and he stepped back into the doorway. I addressed myself to the telephone once more, watching Beverly as I talked.

"The Blaine girl clinched it, of course," I said. "They kept hinting at some mysterious female Annette had been mistaken for, but she was supposed to be a great big secret. I had a hunch, however, that if the whole performance was as phony as I'd begun to suspect, and if I gave them half a chance, they'd actually be happy to drop their red-haired mystery woman into my lap to support their fairy tale—which was exactly what they did, with melodramatic trimmings. Just how many times have we used the ancient gag of roughing up an agent to make him, or her, look good to the other side, sir? And how many times have we had it used on us? Well, chalk up one more occasion, for the record."

I looked at the girl and saw that she was tense, waiting for something. I could guess what it was. She was waiting for the humiliation of having me describe, in front of everybody, her abortive attempt at seduction.

I grinned at her, and went on: "Five will get you twenty, sir, that if we check back on her carefully, we'll find she was a ravishing blonde, or a sultry brunette, who couldn't possibly have been mistaken for our redhead or vice versa, until sometime this morning, many hours after the shooting… What about it, Miss Blaine?"

She hesitated. Then she nodded minutely. It was her way of thanking me for sparing her embarrassment, not that I really needed confirmation. Her hairdo had been just too pretty—too bright and soft and beautiful—for a girl who was supposed to have spent the past twenty-four hours on the run; her clothes too, if you discounted the minor damage incurred in the struggle staged for my benefit. For instance, nobody keeps a white turtleneck immaculate, particularly around the collar, for a hectic day and night in the City of Smog.

It had been a good idea, but Warfel or whoever had

thought it up had been careless about the details. Maybe he'd counted on the fact that when people confess to being involved with murder, the tendency is to accept their stories without too much skepticism.

I looked from the girl, silent, to McConnell, whose expression said he wasn't talking either. I said into the phone: "No, sir, they're not volunteering any information. Warfel's got them in his pocket. Anyway, there's not much chance he told them anything important. They probably don't know enough to make it worth offering asylum or protection or any other kind of a deal. They're just a couple of expendable red herrings... Yes, sir, I'll turn them loose as soon as I'm through here. Warfel may not like them very much, now that his elaborate scheme has flopped, but they'll just have to take their chances. As you say, it's not worth tangling with the mob for nothing. Organized crime is the F.B.I.'s business, not ours."

It didn't work. At least it didn't work immediately. The threat of being turned out on the street, unprotected against syndicate vengeance, didn't bring either of them rushing forward to trade valuable information in exchange for a safe place to stay. I nodded to Charlie Devlin, and she led them away. When the door had closed, I turned back to the phone.

"Okay, sir, I'm alone," I said. "I just wanted them to hear that much of the conversation. I hoped it might persuade them to give us a little help, but either they actually don't know anything worth telling, or Warfel scares them more than I do."

"So I gathered." Mac hesitated, far away on the other side of the continent, and asked with professional caution: "What is the status of your telephone?"

"Our friends assure me that the room and phone are safe as Fort Knox."

"Indeed? Such confidence is touching. But they do seem to be giving you adequate cooperation."

"Yes, sir," I said. "Reluctant but adequate."

"This Mr. Warfel apparently put on quite a show for you. Can you suggest a motive?"

"Yes, sir," I said, "but first I'd like to drop a few names and descriptions into the hopper. I presume you're already digging up what's known on Warfel himself—there should be plenty——but he had two tough gents in his immediate ménage when I saw him, one called Jake and the other nameless. There was also a lousy driver he called Willy, and a guy sitting in the lounge in my motel reading a paper. Then there's a slinky blonde called Roberta Prince, Warfel's current house pet. She's either a dancer or an acrobat or both. Also Lionel McConnell, known as Arthur Brown, known as The Basher; and of course the imitation redhead. And you might as well check out my lady colleague while you're at it, the girl they seem to have assigned to me here, Miss Charlotte Devlin, called Charlie for short…"

He pounced on that. "Do you suspect this Miss Devlin? Of what?"

"Of nothing, really," I said. "But the Blaine girl was kind of surprised to see her. Maybe she was just surprised at seeing a woman—that's what I figured at first—but maybe she had some reason for being surprised to see that particular woman. If so, I'd like to know why. Anyway, if I'm going to be working with Devlin, I'd kind of like to know what her record looks like. I mean, what can I count on her for and what can't I? And has she been doing any work recently that brought her in contact with the Warfel ménage? I mean, maybe her people had some reason for assigning her to me other than pure friendship and cooperation. Could they have an interest in Warfel that might conflict with ours?"

"That would be difficult to determine at this point, since we don't know exactly what our interest is," Mac said slowly. "Very well, I'll try to investigate, although it will be ticklish business. Give me what you have on the rest and I'll set the machinery in motion…" It took a little while for me to describe all the individuals concerned for the tape recorder some three thousand miles away. When I was through, Mac said, "Now what, exactly, are your ideas about Warfel?"

I said, "I figure he must have been trying to cover for the real murderer, who must be somebody important enough to give him orders or rich enough to hire him. I'm no expert on the operations of the syndicate, but I gather it's willing to cater to just about any human weakness. That presumably includes murder. If you happened to shoot somebody, and knew the right people in the right underworld circles, they might just furnish you with a fall guy or two if the price was right."

Mac said thoughtfully, "Of course, there's also the possibility that Warfel himself killed Ruby, or had her killed, and then offered up these sacrificial goats to protect himself."

"Maybe, but why would he kill her?"

"A man like that has many secrets. She could have stumbled onto one of them."

"A man like that keeps his secrets well hidden, sir, and they're generally secrets that wouldn't have interested our girl very much. If she'd stumbled onto one, she'd have minded her own business like a good little government girl, and refused to get involved unless... Is there any indication that Warfel might have political connections overseas? And I don't mean in Sicily or wherever it is so many of these rackets characters seem to originate."

"I see what you have in mind," Mac said slowly. "No, Mr. Warfel plays ball with the local politicians, of course, or they play ball with him, but there's been no hint of any other type of political activity. He's been investigated frequently and thoroughly by competent people who'd have been happy to pin something—anything—on him. No, the idea of Mr. Warfel as the agent of an unfriendly foreign power, or the accomplice of such an agent, is intriguing, Eric, but I'm afraid it's improbable."

"I disagree, sir," I said. "If he's not one, then he's covering up for one, although he may not know it. Our murderer's contact may be somebody higher in the organization. Warfel may simply have got a phone call telling him what to do, and maybe how to do it. He may not even know the name or business of the man he's shielding. If that's the case, I've got a very tough job ahead of me, tracking the guy I want through a forest of high-echelon racketeers."

Mac said, "This is highly theoretical, Eric. You have absolutely no proof—"

"Annette was killed, wasn't she? And a great effort was made to sell us a couple of phony murderers, presumably to take the heat off the real one. You're not thinking, sir. You're not thinking about our girl O'Leary, and what kind of a girl she was, and where she'd been before she came to us, and what frame of mind she was in when she landed in Los Angeles yesterday—well, I guess it's the day before yesterday by now. Of course, you didn't know her as well as I did, sir. All you've got to go on is a couple of interviews and some dry personnel records. I worked against her on one job down in Mexico, and with her on another, remember?"

We're not a buddy-buddy, call-me-Mac kind of outfit. He likes a certain amount of formality and protocol. I guess I'd let myself get carried away, a bit disrespectfully, because his voice was cool when he spoke again.

"And just what do you deduce from your superior knowledge of Ruby's character, Eric?"

I said, "What I'm remembering right now is three things. First of all, the girl was a pro—"

"I wouldn't go so far as to say that." Mac's voice was still rather stiff and severe. "Promising, yes, but she had by no means achieved true professionalism."

I said, "Okay, so she hadn't quite learned how to control her temper, if that's what you mean. But on the whole, when I worked with her, her reactions were pretty sound. She certainly wasn't afflicted with any overpowering, irresistible do-good impulses. Even if I hadn't already figured out that Beverly Blaine had to be lying, I'd have known it when she claimed to have sold Annette a sob story of some kind. The kid would never have fallen for anything like that. She was a pretty tough little cookie, and she wouldn't have stuck her neck out an inch…"

Mac interrupted. "That's more fine-sounding theory, Eric, but the fact is that she obviously did stick her neck out, somehow."

"You didn't let me finish, sir," I said. "I was going to say that she wouldn't have stuck her neck out an inch— *for anything that wasn't in the line of business*. Our business. She wouldn't have got herself involved with any weeping cuties with husband trouble, and if she'd seen a murder being committed, or a suitcase full of dope being smuggled—by Warfel or anybody else—she'd have looked the other way, like any of us would, like the rules require. She would have remembered the standing orders not to risk her effectiveness as an agent, by attracting attention either as the good Samaritan or the public-spirited citizen. To that extent, sir, I say she was a pro."

"Perhaps you're right. But there's still the possibility I suggested earlier, that she was a pro selling out."

"There wasn't time. I'll admit she might have been capable of it under the right circumstances, meaning if she was mad enough, but I think you'll agree that she wasn't a coldblooded traitor with her plans laid in advance. That means she came to L.A. without any prearranged contacts. It takes time to sell out, sir. You've got to find the right people. You've got to convince them of your sincerity. You've got to convince them you've got something worth buying—and then you've got to deliver your information, all of it. If somebody did get one of our people talking about our setup, even a novice agent, would they finish with her and dispose of her in less than a day? You know they wouldn't. They'd want to spend at least a week on thorough debriefing, going over every detail of our training and operations arrangements again and again until they were absolutely sure they'd pumped her dry."

Mac said, a little impatiently, "Very well. Assuming that she wasn't killed because she'd stumbled on some syndicate secrets, or because she'd got involved in a treason scheme that backfired, what do you suggest as a cause of her death?"

"I suggest she was trying to help us. I think what she saw, either on the plane or in the airport, was somebody in whom we're highly interested, somebody on the high-priority list perhaps…"

"Then why didn't she get on the phone and report it before taking action, as the normal procedure requires, particularly of inexperienced young agents in her category?"

"Because, as you point out, she wasn't quite professional enough, sir. Because she had a temper like dynamite and you'd just lit the fuse. Because she was mad at you and was going to show you up, by dealing with the situation herself in her own way. She was going to prove to you that initiative and daring were better than conformity and discipline, and to hell with normal procedure."

Mac said, rather reluctantly, "It's plausible. So your theory is that she spotted somebody important and tried to follow but was detected and killed."

"Yes, sir. Her attitude was professional enough, but her experience was still pretty limited. I think the guy she was tailing set a trap for her, caught her, and took care of her with his overgrown cannon, after first knocking her around just enough to learn that she was operating alone. And then, because his presence in Los Angeles—maybe even in the U.S.—was supposed to be a very hush subject indeed, he got hold of some local underworld talent and arranged for them to make it look as if she'd been killed by mistake, so we'd have no reason to investigate her motives and movements." There was a thoughtful silence. Presently I said, "That's the way I figure it, sir. She was pro enough not to get sidetracked on something that was none of our business, but she was amateur enough to try to handle it alone. There's also a third factor that might be important."

"What's that, Eric?"

"She'd recently been mixed up in a communist operation in this very area, remember? It could be that she ran into somebody she was in a special position to recognize, better than anybody else in our outfit. Remember the assignment on which I met her, sir. Remember the circumstances. Her husband had been killed in Vietnam. She'd blamed this country for sending him to his death, if you recall, and a fast-talking enemy agent—I never learned exactly who—had taken advantage of her resentment to persuade her to help with a fancy anti-U.S. plot they had going below the border in Mexico."

"I remember," Mac said. "What is your point?"

I said, "We broke up the conspiracy, all right, and got all the people immediately concerned, with the help of the Mexican authorities, but we didn't get the ones who'd pulled the strings from up here, north of the border. At least, if we did, I was never told about it."

"We didn't," Mac said.

"Afterwards, when I recruited Annette for that job working on our side—she was pretty disenchanted with the opposition by that time, and she had a Mexican prison staring her in the face—I didn't ask her too many questions. I was too busy telling her things she needed to know for the mission coming up. I just kept an eye on her until I was sure she could be trusted. Actually, knowing her low boiling point, I was careful not to antagonize her by probing into her past. I needed her cheerful and cooperative, and to hell with ancient history. But I presume that after our joint assignment was finished, and she was being considered for permanent employment, she was questioned pretty thoroughly—particularly about the people she'd known during her brief career as a subversive."

"That is correct," Mac said. "And you think she may have come across one of those people again?"

"Well, it would have given her a special reason for lone-wolfing it, sir. This was information only she had. This was a person only she could recognize. Even if she hadn't been mad at you, she'd have been reluctant to call in and let somebody else get the credit for nailing the guy. If you'd check her file—"

"I am checking it," Mac said. "I suppose I should have done it sooner, but I admit I was operating on a different theory... Here we are. She gave us two descriptions and a name. The name, she said, she'd heard only once, but she gathered it was that of the man in charge. You'll recognize it, Eric. We've come up against the gentleman before. The name she heard was Nicholas."

I grimaced. "That's nice. So we could be dealing with old man Santa Claus himself."

"Santa Claus?"

I said, "Just a joke, sir. He doesn't call himself that, as far as I know, but you know how some of our people tend to make up nicknames for members of the opposition, even those they haven't seen. Wait a minute. Nicholas is a man who likes heavy artillery, if I remember the dossier correctly. That fancy new computer should have given him to us by now, just from that angle."

"Unfortunately," Mac said dryly, "that fancy new computer has contracted some kind of electronic indigestion. I'm sending for Nicholas' file but I think you're quite right. As I recall, the lightest pistol he's on record as having used is a Browning 9mm High Power, no Magnum but still something of a handful. In another instance he left a .45 Colt Automatic beside a victim, that's no child's toy, either. Yes, a .44 would suit Nicholas very well, from what we know of his shooting habits."

"But Annette said she never saw him?"

"None of our people has seen him, or questioned anyone who has. So far, his cover has never been broken."

I said, "Then it couldn't have been Nicholas she spotted here in L.A. and tried to follow." I hesitated. "What about the two guys she actually met, the ones she described for you?"

"One was shot and killed by the Mexican police while resisting arrest after that Mazatlán affair. From what she said, I gather he was the one who recruited her in the first place. The other was just a man who drove a car in which she was transported to a rendezvous. He disappeared, like Nicholas himself—we've had no reports on either of them since. The description Annette gave us fits a small-time European motorcycle racer named Willi Keim—Willi, with an 'i'—who got into some trouble with the law and now specializes in driving chores for the opposition…"

"Willi!" I said. "Does he fit the description I just gave you, of the rock-jawed, potato-nosed character in the Ford wagon? Willy, with a 'y'?"

"I'm afraid I didn't monitor what you fed into the recorder. I planned to play it back later. Just a minute." I heard him find the right section of tape and run it through. "Yes. It could very well be the same man."

"My God!" I said. "I should have known nobody could drive that badly without working at it."

"Mr. Keim is apparently an expert at handling all kinds of wheeled machinery."

"And Annette would have recognized him. He's hard to miss. That could be our lead. Suppose Willi-Willy was still driving for Nicholas, either with or without Warfel's knowledge, probably with. Suppose Willy picked up Nicholas at the airport. Say Annette spotted a familiar face and watched to see who joined Willy and was caught doing it. Obviously, she had to be killed. She'd seen old Santa Claus in the flesh and she had enough of the background to know, or at least guess, what she'd seen. So Nicholas took care of the job, arranged for a syndicate cover-up, and had Willy on the spot to see how well it worked out."

"That could be the way it happened, certainly. If it should be Nicholas... Well, you know the standing orders. He is on the high-priority list. We've lost enough good men—and women—to Nicholas."

"Yes, sir."

"However, there's a lot of guesswork involved, Eric. Don't rely too heavily on this one theory."

"No, sir," I said, "but assuming we're on the right track, the big question now is: just what brings Nicholas back to these parts? It must be something fairly important or his superiors wouldn't take the risk of returning him to the scene of a job that flopped as badly as that Mexican operation of his. A lot of underlings were caught and they must know that one might put a finger on their boy somehow—as Annette did. Do we know of anything big brewing down here, big enough to call for a man of Nicholas' talents?"

"No," Mac said, "we don't know, and we don't really care, Eric. Don't let your curiosity get the better of you. Remember that intelligence is the business of other departments. Your job is Nicholas, and whoever killed Ruby, if they are not the same person. Take care of that. If you happen to learn anything interesting in the process, by all means pass it along, but don't let it distract you from your primary mission…"

## 8

As a bodyguard, I was a bust. They took out the black man right under my nose.

I'd been waiting a little ways up the street outside the office when Devlin's people finally turned him loose with the Blaine girl, the way we'd planned it. I'd watched him say good-bye to her politely and assist her into the first to arrive of the two taxis that had been ordered at their request. He'd taken the second, which came along, with standard L.A. punctuality, some fifteen minutes later. I'd tailed him in the rental sedan Charlie herself had promoted for me—apparently her newborn spirit of cooperation didn't extend to furnishing me with company wheels—but he'd stayed with the taxi less than half a dozen blocks.

I didn't think he'd reached his destination, when the cab swung to the curb. I figured he knew, or suspected, that he was being followed, and was about to play some tricks. I pulled into a parking space half a block away, cut my lights, and waited. It wasn't a subtle, high-class, invisible job of surveillance, but I had little hope of staying with him in any case, and none at all if I got cute. He knew me by sight; he probably knew I was there; and it was his city, not mine.

But it had seemed like something that should be tried, both for his sake and for mine. Watching over him, I might be able to save his life, although it wasn't likely— as a matter of fact, I didn't really think Warfel would be fool enough to strike at either McConnell or the girl, despite what I'd said for effect back in the office. Still, if he were attacked, and saved, McConnell might talk, if he had anything to talk about. And even if nobody made a hostile move towards him, he might lead me to something or somebody significant, although I didn't really have much hope of it.

But it was a possible opening, and I didn't have so many I could ignore one, and the others were being covered. I watched the cab pull away. McConnell stood for a moment at the curb, at last putting on the jacket he'd carried around with him all night. He turned and walked straight at me.

There had been, of course, a certain probability that he'd proceed in my direction rather than moving away from me, or ducking into a nearby building, or darting across the street. There were only so many ways he could go. However, I saw from his manner that this had nothing to do with statistical probabilities. He knew where I was parked and he was coming to me, maybe to tell me something important, maybe just to give me hell for shadowing him, probably the latter.

Abruptly he stopped, looking beyond me. There were headlights in my mirrors, coming up fast. McConnell turned to run. I reached over, hit the door handle on the curb side, dove to the sidewalk, rolled, and came up with a gun in my hand, but it was too late.

There were two of them, in one of those fat-tired, souped-up, fast-back little sport coupes, complete with fake racing stripes, that are America's current answer to the true European sports car. You may like them or you may not—I don't, particularly—but you've got to admit that not much can beat them for sheer acceleration. Some of them even have pretty good brakes nowadays, a real innovation for Detroit.

The coupe shot past as I was picking myself off the sidewalk, and slowed sharply beyond me. I saw a short shotgun barrel thrust out the right-hand window. It flamed twice in the night and McConnell fell; then the rub-out men were getting out of there with shrieking tires and snarling exhausts, and I still hadn't had a clear shot at them.

Punching holes in automobiles isn't exactly what the standard short-barreled .38 Special does best. There's something to be said for the big guns after all, and I'd pulled out the .44 I was still lugging around since nobody else seemed to want it. The coupe was receding fast. I cocked the massive revolver as I thrust it out two-handed, and I let it fire when the front sight blade steadied on the left half of the slanting rear window.

Even with two hands gripping it hard, the cannon kicked so hard you wouldn't believe it. The coupe swerved violently across the street and plowed into the parked cars there. After a moment, the right-hand door opened and the shotgunner staggered out, still clutching his weapon, a semi-automatic job that would hold at least three shells, probably more. What I mean is, even if he hadn't managed, to reload, he probably had ammunition left.

I saw no reason why he should get any breaks from me, and shotguns scare hell out of me anyway, so I didn't wait for him to swing the weapon towards me. I just knocked him over while he was still looking for a target. The heavy .44 slug chopped him down like a tree. I waited, but he didn't move, and neither did the driver of the car, as far as I could make out through the damaged rear glass.

My hands were tingling from the kick of the Magnum, and my ears were ringing from the noise, but part of my mind, aloof from the uproar and excitement, reminded me gently that people had been firing that gun, off and on, for a couple of days now, and there couldn't be much left in it—just one live round, if my count was correct. I drew out the fully loaded .38 as reserve artillery and moved up to McConnell, feeling stupid and frustrated standing there, with a pistol in each hand, and the man I was supposed to protect bleeding on the sidewalk at my feet.

The only excuse I could think of was that protection isn't really my racket, quite the contrary. Besides, I hadn't really believed protection would be required here, which only proved that when you tried to second-guess the opposition you generally wound up guessing wrong. I knelt beside the man on the sidewalk, putting my hand on his shoulder. He stirred almost imperceptibly.

"Easy there," he breathed, face down on the concrete. "Don't move me or I'll fall apart. Who…?"

"It's the honkie bastard," I said.

He was silent for a moment; then he whispered, "Jeez, a sensitive whitey! What do you want, apologies? Did I hear some more shooting? If you got them, I'll apologize."

"I got them. A little late, but I got them."

"In that case, I'm extremely sorry I used a bad word on you, Mr. Helm, sir. Can you ever forgive me?"

"Go to hell," I said. "I'm going to stick the gun in your hand, if you don't mind. Save me a lot of trouble with the police. Unless you have objections. Tell me if you have. They'll also pin the O'Leary murder on you when they check out the rifling in ballistics, but you don't mind that, since you've already put your brand on that one. Do you?"

"Hell, no. Any homicides you got lying around. Proud to take the credit, posthumously. Fine word, posthumously. Didn't know I knew words like that, did you?" After a moment, when I didn't speak, he went on chidingly: "You're supposed to tell me I'm going to be all right, man. Aren't you going to lie and tell me I'm going to be all right?"

I said, "If I thought you were going to be all right, I wouldn't leave you holding the baby."

He gave a little sound that was half a sigh, half a

cautious chuckle. "Yeah, we both know buckshot, don't we? From the way, it feels, he must have put almost the whole load of shot into me, both times... Okay, give it to me."

I wiped off the .44 Magnum and put it where he could grasp it. His hand closed on it, sprained thumb and all. We still had the sidewalk, and even the street, to ourselves. Shots had been fired, a car had crashed, but nobody in Los Angeles gave a damn. Well, that was all right with me.

"Do you know anything I ought to know, McConnell?" I asked.

"I don't know anything. That's what I was coming back to tell you, that you were wasting your time tailing me. You know how it is. You know how they are. You get mixed up with them, you do what they tell you. You don't ask questions."

"How did Warfel persuade you to take the rap for Annette O'Leary's murder?"

"Persuade!" he breathed. "Well, you can call it that. There's my wife, Lorraine. There are our two boys, four and six. Hostages to fortune, somebody once said. Fortune, hell. Hostages to Frank Warfel. Of course, he promised to have a good lawyer on the job, when I came to trial." There was a little silence; then McConnell said, "See what you can do for Lorraine and the kids, will you?"

"Where do I find them?" I memorized the address he gave me, and asked, "What about the girl, Beverly Blaine. What did he have on her?"

"Look at her left arm. Warfel gave her a little taste of

acid, and I don't mean LSD. He told her, if a couple of drops will do that to your arm, just think what a pint of it will do to your pretty face… McConnell's voice trailed off. He was silent, breathing shallowly. "You'd better beat it, Helm," he whispered at last. "Don't hang around on my account. Doesn't feel like I'll be around much longer, myself."

I looked down at him for a moment longer. It still seemed like a peculiar thing to do to your hair, for peculiar reasons. I mean, I've never felt any particular urge to assume the shoulder-length locks, horned helmet, chain mail shirt, and battle ax of my Viking ancestors. Well, it was his hair, and his business.

"Okay," I said. "Sorry I wasn't more help."

"So long, secret-agent-man. Don't forget about Lorraine and the boys."

"I won't forget."

There were sirens in the distance now. Apparently, some Los Angeleno had overcome his distaste for involvement long enough to pick up a telephone. Well, it saved me from having to call the police and ambulance, not that I thought an ambulance would do much good. Buckshot is generally for keeps.

I hurried back to the rental car and drove off, passing the wreck and the man with the shotgun lying face up beside it. He was, I saw, the nameless man who'd been standing guard in the room with McConnell up in Warfel's apartment, one of those I'd asked Mac to check on. Well, it still wouldn't hurt to identify him, as well as the one behind the wheel. You hate to get so casual you go around shooting people without bothering to learn their names.

I made it out of sight before the police arrived, and kept going until I was well away from the area. Then I ditched the car and walked half a dozen blocks until I found a phone booth near a filling station that was closed for the night—well, booth is too strong a word for it. The phone company no longer provides its clientele with shelter and privacy. You stand out in the smog and fog and tell your business to anybody hanging around. There's a little plastic box to protect the instrument; the customers can damn well protect themselves.

As you will gather, the weather had closed in once more. The heavy, damp air had a nasty, chemical, ozony tang to it that made my nose run and my eyes water. I called the number Charlie Devlin had given me and asked to be put in touch with her, if possible. This led to all kinds of security-oriented complications, but finally I got a guy who seemed to know something. At least he seemed to know who I was and who Miss Devlin was. He was even willing to stick his neck way out and admit it.

I said, "I just lost my subject, permanently. Two men in a hopped-up Camaro. Twelve-gauge auto-loading shotgun stuffed full of buck, very effective."

"What color car? Did you get the license number? Can you describe either of the men?"

I said, "Cut it out. I'm slow but not that slow. Check with the cops. They were heading that way as I pulled out. I'm sure they'll let you look at the wreck and view the remains in the morgue and make up your own descriptions. One of the men was taking orders from Frank Warfel when I saw him previously, if it matters. I set it up more or less to look as if the black man avenged himself before he keeled over. If you've got any local influence, you might pass a hint to the authorities to let it stand that way, officially, and save us all a lot of trouble. And I made the guy a kind of promise, so would you please put a guard on his family, or take them into protective custody, or something, until the smoke clears. Mrs. Lorraine McConnell…"

"I'm afraid we're not authorized… Oh, to hell with it. Have you got the address?"

I gave it to him. "But first you'd better get in touch with Charlie Devlin, if you can, and tell her what's happened. I don't see what Warfel's so worried about, sending his boys rushing out to silence them, but if he was after McConnell he's almost bound to be after Blaine. At least we'd better operate on that assumption. Charlie'd better keep her eyes open wider than I did, if she wants to keep our phony redhead alive a little longer." The man at the other end of the line didn't respond immediately. I asked, "What's the matter? Don't tell me they've already taken care of Blaine."

"No," he said slowly, "not as far as we know, but we just got a call from Charlie. She's at an all-night garage south of town. A guy in a jeep ran her off the freeway about half an hour ago, while she was tailing Miss Blaine. It must have been just about the time you were having your troubles. I would say their timing was pretty good, wouldn't you, Mr. Helm?"

## 9

Tall, tailored Charlie Devlin had got some mud on her shoes. Otherwise she seemed undamaged by her accident, except that her nose was kind of pink around the edges. She kept dabbing at it with a wad of tissue clutched in her fist.

"No, I didn't hit my nose!" she said irritably. "It's just this damn smog; I've got some kind of an allergy... And don't stand there looking so damn superior, damn you! You haven't done so well, either, from what I hear over the phone. At least my subject wasn't shot down in the street right in front of me."

She started to rest her hand on a nearby workbench, but changed her mind when she saw how greasy it was. The garage was a shabby, unpainted, badly lighted cinder-block building on the small service road that ran parallel to the freeway. From outside came the steady roar of fast night traffic heading from Los Angeles to San Diego and vice versa. At the other side of the garage, an elderly mechanic in greasy coveralls was investigating the beat-up front suspension of the big, dark blue, Ford station wagon on the hoist, with the reproving attitude of a surgeon examining a compound fracture: people really shouldn't do such things to themselves, or their cars.

"You've got a point," I said to the girl beside me, "but I wouldn't lean on it too hard if I were you. Not until we find the ersatz redhead. Alive."

Charlie sighed. "I know. I didn't really mean..."

"What happened?"

"Oh, I just goofed, that's all," she said wryly. "The visibility was terrible—well, you just came down the freeway yourself, you know how it is up there. I guess I was so busy trying to keep track of the girl's car in the mist, in all that traffic, without tipping her off that she was being followed, that I didn't check my mirrors the way I should have. All of a sudden, there he was with his damn jeep, cutting right in on me. I was out in the mud and rocks of the construction zone before I knew it. I thought I'd torn the whole car to pieces, the way it handled when I finally got it backed out of there, but the old man says it looks as if I just bent up the front end a bit." She hesitated, and glanced at me. "Did McConnell tell you anything useful before he died?"

I shook my head. "He said he didn't know anything."

"Then why would Warfel have him killed?"

"That," I said, "is a damn good question. Of course, he may have known more than he knew he knew, if you know what I mean, but he's not going to remember it for us now, whatever it was. Which makes the girl fairly important. She had even more opportunities for observation than the hired help. She admitted she'd seen and heard a few things as Warfel's girlfriend, if that part of her story was straight...

"It was. He's been paying the rent on her apartment for a couple of years."

"Then she's even more likely than McConnell to have been exposed to some significant piece of information, whether she knows what it is or not... Hell, *somewhere* there's got to be a connection between that two-bit hoodlum and somebody really dangerous!" I went on, making the question very casual, like an afterthought: "How did you know Warfel had been paying the Blaine girl's rent?"

She glanced at me, and said smoothly, "After all, this is our territory, Mr. Helm. We try to keep track of the people in it, particularly those with whom we may someday be professionally concerned..."

I said, "Cut it out, Charlie-girl."

"What's the matter?" She tried to make her tone very innocent, but she didn't succeed very well.

"Not someday," I said. "You're professionally concerned with Warfel and company right now."

"Well," she said, "well, of course, since we're working with you on this business..."

I shook my head. "You were working on Warfel before I ever came on the scene, sweetheart. It's the only answer that makes sense. His girl did a double take when she saw you; she knew who you were. And we were very careful to shake our shadow when we went out to that pistol range of yours, but we were picked up again immediately when we got back to your office..."

"What makes you think so?" She was stubbornly ignoring the obvious because she didn't want to confess to the truth.

I said patiently, "Because, doll, there was a driver and shotgunner waiting for me outside, and a jeep jockey waiting for you. Remember? Now, how did all those people of Warfel's know where to find us again after we'd given them the slip? They knew—they had to know—because they knew you, Miss Devlin; and they figured you'd bring us all back to your home base, as you did. *And* they knew where it was. And why did they know all that? Because people like Frank Warfel make a point of knowing who's trying to get something on them. They can't keep track of every agent employed by the U.S. government, but they can sure spot the ones who are currently snooping around, like you've apparently been doing. Haven't you?" She didn't answer, but she didn't have to. I said, "That's why you were chosen to 'help' me when my boss asked your outfit to give me a hand; and why you weren't very happy about it. Wasn't it? I was poaching on your Warfel territory and you were afraid I might louse things up for you. Am I right?"

She drew a long breath. "Maybe. If so, do you mind?"

"Not a bit, as long as your business doesn't interfere with my business."

She hesitated. "What about your business interfering with mine, Mr. Helm?"

"Such as how?"

"We want to get the goods on Warfel. Legally."

"How far have you got?"

"Not very far as yet, but sooner or later he'll make a mistake, and we'll catch him at it." She paused once more. When she continued, her voice was kind of harsh and challenging: "And we don't want some trigger-happy super-spook shooting him down for vengeance purposes so he can't stand trial! We want to make a public example of Mr. Frankie-boy Warfel, not a martyr!"

I ignored the final half of what she'd said, and asked, "At what?"

"I… I don't understand," she said, disconcerted. "At what are you planning to catch Mr. Warfel?"

"At… well, at anything illegal. Just let him spit on the sidewalk in front of witnesses… Why are you shaking your head like that?"

I waited while the elderly mechanic went into a spasm of frantic hammering. When relative silence descended once more, I said, "It won't do, Charlie. You're not the lady gangbuster type."

"Well," she said, "well, I try not to be, of course. Just as you try not to look too much like—"

"Like a trigger-happy super-spook?"

She had the grace to flush slightly. "I didn't really mean—"

"The hell you didn't," I said. "But don't try to convince

me you want to bust Frank Warfel just because he's Frank Warfel. You reek of high moral purpose, sweetheart. There's some peculiarly atrocious crime you're concerned with, not just jailing one racketeer because he's a racketeer."

She drew in her breath sharply. "You have no right to make fun of—"

"And you have no right to hold out on me," I said. "You're supposed to be helping me, not obstructing me. Okay, start helping by telling me what Frankie's been up to that's so naughty that you get that holy, dedicated look in your eyes when you speak of making an example of him."

"Damn you, Helm—"

She stopped while the phone rang in the tiny corner office, and the mechanic walked past us to take the call, wiping his hands on a greasy rag. When he'd finished talking, and returned to the car on the hoist, I looked grimly at my female companion.

"All right, let's do it the hard way," I said. "Let's use the old word-association technique. I've been reading your West Coast news the last day or so. Maybe there's been something in the papers that relates to our problem." I stared at her so intently that she squirmed. It was just part of the act, of course. I had a pretty good idea of the answer I wanted already; but I wanted to get it from her so we could talk about it rationally. I said, "What about mud slides, earthquakes—"

"You're being ridiculous!"

I watched her eyes. "Smog," I said, "drugs, missing scientists—"

"What missing scientists?" she demanded quickly.

"Actually, just one that I know of," I said. "A Dr. Osbert Sorenson, meteorologist at UCLA, who recently turned up vanished, according to last night's Los Angeles paper."

"Sorenson? Isn't he the crackpot who wants to abolish the automobile?"

"One of them. And his associates in the Anti-Internal-Combustion-League, or whatever they call it, seem to think the big car manufacturers did him in, to stop him, Would that have anything to do with your Warfel problem?"

"Why, that's just silly!" she said. "What could Frank Warfel possibly have to do with a crazy program like that? And can you really imagine General Motors—"

"No," I said, permitting myself a grin, "not really, and neither can I imagine you giving a damn about Dr. Osbert Sorenson, lost or found. He's just a red herring, isn't he? The word that made your eyelids wiggle, just a little, was the obvious one: drugs." I sighed. "Well, I figured it would be. It had to be, to explain your semi-religious fervor. There's something about dope that seems to arouse the fanatic in a lot of people, including some supposedly sane and objective law-enforcement characters."

She said sharply, "How can *anybody* be objective about a traffic as filthy and degrading as…"

She stopped, realizing that I'd been needling her deliberately to get her to betray herself. Angry, she started to speak once more, but checked herself. We faced each other for a long moment.

I said, "For a dope cop, you've got a mighty thin

skin, doll. What are you people, anyway, some special agency helping out the Customs and Treasury boys?" She remained silent. It was really none of my business, so I went on: "Well, never mind... So Frankie's been playing around with drugs, has he? I thought the syndicate had made a big point of getting out of that racket. I thought they'd decided it brought them more trouble and adverse publicity than the profits justified."

"That's what they said, but we don't have to believe they meant it. Certainly their boy Warfel doesn't seem to!" Charlie drew a long breath. "Oh, all right. I suppose there's really no reason I shouldn't tell you about it. You've heard of Operation Guillotine, I suppose."

"Sorry," I said. "I can't keep track of all the fancy code names. What's this one supposed to signify?"

"A guillotine is a machine for severing the head from the body, isn't it? Well, that's what we're going to do with this dirty business! We're going to separate the great, sprawling, ugly bodies of foreign dope production from the greedy, profit-seeking heads—the importers and distributors—in this country. And one of the heads we're going to chop off is Frank Warfel, to show that even the all-powerful syndicate can't get away with flooding. this nation with insidious poison... What are you grinning at *now*, Mr. Helm?"

"Sweetheart, I'm a pro, remember?" I said. "You don't have to beat me over the head with all the propaganda clichés. Okay, it's a filthy and degrading traffic in insidious poison, but let's just try to consider it calmly, like an ordinary racket, like protection or extortion or white slavery. How about it?"

She said severely, "You seem to think it's something to joke about! Do you think it's humorous that we're trying to protect innocent people from—"

"From their own bad habits?" I said deliberately. "Hell, no. I think it's serious as hell: protecting kids from the evils of marihuana by subjecting them to the evils of jail. Of course, it's rather like protecting the baby from colic by administering a massive dose of strychnine, but I agree there's nothing funny about it."

She started to react, instantly and indignantly. She was so easy to tease it was hardly sporting. I held up a hand, quickly, to check the impending outburst of righteousness.

"Okay, okay, simmer down," I said. "I'm just needling you again, Charlie. I'm sorry. I apologize. The drug traffic is a dreadful thing, and I'm glad we have fine people like you fighting against it. Now tell me all about Frank Warfel's connection with it."

She disregarded my request, and said stiffly: "I see absolutely no justification for your sarcasm, Mr. Helm, or your air of tolerant superiority. Unless you're one of the misguided people who think—"

"Who think a joint of grass is no worse than a dry martini?" I shrugged. "Hell, I don't know a thing about it. I'm a martini man myself. I've never tried the other stuff. Honest Dope-wise, I'm pure as a mountain spring—well, as a mountain spring used to be." I drew a long breath. "Look, Charlie, you've got your hangups and I've got mine, one of which is that I feel strangely compelled to discourage people from shooting at me or my colleagues in a fatal sort of way. And even if I didn't feel that way, my boss does, and he's the boss. Since Frank Warfel is involved in the current incident of this kind, could we please discuss him dispassionately just for a minute."

The mechanic went back to work again with his little hammer, and for a minute or two conversation was impossible.

When we could hear again, Charlie said stiffly, "You've referred to marihuana, Mr. Helm, as if nothing else was ever smuggled across the Mexican border, but Frank Warfel isn't interested in that weed. There's not enough profit in it, and the amateur competition is too great. Every long-haired hippie who manages to get into Mexico tries to come back with a car full of pot."

I couldn't help a quick glance at her crisp, clipped hair, realizing now that it was an anti-revolutionary symbol: as long as the unwashed, protesting, drug-absorbing young wore their hair long, she'd wear hers short.

"What's Frankie's bag, then?" I asked. "Coke or heroin?"

"The coca leaf grows only in South America, Mr. Helm," she said rather pedantically. "Frankie would want his source closer at hand. The opium poppy, on the other hand, grows quite well in Mexico. That's where the gum comes from. The Chinese opium addicts use it straight, or did before they were corrupted by Western bad habits, but most other users prefer to get their kicks in more concentrated form. Extracting the morphine base from the gum is a fairly simple process; the catch is refining the base into high-grade heroin. The Mexican product has traditionally been pretty poor. They haven't had the technicians or the equipment, so they haven't been able to compete with the pure stuff refined in Europe. It takes a real chemist with good laboratory facilities—"

"A real chemist?" I said, frowning. "I don't suppose a meteorologist would have an adequate chemical background."

Charlie frowned at the interruption. "You've got a fixation on this missing Sorenson man, haven't you? Or do you know something about him you haven't told me?"

"Not a thing," I said honestly. Then I grimaced, and said, a little embarrassed: "Hell, Charlie, I'm a hunch player. Most agents are. I got vibrations when I read that squib in the paper. Humor me and check on Sorenson's scientific training when you get a chance, will you?"

She wasn't impressed. "Well, if you think it's important," she said negligently. "Anyway, the border traffic in hard drugs has been relatively unorganized in this area, but we have reason to think Frank Warfel intends to change all that. There are indications that he's trying to set up a smuggling route between some place here in southern California, and some below the border down along the Baja coast, probably in the neighborhood of Ensenada. Hundreds of pleasure boats wander between U.S. and Mexican waters on a good summer weekend; nobody can really check them all."

"Has he got a boat of his own?" I asked. "He didn't look like a yachting type to me."

"That's more or less what put us onto it," she said. "He bought a yachting cap and a big seagoing motorsailer a couple of years ago and started getting very nautical indeed. Since then he's been running down to the Ensenada area quite frequently. Ostensibly it's just a matter of booze and broads, if you know what I mean—the shipboard parties get pretty noisy sometimes. We have a hunch some of that noise is generated for public consumption, so to speak, and the parties have actually been a cover for some trial runs. Naturally, we've left him strictly alone so far. We've been trying to determine just how many boats besides the *Fleetwind* are involved; and where the actual southern terminus is located."

"So you've got the probable route pinned down," I said. "Have you any line on the laboratory, and the source of supply?"

"The source is easy, and at the same time impossible," she said wryly. "What I mean is, there are hundreds, maybe thousands, of Mexican farmers back in the hills growing the poppies on a small scale. There are dozens, maybe hundreds, of independent collectors buying the gum from them and boiling it up to get the morphine base, which they'll sell to anyone who'll pay the going price—"

She had to stop as the elderly gent in coveralls passed us once more, heading for a grimy door next to the office, presumably the john.

"It would take the Mexican Army to make an impression at that end," Charlie said when the old man was back on the job once more. "As a matter of fact, the crackdown by our brother agencies along the border has kind of jogged them into taking a little action: burning a few fields and arresting a few peasants. It won't last, of course; it never does; but it's the best we can hope for right now. The laboratory is a different matter. Frankie has got to set up a good one somewhere, if he wants to market a high-class product. We think he must have it just about ready to go."

"Have you any idea where?"

She moved her shoulders half-helplessly. "Not really, except that it will undoubtedly be in Mexico. The surveillance problems are smaller there; besides, the refined heroin takes up less room than the morphine base and is easier to smuggle. We figure it's either in Ensenada or between there and the border, but Frankie's been very careful on his south-of-the-border cruises and we've had to do our watching from a distance so as not to tip him off. Once we locate the lab, we can get the Mexican authorities to close it down for us—but of course we don't really want that to happen until the timing is just right. We want to be certain that the place is in actual production, and that Frankie himself has taken delivery of a few kilos and brought them up here, where we'll be waiting."

"What makes you think he'll handle the smuggling himself?" I asked. "Most of those big boys make a point of keeping their hands clean of everything connected with drugs except the money."

"Frankie's got a problem," she said. "The syndicate *does* frown on the dope trade these days, officially, for public relations motives. That means that Frankie's got to keep his activities secret not only from us, but from his Mafia associates and superiors as well. I don't think he'll trust any underlings to handle the first few shipments. He'll take as few syndicate people into his confidence as possible until he's got things running smoothly and profitably."

"It sounds reasonable," I said. "But you're going to a hell of a lot of trouble, it seems to me, to catch just one man with a few pounds of happy-dust."

She hesitated. "You don't understand; it's not just one man we're concerned with. At present, the syndicate is more or less out of the drug business, except for a few greedy, rebellious individuals like Frank Warfel. Right now, Frankie's superiors would certainly crack down on him if they knew he was planning to involve the organization in a risky gamble with dope. But suppose he manages to hold them off until he can show them a smoothly functioning gold mine from which they can all profit? In that case, they'll be much less likely to chastise him, won't they? They may even be tempted to change their official policy once more. And even if they don't, they may find more and more backsliders like Frankie defying their edict—"

"Actually, from what little I know about them, I gather the various families don't really have much authority over each other."

"That's right." Charlie looked at me almost pleadingly. "You see how important it is, Matt? You see that it's got to take precedence over your quest for vengeance. I mean, thousands of lives will be ruined by drugs if Frankie succeeds; or if… if somebody kills him so we can't catch him red-handed and make such a big public stink that his Cosa Nostra friends will continue to stay out of the drug business, permanently."

Well, she had a point. I might kid her about the strange legal logic that tries to cure an addict by making a criminal of him, but I hold no brief for anyone who tries to cash in on his addiction.

I said, "Well, to the best of my knowledge, I'm not really after Frank Warfel."

"Perhaps not. But judging by your record, which I've read with great interest—the parts we were able to obtain—you certainly wouldn't hesitate to shoot him if he got in your way. And that mustn't happen." She drew a long breath. "Look, I'll make a bargain with you. You leave us our Frankie and we'll do our best to get you your Nicholas. Okay?"

I said, "Some bargain. You've got instructions to assist me. I've got no instructions to assist you—" It hit me belatedly, and I stopped and stared hard at her. "Just what do you know about Nicholas, sweetheart? As far as we know, he's never been connected with dope, so where did you get the name?"

She looked down, clearly embarrassed. "Well, I… I just heard something…"

"Heard?" I said grimly. "Oh, I see. Over the phone." After a moment, I couldn't help grinning. "Charlie, I'm surprised and shocked at you, eavesdropping like that. And there I thought you were being so kind and cooperative, saving me from wearing out my dime in a public booth."

She said without meeting my eyes, "All our phones are monitored, naturally."

"Oh, naturally."

"You asked your chief to check up on me. I heard you. Did you think I wouldn't check up on you?" She forced herself to look at me defiantly. "Do we have a deal, Matt? Frankie for Nicholas and whoever else was involved in killing your girl—as long as it isn't Frankie."

I said, "Hell, I'm not a homicidal maniac, doll, whatever you may have read in my record. If it *is* Frankie, and you put him away on drug charges, that'll serve our purpose just as well as shooting him. It's a deal." I held out my hand and she shook it. "Okay," I said, "that's settled. Now you'd better give me some license numbers and descriptions. Did you recognize the man who ran you off the road?"

"Yes, it was the ugly one who was driving you around earlier in that beat-up old station wagon."

"Willi Keim?"

"Willy Hansen is the name we know him by."

"What model jeep?"

"It wasn't the little Universal, but the longer one, kind of fancy, they call a Jeepster. White. California plates." She gave me the number.

"And Blame's wheels?"

"A sporty convertible, gold with a black top, that she

picked up at the airport. She had the top up, of course, in this weather. One of the Pontiacs. I can't remember all the jazzy names. A Firebird?" She gave me that number, too, and said a little warily: "You sound as if you were planning to take off after her by yourself and leave me here."

"That's right," I said. "Somebody's got to keep in touch with home base, in case the police report a bad accident involving a gold convertible, or a dead redheaded female body, or something. And you were going to do some research on Sorenson, remember? I'll head south and check back with you. Have you got anybody at the border to see who goes through?"

"We've always got somebody at the border to see who goes through, Mr. Helm. And in answer to your next question, yes, they've been alerted and given all available information. But they can't take action without bringing in the police officially; that's not their job."

I regarded her for a moment. I would have been happy to trade her for a certain tough, unscrupulous, hot-tempered, redheaded little girl with whom I'd once worked, but that girl was dead. What I had to back me up now was a lady dope cop with ideals, and in this business nothing will kill you faster or deader than ideals. It wasn't a happy thought.

"No," I said, "it's my job, Charlie. And yours."

## 10

When I came outside, the mist was just as thick as it had been, or a little thicker, and it smelled just as bad, or a little worse. I went over to the new rental car that had been brought to me by Devlin's people after I'd explained to the guy on the phone that I'd ditched the other one, because somebody might have seen the license plate at the scene of the shooting and mentioned it to the police. He'd promised to deal with the problem, if it turned out to be a problem.

I'd already driven the replacement far enough to know that it was never going to become my favorite vehicle: a commuter's special with too many power gadgets and too little character. It had one of those space-age names—Satellite—that they like to give to cars nowadays when they're not naming them after animals, birds, or poisonous reptiles.

Getting into the shiny sedan, I heard a siren on the freeway and saw an ambulance go by up there, heading

for Los Angeles. It was the third such emergency vehicle
I'd encountered since starting south. Well, it was a bad
night for driving. There was bound to be some breakage.
With that thought, I slid behind the wheel, swung the car
around jerkily—a sports car man at heart, I'm not at my
best with automatic transmissions and power brakes—
and headed for the nearest on-ramp to join the fun.

Southern California drivers are a courageous lot. You
might even call them reckless—perhaps life has lost its
meaning down there without real air to breathe. By the
time I'd raced that headlong, suicidal traffic through the
gradually lessening fog to the outskirts of San Diego, I
was happy to pull off the freeway and find a phone. When
I called the garage, Charlie Devlin answered promptly.

"McGrory's Motor Service."

"Hi," I said.

"Oh, it's you. Where are you now?" I told her, and she
said: "No farther than that? Well, your subject crossed
the border at Tijuana, some twenty miles ahead of you,
almost an hour ago. She headed south towards Ensenada,
our people report. The white Jeepster was two cars behind
her going through the international gate."

"Your people couldn't stick a pin in his tire to stop him,
or plant some marihuana under his seat, or something?"

"Don't be silly, nobody cares about marihuana
smuggled *into* Mexico. And I told you, these are
information people, not action people. When they need
muscle they call the police. Or us. Did you want the
police dragged into this?"

"I guess not." Obviously, if I'd wanted the police, I should have made up my mind earlier. "You're sure she's on her way to Ensenada?"

"No, of course I'm not sure. She could have doubled back, although she wasn't seen recrossing the border. But she could have swung east towards Mexicali; there's a good highway just south of the line that runs well over by Arizona. However, when last seen, she was barreling out on Mexico Highway 1, the road that'll take you clear down Baja California to La Paz, if you and your vehicle are tough enough to make it. It's about eight hundred miles. The pavement ends about ninety miles south of Ensenada at present. After that, things get pretty rough."

I'd heard about that rugged peninsula road before—they run well-publicized races down it for trail-type vehicles, and a lot of them fall by the wayside—but I let her finish the geography lesson anyway.

Then I said, "Well, Beverly's not likely to try the Baja boondocks in her flossy convertible, but Willy's all set to make the run with that four-wheel-drive heap, once he does his job. Maybe that's the idea."

"Or maybe we're just supposed to think that's the idea."

"I'll keep both possibilities in mind. How's your car coming?"

"It'll be another hour or so. I had them wake up somebody to get the parts in LA. and run them down here…"

She stopped abruptly. I heard some odd, choking sounds over the phone.

"What's the matter?" I asked quickly. "Miss Devlin? Charlie?"

Her voice came back on the line sounding kind of hoarse and strangled. "Just this damn allergy. Don't get excited. As I was saying, we've got the parts now, but the man's just started putting them in. As soon as he's finished, I'll come after you."

"Name a rendezvous," I said. "I don't know the area."

"The Bahia Hotel in Ensenada. It's on the main tourist drag, on the right-hand side of the street going south; you can't miss it."

I said, "Okay. Incidentally, I've switched cars. Look for a Plymouth Satellite four-door, kind of reddish-brown. If the sun visors are down, you make contact with me as soon as possible. If they're up, stay clear and wait until you hear from me. Watch that allergy, Charlie."

"Thanks," she said. "You be careful, too. Oh, I've ordered LA to check on Dr. Sorenson for you."

"Thanks."

Getting into Mexico was no problem; the uniformed officials at the gate just glanced at my identification and waved me through. Coming back, however, promised to be a different proposition, judging by the line of backed-up traffic waiting to be searched for drugs on the U.S. side. Considering that any smart smuggler would have the word by now, it seemed unlikely that the Customs boys were making any great hauls to justify the unpopularity they were generating on both sides of the border, but maybe they were hardened types who didn't care whether or not people loved them.

I followed the sparse highway signs through Tijuana in the dark without learning much about that colorful, wide-open town except that it doesn't spend much money keeping up its streets. Shortly after leaving the city limits, however, I found myself paying toll for the privilege of driving down an excellent four-lane highway at the legal speed of a hundred and ten kilometers per hour, roughly seventy m.p.h.

I could see the ocean on my right, now, in the growing dawn light. Down here the air was clear, and it looked like a beautiful morning coming up, with only a few clouds in the sky. It was like driving out from under a moist, stinking, gray blanket; but that ocean bothered me. Some people, I know, think of oceans in terms of pleasure boats, or sport fishing, or surfboards, or just plain happy swimming; but in my line of work we tend to regard any large body of water primarily as a tempting place to ditch a corpse.

Beyond the southern fringes of Tijuana, there wasn't much in the way of human habitation to embarrass anyone planning a burial at sea—or a heroin pickup, I reflected. Infrequent highway signs indicated turnoffs to villages that, as far as I could make out from the highway, were largely collections of shabby house trailers parked along the shore for the convenience of fishermen from the north. At least they looked very much like the seaside slums I'd seen elsewhere in Mexico, inhabited, during the season, by dedicated Yankee anglers. At this time of year, in the middle of the week, the villages were mostly deserted. They became more infrequent the farther south I drove.

Seeing the lonely road, and the empty, rocky coastline, I decided that Willy had deliberately waited for his victim—we prefer the word subject—to get down into Mexico where he could do his work conveniently and unobserved. Driving along, I watched the pavement for signs of hard, emergency braking, and the shoulder for tracks leading off the road.

I found them. You'd be surprised how many double streaks of rubber leading away into nothing you'll see on any highway if you really look; and how many wheel tracks run right off the edge of the road embankment without further traces of the vehicles that made them. I must have stopped half a dozen times in forty miles, quite sure that I'd come upon a broken convertible beyond those swerving tiremarks leading into empty space, only to find myself looking at a virgin hillside or an unmarked cliff, with no signs of wreckage below.

The last time, however, as I was turning back to the car, I saw what I was looking for on the distant rocks beyond the small bay ahead: a pile of twisted metal with gold paint, on it, gleaming dully in the shadow of the coastal hills. Well, at least it hadn't burned.

I drove over, there and parked above the place and sat a moment in my car, not particularly wanting to see what was down there. I mean, it was too bad about McConnell, I'd been a little slow there, they'd caught me by surprise, but at least I'd been present and trying. Here I might have saved a life by calling in the police and having Willy Hansen picked up on some pretext or other before he crossed the border. Or I could have had the girl picked up and held in protective custody.

It would have involved a lot of explanations and formalities afterwards; it might even have loused up the mission completely. Mac would have been annoyed, but that wasn't why I hadn't done it. The fact is, I hadn't really thought of it until too late. People like me just don't think in terms of police; and because of my lone-wolf working habits, a girl was dead. There was nothing left for me to do but go look at what was left.

I got out of the car. At this point, the lanes of the dual highway were cut into the steeply sloping hillside at different levels. There was a masonry retaining wall to keep the upper northbound lane from sliding down onto the lower southbound lane on which I stood. There were plenty of signs to indicate what had happened.

Beverly had simply failed to make the sweeping right-hand turn around the head of the bay. She'd lost control of her car somehow and gone clear across the road to the left. She'd caromed off the stone retaining wall, leaving gold paint and chipped stonework behind her. Still fighting helplessly for control, perhaps, she had bounced back across the highway and over the edge. The tracks were clear in the dirt of the highway shoulder.

Professionally speaking, I had to admit that it was a good job. It looked like a simple matter of too much speed and too little driving ability. Well, if Willy was anything, he was a pro in automotive matters. I wondered just how he'd managed to work this.

I started for the edge and paused to study the tracks of a four-wheel-drive vehicle with cleated tires on all wheels. Then I saw a small green suede shoe beyond. I picked it up, frowning. Its presence up here could only mean that Beverly had jumped clear when she saw the precipice ahead, and her shoe had come off in the fall…

I hurried to the edge and looked down. It wasn't really a precipice, just a steep incline of rocky rubble and tough little bushes, but quite a scramble for a man with city clothes on. I found the other shoe about a quarter of the way down, and some scraps of green wool cloth snagged on the brush, but I didn't find her. There was other stuff all down the slope, including seat cushions, broken glass, and one door of the convertible. There was also a familiar leather purse, which I picked up. It had gotten badly scratched but it had stayed closed.

There was no girl, alive or dead. I made sure of this, and went over to the car. It was a total loss, smashed and battered into shapelessness, having rolled down a couple of hundred feet of hillside before coming to a sudden stop against the black rocks of the shore. It had ended right side up and the top had been ripped off. There was nobody inside and no blood on the upholstery, which fitted the theory that she'd unloaded before the vehicle went over the edge, but where was she?

That was, of course, a stupid question. I knew where she was, and I laid down the purse and shoes I'd collected, and walked to the edge of the rocks and looked down. Slow, heavy waves broke into foam twenty feet below, and I could feel a little spray blow up against my face. There was nothing washing around down there, of course. Willy, coming along right after the crash, however he'd made it happen, would have cleaned up tidily. The weighted body he'd dumped off the rocks might break loose and come ashore eventually, but not so soon and probably not here.

I looked out to sea where the waves were breaking over other black rocks, a hundred yards out in the bay. They looked sinister and dangerous out there. I wondered why Willy had bothered to dispose of the body. It would have made a better picture for the authorities, when they arrived on the scene, if he'd left her wherever her headlong dive from the doomed car had deposited her— after, of course, making quite sure she was dead. But maybe he'd had to put a tell-tale bullet into her to keep her from getting away…

Some impulse of anger made me pick up a chunk of rock and pitch it at the water below.

"Help!" The weak voice seemed to come out of the cliff at my feet "Who's up there? Oh, please won't you help me! Somebody, please get me out of here—"

## 11

Getting her out of there promised to be something of a job. First, I tried to pinpoint her location, to see just what I'd be getting myself into by going after her. I couldn't spot the area at the foot of the overhanging rocks from where the pleading, disembodied voice seemed to come. Well, that figured. If she could have been seen, Willy would have seen her; and disposed of her.

I glanced around warily. Apparently Beverly had managed to survive the crash and conceal herself from her pursuer, which was nice, but if Willy was a patient man, he could be waiting around to catch her coming out of hiding when she thought herself safe. I had an uneasy feeling of being watched…

"Help!" the voice called from below, as the noise of the surf subsided briefly. "Please don't go away, whoever you are! Help me!"

To hell with Willy. "Hold on, down there," I shouted. "I'll be right with you."

It was an easy promise to make. Living up to it posed a few problems. There was obviously no sense in my diving heedlessly and heroically off the rocks to join her. That would just make two of us at the bottom of the junior-grade cliff, neither knowing a way back up to the top. Besides, I'm not much for making twenty-foot dives into unknown waters off an unknown coast. In fact, I'm a mediocre swimmer; but clearly I was going to have to exercise my limited talents in that direction whether I wanted to or not.

Exploring hastily, I found a crevice some fifty yards off to the right that led down to a kind of shelf less than a foot above the water. As I undressed, I looked around dubiously once more. I'd be in a poor position for self-defense if Willy should appear on the rocky shore above me while I was paddling around in the surf in my shorts. Well, apparently it had to be done, and I was the only guy around to do it.

Taking my gun, I made my way down into the crack. The breeze off the sea was chilly enough to remind me that it was too damn early in the spring for any sensible person to get wet all over in anything but a nice warm bath— well, a hot shower, maybe, but I'm a tub man myself, when I can find a tub long enough. I hid the gun among the rocks down there and approached the launching pad. A wave broke into the entrance and washed about my ankles, letting me know that the water was even colder than the air, but there was nothing to do but go into it, so I went. The shock was breathtaking. I stroked clumsily off to the left, hoping the exercise would warm me. It didn't.

I found her huddled in a shallow cave, little more than a niche washed out by the waves, at the bottom of the rocky point on which I'd been standing when I heard her voice. The sea sloshed right into the little hollow, drenching her with metronome regularity where she clung to a stone outcropping. I got an impression of a dead-white face, tangled hair, and torn clothing that streamed like seaweed from a small, half-naked body, but at least she was alive enough to watch me hopefully as I came in for a landing.

She tried to say something; but the roar of the surf blotted it out. I was too busy keeping myself from being washed back out to sea to listen, anyway. It was a tougher rescue operation than the previous one in which we'd participated, I reflected grimly. I pried her loose, between waves, shoved her out of there, and dove after her. She started swimming, but feebly and ineffectually. I got hold of some cloth that ripped when the strain of the next wave came on it; then I got a fistful that didn't Kicking desperately, paddling one-handed, I managed to tow her clear of the rocks. Some time later, I boosted her onto the shelf from which I'd come—with, I was glad to note, some token help from her. At least she was still present and voting.

Climbing up beside her, with no help from her, was harder than it should have been for a healthy man in good condition. I dragged her out of the reach of the waves and crouched there, panting and dripping and trying to keep my teeth from chattering. After a little while, I remembered the gun and found it. If Willy was lying in wait for us above, I was once more in a position to shoot back, even if my chances of hitting anything were slight, the way I was shivering.

Beverly rolled over weakly to look at me through the hair that veiled her face. I reached out and parted the wet strands with a forefinger, so that I could look in as well as she could look out. Her lips moved stiffly.

"Mr. Helm!" she whispered. "I d-didn't really recog… recognize…" She couldn't finish. She just curled up into a ball and hugged herself, shaking with cold.

"Are you hurt?" I asked.

It was a stupid question. What I'd meant to ask, I guess, was if she was too badly hurt to proceed under her own power.

"Sure I'm hurt… I hurt all over," she breathed. Her voice was stronger and steadier. "Or I did before I f-froze to d-death." She made an effort to sit up, succeeded with my help, and went on: "But I don't seem to have b-broken anything ess-ess-essential." The shakes hit her again, so violently that she could hardly get the last word out.

"Can you make that?" I asked, after the spasm had passed. I indicated the cleft up which we still had to climb.

"I… I think so, Mr. Helm. Matt…"

"What?"

Her greenish-hazel eyes regarded me with disconcerting steadiness out of her pale, wet face. "You're b-beautiful," she said softly. "You're the p-prettiest man I ever saw, even if your knees are b-b-bony. I'd given up, I guess. I'd have d-d-died there if you hadn't come after me. Th-thanks."

"Go to hell," I said. "If you're strong enough to make speeches you're strong enough to start climbing."

I still had the uneasy sensation that someone was watching and, at the top, I checked the surroundings carefully, gun in hand, but there was no Willy in sight. That was fine with me. I reached down to help Beverly over the last rocks, left her catching her breath, and went over to get her purse and shoes. I brought them back and dropped them beside her.

Then I went to my own clothes, mopped myself off a bit with my undershirt, and tossed the damp garment to her for similar employment. I got dressed except for my jacket. Its warmth tempted me strongly, but there are times when a man has to prove, to himself and to others, that he really is a gentleman at heart, all evidence to the contrary notwithstanding. Besides, I needed a way to show—call it a symbol—that I really was very glad to have found her alive. It was a weight off my conscience, or a stain off my soul, or something.

Tucking my gun back under my waistband, I carried the coat over to where she was standing, a little unsteadily, vaguely rubbing at her hair with my undershirt. It wasn't very nice of me, under the circumstances, but I couldn't help pausing to get the full effect. It was pretty spectacular. I'd encountered a lot of beat-up characters in my undercover career, but I'd seldom met a lady who was so literally in rags.

Her neat little wool pantsuit, never designed for

hardship, had disintegrated into a scarecrow collection of flaps and, loops and pennants of torn green cloth, sodden and dark with seawater. One arm and leg were almost totally bare, and sizeable anatomical areas were raggedly exposed elsewhere. Apparently, the dive from the doomed convertible had scraped most of the clothing, and a good deal of skin, from her right side. The hasty scramble down the slope, and the ocean swim, had completed the job of demolition all around. She was so tattered it was almost funny.

She stopped drying her hair and glanced at me in a puzzled way, as if wondering why I was staring. Then she looked down at herself, becoming suddenly aware of, and aghast at, her shipwrecked appearance.

"God, I'm a clown!" she gasped. "I'm a… a disaster area! I didn't realize… Matt, what am I going to do? I can't show myself anywhere like this!"

"We'll get you some clothes," I said. "Meanwhile, here's something to keep you warm—"

"No, wait a minute, please."

She tossed aside the undershirt she'd been using as a towel, struggled out of the clinging remains of the jacket, and untangled herself from the trailing remnants of the pants. Rolling the garments into a ball, she walked gingerly, barefooted, to the edge of the rocks, and pitched them into the sea.

She came back to me, no longer a comic figure in flapping rags, just a pretty girl who'd got herself kind of wet and scratched and dirty, in a costume that now consisted of a sleeveless white turtleneck jersey and a pair of brief white nylon pants—little more than she'd been wearing in our abortive seduction scene of the previous evening. The scanty outfit wasn't clean, dry, or even wholly intact, but it wasn't a cruel joke.

"I'll take that coat now, thanks," she said.

I hesitated, frowning at the blood-caked lacerations that seemed to reach almost from shoulder to elbow, and from hip to knee, although it was a little hard to tell how much was injury and how much was just clotted gore.

"First you'd better let me have a look at that arm—"

"There's nothing you can do about it here, so why make like Dr. Kildare?" she said a bit sharply. "I'll live, if you don't keep me standing in this wind all day."

"Sure," I said, wrapping the coat around her. "Put on your shoes and let's go. Here's your purse."

As an afterthought, I went back and picked up the wet undershirt she'd thrown aside. It might come in handy for bandages or something; besides, if I left it there, the Mexican authorities might think it was a clue. When I caught up with her, she'd paused by the wrecked convertible. She reached in to take the keys, still in the lock, and dropped them into her Mexican-leather purse.

I grinned, regarding the battered hulk. "What's the matter, are you afraid somebody's going to stick the wheels back on and drive off with it?"

She didn't smile. "Besides the car keys, there's also my apartment key, and the key to a safe-deposit box, if I ever dare go back to get what's in them. Like a nice mink coat and some jewelry..." She grimaced, and frowned at what was left of her car. "Do you know, that damn thing almost *killed* me?" she said in a wondering voice. "Wouldn't you think they'd make them so you could get *out* of them in a pinch?"

"Exactly what happened?"

She shook her head quickly. "Not here, Matt. Wait till we're safe in your car with the heater going."

We made it up to the highway without any further trouble. As I unlocked the door of the sedan, the first traffic of the day came by, but it was no Jeepster, just a Chevy pickup truck with the cab crammed full of assorted Mexicans, adults and children, who stared at us so curiously that I was afraid they'd spotted the wreck below. Then I saw that they were looking at Beverly's wet hair and abbreviated costume, which apparently they took for a bathing suit.

They drove past, laughing at the crazy *gringos* who couldn't wait till summer for an early-morning swim.

## 12

"You warned me," Beverly said at last, breaking the comfortable, silence that had settled over us as the warmth of the car's heater began to take effect. "I suppose it was my fault for not listening to you."

I was again driving at the legal speed of a hundred and ten kilometers per hour, seventy m.p.h. to you—well, I suppose I should actually have held it at sixty-eight and four-tenths, but nobody's got a speedometer that accurate, not even, I hoped, the Mexican police. I took my eyes off the road to glance at my companion, finding her bare legs only mildly distracting. I guess I still hadn't thawed out completely.

She'd gotten a comb from her scarred purse, and a mirror that had miraculously survived the crash intact except for a broken corner. She was fighting the snarls out of the darkened red-gold hair that, as it dried, was lightening once more and reverting to its former glorious, if artificial, color. The dead-white pallor had left her face, and she'd treated herself to a touch of lipstick. Even beat-up and waterlogged—or at least not thoroughly dried out yet—she was quite an attractive little person.

"What did I warn you about?" I asked.

"Don't you remember what you said when you were calling a taxi from that motel room, about cars that might be gimmicked so the brakes wouldn't brake and the steering wouldn't steer? But you were talking about that rental car, the one I was supposed to have borrowed from your girl agent, and by the time I got around to picking up my own convertible, I'd forgotten all about it. It never occurred to me... They must have sabotaged it while it was standing at the airport. Of course they had all the time in the world."

We were still driving along the edge of the Pacific. Baja California was beginning to wake up, and there were a few cars on the four-lane toll road, although there weren't many signs of habitation around to indicate where they might have come from, just the rugged coastal hills up to the left, and the rocky shoreline, and the ocean, down to the right.

I said, "So your steering went out, or was it the brakes?"

"Both," she said. "It was... it was like a bad dream. There was a man right behind me all the way from the border. I'd spotted him earlier, he wasn't even trying to be inconspicuous. He was practically riding my rear bumper. I kept jacking up the speed, thinking I ought to be able to outrun a lousy little jeep..."

"Did you know the driver?"

"Sure. I got a glimpse of him under the lights, going through Tijuana: a rock-faced character named Willy Hansen. Among other things, he drives for Frankie, although I don't know why. The few times Frankie had him chauffeur me around—while I was still the golden girl around the place—he scared me stiff. He acted like he'd never even seen a horseless carriage before."

I said, "I know. I rode with him a couple of times myself."

Beverly shrugged her small shoulders under the sports coat she was still wearing like a cape. "Maybe he's better on the open road than in city traffic. Anyway, I couldn't seem to gain on him much, and that glamor-buggy of mine is... was supposed to be fast, a real bomb. That's what Frankie-boy said when he presented it to me, and don't think I didn't have to pay for it like all his presents. Ugh." She was silent briefly, her face bleak with memory. "The wages of sin," she murmured. "So now I'm sitting here practically naked, with less than fifty bucks in my purse, and no safe way of getting at all that lovely loot back in L.A. for which I sold my innocent body. Well, almost innocent. That should be an object lesson to little girls who think... Ah, hell!"

"Sure," I said. "We left the heroine pouring the high-test fuel to her high-powered convertible with the villain in hot pursuit. The suspense is terrific."

Beverly laughed. "Sorry, I didn't mean to moralize," she said. "Anyway, I tried to shake him, and I did gain a little, maybe half a mile. I really had those tires smoking in the curves. I guess that's what he wanted. They must have fixed everything to fail when I put a lot of strain on it. Up above the border, in the fog, I'd been taking it pretty easy. I guess that's why I got as far as I did without anything happening." She looked around and sighed. "It certainly is nice to see blue sky for a change. That damn smog gets me down."

I made a face at her. "As a storyteller, sweetheart, you make a swell movie star. Along with the morality lectures, let's just skip the atmospheric conditions and their psychological effects, huh?"

She laughed again. "All right. I hit that sharp curve going into the bay where you found me, and I really had to lean on the wheel to pull her around. As I came out of the turn, I felt things let go, power steering and all. There just wasn't anything left in that department. So of course I stood on the brakes as hard as I dared, and they went out, too. The pedal held up for a moment and then went clear to the floor. The car was still holding the road with nobody steering it, but that long curve was coming up, the one at the head of the bay where you had your car parked. I knew I had to jump and take a chance of being smeared all over the pavement—"

I said, "So you went out the right-hand door. Why?"

She glanced at me. "Matt, what—"

"A man can't help wondering," I said. "The lady is driving the car. This is customarily done from beneath the steering wheel, usually located on the left side of the vehicle here in the U.S. of A. She decides to unload, and the *right* side of her costume and anatomy takes the brunt of the landing. A man experienced in drawing large deductions from small clues, like me, can't help but wonder why."

Beverly grinned. "You're so cute when you're suspicious, darling. I *thought* you were looking at me awfully hard down there. Well, believe it or not, I went out the right-hand door simply because I didn't want to risk being caught between the car and the bank—we were drifting over to the left pretty fast—or that damn stone retaining wall, either. Okay?"

"Okay," I said. "I just have to go into my pro act now and then, to keep in practice."

"I mean," the girl beside me said grimly, "I tried to go out the right-hand door, but it wouldn't open. That damn little lock button was down, for Christ's sake, and if you start by pulling at the door handle the crazy button won't come up until you let go, and of course in my panic I got them in the wrong order. While I was fighting it, we bounced off the wall, and then I finally got it open and kicked myself out—and what the hell ever happened to nice sensible door locks that unlock when you pull the inside handle. We used to have them, didn't we?"

"They aren't safe. Some guy in Washington said so."

"Well, I'd like to put that guy in Washington into one of these super-locked death-traps heading straight for a two-hundred-foot drop and see how safe he feels!" She shook her head angrily. "Anyway, when I stopped bouncing and flopping and sliding around, I was still alive. I'd lost a lot of skin, and my clothes were in shreds, and everything was kind of vague and hazy, but my arms and legs seemed to work all right although I hurt like hell in a dozen places. I knew there was something I had to do, somebody I had to get away from…"

"Where was Willy with the jeep?"

"I could see his headlights coming around the point. I knew I had to get out of there before he found me and finished me off, and I just slid and rolled and crawled and scrambled down through the rocks and brush, and staggered to the shore and threw myself off the edge, hoping the water was deep enough so I wouldn't knock out my brains. I guess I had some vague idea of swimming to those rocks way offshore that I could barely see—it was just starting to get light—but when I got into the water I knew I didn't have the strength to make it, cold as it was. Besides, he'd see me swimming long before I got out there, and either shoot me from the shore or come after me. I spotted that hollow at the foot of the cliff and paddled back and crawled into it. It felt like hours, clinging there, with those damn waves splashing over me every few seconds. When I saw a stone hit the water from above, and knew somebody was up there—"

"How did you know it wasn't Willy?"

"I didn't," she said. "But it had been a long time. He should have given up and gone away; and I knew I couldn't last much longer. I had to take a chance. I knew I'd never make it out of there without help, so I yelled with all the strength I had left. And you came."

"Yeah," I said. "I came."

I touched the brake warily, so as not to arouse to anger the short-tempered hydraulic gremlins lurking in the power-assist machinery. I brought the sedan to a halt on the shoulder of the highway, and switched off the engine, and looked at her.

"What would you have done if I hadn't come?" I asked.

"What's the matter, why are we stopping?" Beverly glanced at me, puzzled. "What do you mean, Matt? I... I'd have died there, I suppose."

"Maybe, but I kind of doubt it," I said. "But what if you'd had somebody else to deal with? Say that tall young lady agent, my associate—but of course Willy ran her off the road north of San Diego to get her out of the way. But what about the Mexican police? Willy couldn't very well run interference for you there. What kind of an act would you have put on if they'd got there before me?"

Beverly was frowning in a bewildered way. "Matt, I don't understand! What—" Casually, her hands grasped the purse in her lap as she turned to face me.

"No, sweetheart," I said, and I showed her my left hand aiming the snub-nosed .38 across my body. "No, leave that purse strictly alone, please."

"Matt, *darling*—" Her voice expressed only surprise and hurt. Her fingers opened obediently and released the purse. Her eyes were big and bewildered. She was a very pretty thing and a good actress. It was a pity she hadn't made it in Hollywood, but perhaps she hadn't really tried. Perhaps she'd had other business in California that seemed more important. Maybe it even paid pretty well, although none of us get rich in this business—at least we're not supposed to. "I don't know what you're driving at!" she said with a nice little touch of anger.

"Sure you do," I said. "It was the blood, you know."

"What?"

"The blood," I said. "I mean, in case you're wondering what finally tipped me off, slow and stupid as I am. All that crusted gore on your arm and leg, very painful-looking and convincing. Except that a girl who jumps into the ocean immediately after she's been hurt, and then hangs onto a rock with the waves washing over her constantly—every few seconds, I believe you said—well, her blood just isn't going to stick to her long enough to coagulate like that, is it?"

Beverly licked her lips. "Matt, you're crazy! I don't know what you're thinking, but—"

I said, "I'm thinking I've seen this show before, somewhere. Like back at that motel where you did your maiden-in-distress act for me the first time, with kind of the same costume and makeup, although not nearly so elaborate, just a few smudges and tears, and some convincingly disheveled hair."

"Darling, you can't really believe—"

"This time, of course, you knew you had to make it look very good to convince me. So you set it up right, you and Willy; but it was a damn cold ocean on a damn cold morning and you didn't know how long it would be before I, or somebody, came along to find you, down there under the cliff. You might have frozen to death by that time, waiting down in that hollow, constantly soaked to the skin. Besides, from down there, you couldn't see who was coming. So you hid in the rocks up above, I figure, where you could watch the highway, with your clothes dramatically ripped and your skin convincingly lacerated—"

"Matt, really!" she protested. "You can't believe I did *that* to myself!"

"With some help from Willy," I said. "Sure I believe it, and it was a swell job, and it must have hurt like hell. You're a pro, baby. I'll give you a testimonial any time you want it. Then you sent Willy on his way and waited. It must have been kind of chilly with the wind blowing through those spectacular rags you'd prepared for my benefit, but at least you weren't being continually soaked with ice water."

Beverly said firmly, "You're being utterly ridiculous!"

"When you saw me stop my car," I said, ignoring her, "and start down the slope towards you, *then* you slipped into the water and got into position to be rescued, not realizing that by that time the blood and stuff had caked too hard to wash away." I drew a long breath. "I let you talk just now to see if you had an explanation, but you didn't. Of course, you'd have had a hard time, anyway, explaining the gun in your purse…" I made a warning gesture with the .38. "Easy there, doll. This may not be a .44 Magnum, but it makes a nasty hole at short range."

Beverly moistened her lips once more. "Matt," she said, "Matt, I—"

I said, "I saw you get it out of the wreck when you pretended to be so concerned about your keys. I was watching you pretty closely by that time. It seemed to be quite a firearm. Do you mind if I have a look at it?"

She didn't speak. I reached over cautiously and took the carved leather purse. It was heavy now, heavier by several pounds than when I'd handed it to her down by the shore. I opened the flap and looked at the big Colt .45 automatic resting among all the feminine accessories, like a bull in a boudoir.

I frowned at the weapon for a moment, remembering a small girl with a dirty face, very shocked, telling me that, Heavens, she didn't know anything about guns! Now the same little girl had a .45 in her purse, a purse that was big enough to pack even larger artillery, say the Magnum variety. It had a husky shoulder-strap to bear the weight. That way, even a small female person could lug around a heavy revolver without bulging in any unusual places...

I heard Beverly laugh oddly, and looked at her. "You men!" she said after a long moment. Her voice had changed. It was no longer helpless and innocent, but sharp and scornful. "It's really quite infuriating, dearie, the way you hulking males all take it for granted that nobody else can fire your big pistols and revolvers. But it certainly makes a fine cover for a girl who can stand a little recoil." She smiled at me crookedly. "Actually, the kick never bothered me much. It was the noise I had some trouble getting used to."

She was a little ahead of me. I'd figured it out only far

enough to know that she wasn't the poor little victim of circumstances she'd wanted me to think her. She wasn't just another pretty Hollywood hopeful gone astray in tinseltown. I hadn't yet had time to do much work on the problem of who she might be, if she wasn't Mary Sokolnicek or Beverly Blaine. I'd been sneaking up on the answer, after seeing the big pistol, but the idea she presented still came as something of a shock.

I whistled softly. "Don't tell me! It's old Santa Claus himself. I mean, herself."

She frowned. "Santa Claus? What does that mean? Oh, of course: St. Nicholas. Is that what you call me?"

"If that's who you are," I said, watching her. "If you're the mysterious Nicholas we've been looking for all this time."

"Why should you doubt it, darling?"

"Why should you admit it?"

"Why not? You have caught me. You have orders to kill me, do you not?"

"That's what the head man said. If you're really Nicholas."

"My actual code name," she said calmly, "is Nicole. We just changed it to Nicholas for one assignment, where it was important that I be taken for a man. We never expected that I'd be able to keep up the masquerade indefinitely, but somehow nobody ever caught on to the fact that Nicholas was a woman, not until Willy got careless and led that redheaded ingenue of yours, the one with the Irish name, straight to me. She knew enough, from her previous involvement in our affairs, to make the connection. I had to kill her before she revealed who Nicholas really was. There wasn't anything else to do."

"No," I said. "No, I can see that. It was necessary."

"Yes," she said softly, "necessary. So many things are necessary in this business, aren't they, Matthew Helm?"

She was still a little ahead of me. I should have known what came next, after the confession, but she got her hand to her mouth before I could stop her. Perhaps I didn't try as hard as I might have. After all, while Mac had said that retribution wasn't our business, he'd also said that there was no reason for the person responsible for Annette's death to survive.

She didn't.

# 13

Mexico boasts some very picturesque cities and towns, but Ensenada isn't one of them. Although it's within easy driving distance of the border, it lacks much of the stimulating, honky-tonk atmosphere of the true border towns. On the other hand, unlike some spectacular examples farther south and east, Ensenada displays nothing very interesting in the way of history or architecture. At least, if there were any ancient ruins or towering cathedrals around, they were well hidden from the main thoroughfare I used.

The impression I got was of a crowded, bright, busy, dusty community, peopled by dark-faced citizens who had their own affairs to think about and, for the most part, weren't tremendously interested in visitors from the north. Even the setting wasn't remarkable, since here the coastal hills had drawn back a bit from the sea, leaving the town sitting on a fairly flat piece of shore facing a large bay—the *bahia* for which, presumably, my hotel was named.

I had no trouble finding it. As Charlie Devlin had indicated, it was right on the main drag. When I pulled up in front, a boy came out to help with the luggage, but he didn't seem very disturbed to find I didn't have any. Apparently the situation had arisen before, and he was used to mad *Americanos* who'd suddenly decided to dash down to Ensenada for a day or two with nothing but what was in their pockets.

At the desk, a pretty, black-haired señorita whose English was intelligible but far from perfect assigned me to a room and passed the key to the boy. He pointed out the bar and restaurant, and then led me down a long corridor and exhibited my quarters with a thoroughness, and a proprietary air of pride, that earned him a buck, although he'd had nothing to carry. A reputation for generosity isn't a bad thing to establish in a strange foreign town; and actually it was a pretty good room, and everything worked.

Having made sure of this—Mexican plumbing tends to be temperamental—I went back out to the car and drove it around to the parking area behind the building. Before locking up, I carefully turned down both sun visors for Charlie Devlin's benefit: our prearranged let's-make-contact signal. In my room once more, I pulled off my shoes and lay down on the bed to wait.

It had not been my intention to do any heavy thinking. There seemed to be no constructive cerebration left to be done. To all appearances my job was finished. I should have been happy. All that remained was to buy

my idealistic colleague a drink when she arrived, thank
her for her help, wish her luck with her job, and wrap up
the whole assignment with a report to Washington, where
they'd complete the dossier on Nicholas and consign it to
the permanently inactive file...

The trouble was, for one thing, I don't really like to
see people die, and there aren't so many pretty, spunky
little girls around that we can afford to lose one, no matter
what her politics. Of course, personal likes and dislikes
don't figure largely in this business, or shouldn't. More,
to the point was the fact that it had been too easy.

A good many years of experience have taught me
to view with suspicion difficult cases that conveniently
and unexpectedly solve themselves, and villains—or
villainesses—who are obliging enough to kill themselves
after kindly confessing their guilt. Anyway, the cerebral
machinery kept spinning busily, reviewing the events of
the past few days.

Lying there, I had to relive the whole affair, including
the final ghoulish details involved in putting back into
the sea, dead, the small female body I had so recently
fished out of it alive; I hadn't enjoyed the task, but it had
seemed like the logical solution. Mac had wanted it done
inconspicuously, and with a little luck, this should be
inconspicuous enough for anybody.

The authorities would find the wrecked car. Nearby,
they'd probably find, washed up on the rocks, some scraps at
least of the artistically tattered costume Beverly had thrown
into the sea. They would assume that the dazed—perhaps

hysterical—owner of the smashed automobile, stumbling about on the low cliffs in the early morning darkness, had managed to fall over the edge, and had then shed her hampering garments in her futile efforts to swim to safety.

A little farther down the coast, depending on the currents—I'd brought her back as near to the scene as I'd dared—they might or might not find the body. If they did, there would be no obvious signs of poison, I was fairly sure. She'd been a pro working for pros. What she'd used had been fast, effective, and undoubtedly reasonably undetectable.

A county coroner, or whoever performed the duties of that office here in Mexico, would be unlikely to spot it. I didn't think anybody would even notice that there was less water in the lungs than usual in cases of drowning. If they did, well, she'd been through a serious crash before she hit the water; she could have died as a belated result of internal injuries. Scratch one *turista*, possibly drunk, who'd failed to negotiate a curve in her expensive Yankee convertible.

A knock on the door made me sit up and swing my stockinged feet to the floor. "Just a minute," I called. "I'll be right there, Miss Devlin."

Of course, it didn't have to be Charlie Devlin, although it was time she arrived. It could be the Mexican police, perhaps having obtained my description and license number from the pickup-truck-load of native citizens who'd seen Beverly and me by the roadside near the wreck.

I didn't really think those citizens would volunteer information to the cops even if they heard it was wanted. Mexicans, as far as I know, have no more love for getting involved than anyone else. Nevertheless, I had to keep in mind the possibility that the local law was smarter and more suspicious than I'd hoped, and had traced me here somehow—in which case I could only act as much as possible as if the last thing in the world I was expecting to see, when I opened the door, was a policeman. The knock came again, more impatiently, as I finished tying my shoestrings.

"Okay, okay, I'm coming, Charlie!" I shouted. "Let a man put his shoes on, will…!"

Speaking, I crossed the room and yanked open the door, and stopped without completing the sentence. It wasn't Charlie Devlin, standing there in the hall. It wasn't the Mexican constabulary, either. It was the willowy blonde, the elongated acrobatic dancer, Frank Warfel's current playmate. Her presence didn't make a hell of a lot of sense to me, although she was certainly preferable to a policeman. We faced each other in silence for a moment.

Then she asked, "Who's Charlie?"

"Just a girl I know," I said.

"Lucky you," she said brightly, "to know a girl named Charlie."

"I also know a girl named Bobbie," I said, since it seemed to be that kind of a conversation. "What can I do for you, Bobbie? Excuse me. I mean, of course, Miss Prince."

She gave me her wide, delicious, sexy, meaningless Hollywood smile. "Probably you can do lots of things for me, darling. We'll have to talk about it some time. But right now, The Man wants to see you."

I studied her for a moment, dubiously. She wasn't really a bad-looking girl, and I don't want to give the impression that I like them fat, or even pleasantly plump. I just felt she was overdoing the hipless, bustless bit. Actually, she looked better in street clothes than in the sexy satin lounging pajamas in which I'd last seen her, which had emphasized her narrowness.

Now she had on a checked black-and-white pantsuit that would have made any other woman look broad as a barge; it only made her transverse dimensions seem practically normal. There were wide, floppy trousers and a long jacket thing without sleeves—maybe it qualified as an overgrown vest—and a soft white silk blouse. Her shoes were the square-toed, square-heeled jobs dictated by current fashion; apparently Frank Warfel only demanded spike heels at home. Her face was made up so dramatically that, with the striking blonde hair—now worn seductively loose down her shoulders—you just knew she had to be a big movie star. The game was to determine which one she was being this week.

"Frankie wants to see me?" I said. "What about?"

She gave me the wide, wet, irresistible movie smile once more. "Who reads minds?" she asked. "He takes me into his bed, not into his confidence, darling. I don't know what the hell he wants to see you about. Why don't you ask him?"

"Where?"

"In my room. Right down the hall, darling."

It wasn't right. I mean, her eyes weren't right and her

casual manner wasn't right, and she was hitting me over the head with too many darlings. It was a set-up, a deadfall, a trap. I'd been around long enough to smell them, and this one had the characteristic sour stink of betrayal.

Anyway, if Frank Warfel had wanted me for casual conversation, he wouldn't have used his special, acrobatic blonde as a messenger. He'd have sent one of his ordinary errand boys as he had before. The presence of the girl meant that, for some, reason, he felt that a little sex appeal was advisable this time to render me unsuspicious and vulnerable. On the other hand, I reflected, with all of desolate Baja California outside to choose from, it seemed unlikely that he'd pick a public hostelry to murder me in.

Anyway, as I've said, I wasn't happy with the case, even though my part of it should have been at an end. If Frank Warfel was setting traps for agents of the U.S. government, it might be interesting to know why. Idle curiosity isn't encouraged in the profession, but this seemed like a justifiable bit of research.

"Lead the way," I told the girl cheerfully.

She didn't move at once. She hesitated, studying my face. I had a hunch she was toying with the idea of issuing a warning. Then she moved her narrow shoulders in the minutest of shrugs, turned, and walked ahead of me down the hall. She stopped in front of a door, knocked, and turned to give me her photogenic smile once more. Still smiling, with no change of expression whatever, she kicked me hard on the shin.

The toe of her fashionable shoe must have been

reinforced for just that purpose. As I bent over with the sudden pain, the door opened, and a big man reached out to chop with his hand at the back of my neck. He caught me as I fell and dragged me inside.

**14**

I lay on the bed where I'd been dumped and listened to the voices. One was familiar. I'd heard it only once before, in a Los Angeles apartment, but after a little I placed it as belonging to the man called Jake, official frisker and bodyguard to Frank Warfel. Well, that figured.

This voice said, "Here you are, sir. One snub-nosed .38, one wallet with cards identifying a Mr. Matthew Helm, one customer's copy of a rental-car agreement paid up by credit card in Albuquerque, New Mexico, and one used one-way TWA ticket from Albuquerque to Los Angeles."

The second voice, responding, didn't figure at all. It was not Frank Warfel's voice. It was higher and shriller, kind of peevish. After a rustle of paper, it said: "New Mexico. Looks like he did a lot of driving there the last few weeks. Could there be a connection? Has Frankie been doing any visiting a couple of states to the east, recently?"

"No, but his girl could have, the Blaine dame," Jake said. "Three times in the last couple of months Frankie lent her a driver and she took off in that hopped-up little Pontiac with the fat tires. We never could manage to tail them. That Willy Hansen's lousy in traffic, or pretends to be, but give him an open road and nothing can catch him. I mean, he flies low and fast. But they were always heading east when the boys lost them."

"But that's not the way Frankie was heading just now when you lost *him*." The unknown man's voice had a tart, sarcastic sound.

Jake was apologetic. "Hell, Mr. Tillery, it's a big ocean, and keeping track of a boat in all that fog and mist… Anyway, there was a heavy swell running, nothing to bother a vessel the size of the *Fleetwind*, but the boys in their little power cruiser took quite a beating."

"Extend to them my sincere sympathy," said the man called Tillery, "and then fire them and get yourself some real sailors. And maybe some real drivers, too." There was a little pause. "I thought you told me the *Fleetwind* was tied up for repairs."

"That's what I heard Frankie say. Something about needing a new generator fitting, or something. That's why the boys weren't quite ready to—"

"In other words, Frankie made monkeys of you."

"Maybe so, Mr. Tillery," said Jake doggedly, "but we did manage to find where he's going and when he'll be back. He's planning to make his first dope pickup at Bernardo tonight. He'll be back at his usual dock tomorrow night like nothing had happened, like he's been doing ever since he got the boat. If he's left alone, he'll land the shipment in a day or two. If the law comes aboard, he'll pump it out the trick seagoing john he's got rigged. I hate to think of it, considering what the stuff is worth."

"I hate worse to think of his being caught with it, and so do the directors of the corporation. We'll have to make sure it doesn't happen." Tillery was silent briefly; then he asked: "Did you find anything else on this man?"

"Just the usual keys and change and matches and stuff. Oh, and a good-sized pocket knife, nice and sharp. I don't figure he uses it just to trim his nails."

"You say he's a government man. How do you know? There's no badge or I.D. card here."

"Frankie had his motel room and phone bugged. The boys heard him calling Washington, D.C., checking in with the guy he works for. The name wasn't mentioned, or the department, but Frankie seemed to think it was spy stuff, like C.I.A. or something."

"The damn fool!" Tillery's voice was definitely peevish now. "It's not enough that he gets himself and the corporation mixed up in some far-out dope-smuggling deal; he's got to get us all involved with a female foreign spook as well—*and* help her kill a U.S. agent. Don't we have government trouble enough without getting the cloak-and-dagger boys down on us? Damn it, Jake, I wish you'd alerted me sooner!"

Jake was still on the defensive. "I called as soon as I had something definite to report, just like you told me, Mr. Tillery. I'd already warned you about the dope angle, way back when Frankie started fooling with the boat and all. And I'd told you the girl he was playing footsie with wasn't exactly the little Hollywood tramp she pretended to be, not with the hardware she was packing and the contacts she kept slipping off to make."

"But you never did manage to identify any of her contacts, did you?"

"Hell, the girl is… was a professional, Mr. Tillery; and you said we should be careful not to alert either her or Frankie. We did manage to catch a glimpse of her with one man, a Chinese character, kind of a Charlie Chan type, big and smooth and plump with a little mustache—"

It was the most interesting piece of information I'd received since arriving on the West Coast. It scrambled all my previous ideas about the assignment so thoroughly that, trying to sort them out once more, I missed some of what Jake was saying.

"…no, sir, we never identified him," he finished up. "Hell, who's going to tail a chink in that part of San Francisco? Might as well try to shadow a nigger through Harlem."

"A black man, Jake, please. We must display no prejudice these days. What about our guest here? You're certain it was the murder that brought him on the scene?"

"Yes, sir. He went straight to the hospital when he got to L.A. Seems like the redhead who was shot belonged to his government department or bureau or whatever they call it—the real redhead, not Frankie's little dame with a dye job, the one who did the shooting. This guy was sent to find out who killed their girl and settle the account. It was a definite contract. The boys heard him get his orders over the phone. It shook up Frankie and his dame, they hadn't expected anything like that from the government, I guess, at least Frankie hadn't. They tried some fancy play-acting to throw our friend here off the scent, using Basher Brown as a patsy, but this government character was too smart to buy their script—"

Roberta Prince's sultry voice broke in, sounding offended: "Who're you calling Frankie's dame? Frankie's ex-dame, *if* you please! I'm Frankie's dame now, and God help me if he learns I've sold him out."

"Sweetheart, you're just camouflage," Jake said bluntly. "I heard them talking. The other chick was planning to leave, even before the shooting happened. She had important business somewhere else—"

"You couldn't find out where, Jake?" This was Tillery. "It might give us a lead."

"To what? We know definitely that the lab is somewhere in that crummy Bernardo trailer village up the coast. We know Frankie's on his way there with his boat to pick up a load—"

"What I want to know is what else he's got us mixed up in *besides* dope!"

"I wouldn't know that, Mr. Tillery," Jake said. "I just know Frankie picked this kid, here, out of her night club act to make it look like he'd got tired of the other one and booted her out. That way there wouldn't be any questions asked when she turned up missing."

"Gee, thanks a lot for the compliment!" Roberta's

voice was sharp. "Just the same, if he knew where I was and what I was doing here, he'd kill me!"

Tillery said, "You've been promised protection and an adequate sum of money, Miss Prince. You'll get both, if you continue to cooperate." There was a brief silence; then his voice came again. "I gather from what you've reported, Jake, that our guest has just fulfilled his government contract."

"Yes, sir," Jake said. "We kept an eye on him all the way down, after he made contact with the female fuzz in that garage near L.A. where she was having her car fixed. We saw him ditch the Blaine girl's body. It was kind of funny, since he'd just got all wet saving her life." I remembered my uneasy feeling of being watched down there among the rocks. Jake went on: "At least I figure he thought he was saving her life, to start with, but something must have tipped him off she was just playing the same old please-rescue-me record all over again—"

"Which brings up the question," Tillery interrupted, "after the failure of the original charade she and Warfel had set up to fool him, why should Miss Beverly Blaine still have been trying to gain the confidence of this government man? Why did she stay behind and put on an elaborate act for his benefit? She even had Frankie send the rub-out men after The Basher just to make it look as if she were in real danger! Why?" Jake didn't answer, and after a moment, Tillery went on thoughtfully: "The three of them. Warfel and the girl, using Warfel's corporation contacts to set up something big—maybe on instructions from that fat Chinaman you saw—with Hansen to supply the muscle and do the driving. But just what the hell are they after besides dope, Jake?"

"I'm sorry, Mr. Tillery. I never heard anything that would help. Frankie always had something for me to do somewhere else when they started talking real seriously."

"Warfel heads south towards Baja California in his boat," Tillery said in the same musing voice. "Hansen heads south in a jeep. The girl heads south in her convertible—but she wrecks it deliberately, with Hansen's help, and stays behind to be rescued by this employee of Uncle Sam. Why? It looks as if they were afraid of Mr. Matthew Helm and wanted to have one person keeping an eye on him—or a gun on him—while the others carried out the operation, whatever it is. Which in turn kind of indicates that our so-unconscious friend here must know *something* about what they're planning, enough to worry them. What about it, Mr. Helm?" There was a sharp little laugh. "Come on, Mr. Helm. I've been letting you lie there and listen to save explanations, but that's enough of a nap. You can catch up on the rest of your sleep tonight Wake up now and join us."

I opened my eyes obediently. I'd figured him for a small man, with his squeaky voice, and I was right in a way. He wasn't very tall. However, he was pudgy enough to outweigh a lot of taller men, a pink-faced butterball character with a little round head on a little round body. He was dressed in the informal West Coast fashion: slacks, sports coat, sports shirt, and a natty little cocoa-straw hat with a brim too small to keep the sun off anything, but maybe he wasn't planning to spend much time out in the sun. He looked like a pink, plump cherub except for his eyes, which were small and mean.

I looked at him, and I looked at big Jake watching me hopefully, obviously wishing I'd be foolish enough to make trouble, and I glanced over at the limber blonde in the loudly checked pants outfit, sprawled bonelessly across the armchair in the corner. Then I looked at the fourth person in the room, whose presence I hadn't even suspected until now, because he'd made no sound.

I should have guessed there was somebody else present, of course, somebody important, from the way they'd all seemed to be making speeches to the gallery instead of to each other, bringing each other up to date on stuff they should all have known without telling. He stood by the door, a solid, dark-haired man with a meaty, dark face. He was dressed like a big-city character from the east, complete with a big-city shirt and tie, a gabardine topcoat, a small felt hat, and big dark glasses to shield his eyes from our dangerous western sun. I knew at once that this was a different and tougher breed of predator from Butterball Tillery.

This man, I knew instinctively, represented the "corporation" to which Tillery had referred, the giant underworld organization to which Frank Warfel also belonged, which he now seemed to have embarrassed by his extracurricular activities. Apparently, it was the job of Tillery, the local troubleshooter, to terminate the embarrassment and, probably, the man who had caused it; but an eastern representative had been sent along as official observer for the board of directors, to make certain the corporation's interests were properly safeguarded.

"Mr. Helm." Tillery's voice drew my attention from the silent figure in the corner. "My apologies for the violent greeting, Mr. Helm, but we knew you to be armed and we didn't know how you'd react. Allow me to return your belongings. Please place the revolver, and the cartridges I have removed from it, in different pockets. You can reload when you leave here."

"And when," I asked, "will that be, Mr. Tillery?"

"That depends on you, Mr. Helm," he said smoothly. "All you have to do is answer a question and you're free to go. As you'll have gathered from what we let you overhear, we know all we need to about Frank Warfel's proposed heroin operation. We can take care of that, and will. But the corporation that employs me—you may know it by other names—cannot afford to become involved in treason, for exactly the same reason it no longer deals in drugs. When an activity becomes too unpopular, it also becomes unprofitable."

I said, "That's a nice, patriotic viewpoint."

"Let's not wave the flag. I believe we are both on the same side in this. Why quibble about motives? What we want from you is one single piece of information: just what kind of international monkey business has that little red-haired girl put Frankie up to, Mr. Helm?"

"I don't know," I said.

"Hit him, Jake."

The plump little man's voice didn't change as he said it. Jake yanked me off the bed and slugged me hard at diaphragm level, so I sat back down again, breathless.

"Let me remind you, Mr. Helm," Tillery said gently, "that being a U.S. agent gives you no privileges here, quite the contrary. You are not in the United States now. You are a sneaky *gringo* spy who has just committed a brutal murder on Mexican soil—"

I said, "Hell, I didn't kill the girl. I might have, but she saved me the trouble. She was a pro; she was also a murderess. She knew that once she was caught, she was dead, whether I did the job myself or took her back across the border for trial. She preferred to get it over quickly; or maybe she had orders not to be taken alive. They often do. Anyway, as soon as she knew for sure I was onto her, she popped the kill-me capsule into her mouth and bit down hard. All I did was get rid of the body."

"Nevertheless, I don't think you'd like to have your activities called to the attention of the Mexican authorities, which is why you will not scream for help or do anything else to cause us trouble while we're questioning you. Let me ask you something else: just what were you doing in New Mexico recently that involved a lot of driving?"

"Fishing," I said truthfully.

I knew he wouldn't believe me, but I couldn't, at the moment, think up a lie he would believe. The truth was easier to work with.

"Fishing, Mr. Helm?" Tillery's tone was skeptical.

"I was on leave," I said. "I used to live in Santa Fe. I came back to visit some friends and catch some fish."

"And you covered over a thousand miles—"

"Navajo Lake and the San Juan River are way up north in the state; Elephant Butte Reservoir is pretty far to the south. Then there are Conchos Lake, and Miami Lake, and the Chama River and the Rio Grande, and Stone Lake out on the Jicarilla Apache reservation. Look at the map. A man can log a lot of miles in New Mexico, fishing practically every day for a couple of weeks."

Tillery smiled thinly. "I'm sure he can, Mr. Helm. I'm not so sure you did. I'm not so sure you were not carrying out a preliminary investigation around Albuquerque, say, that later led you to Los Angeles and Frank Warfel, or the girl calling herself Beverly Blaine."

I said, "I was on leave. They called me up and told me one of our people had been shot in LA. and I'd better grab my secret-agent hat and get out there."

"And of course you'd never heard of Frank Warfel before, and therefore you can't possibly tell us what he and the redhead were up to besides dope." Tillery's voice was sour.

"That's right."

"Hit him, Jake."

Jake went through the haul-me-up-and-knock-me-down routine once more.

Tillery said calmly, "You must have some information. It makes no sense otherwise. The Blaine girl was obviously under the impression that you were dangerous to her and Frankie and their mission in some way, otherwise why would she have taken the risk of trying to get close to you once more, as an innocent victim of gang vengeance? At the very least, we can figure that she stayed behind to find out how much you knew, which indicates that you must know something, enough to worry them all. What is it, Mr. Helm?"

I said truthfully, "If I have any information dangerous to them, I don't know what the hell it could be."

"Hit him, Jake."

We played variations on this theme for a while. It got a little rough, but there was nothing to do but take it. I mean, if I'd thought they were planning to kill me, or work me over hard enough to cripple me, I might have tried something violent to break it up, but that would have involved noise and, probably, dead men on the floor, and Mexican policemen all over the place. As long as it was no more serious than a bunch of hoods demonstrating their touching faith in the power of knuckles, I could ride along with it, amusing myself in the usual way—under such circumstances—by thinking about the excruciating deaths they were all going to die when I caught up with them, later...

"*Stop it!*"

It was Roberta Prince, coming abruptly out of the chair from which she'd been watching the show. She darted across the room to grab Jake's arm, cocked to slug me once more.

"Oh, stop it, stop it, stop it!" she cried. "What are you

trying to do, kill him? He's a government agent, you can't just… Mr. Tillery, you told me if I got him here there'd be no rough stuff. You promised—"

Jake flung her off. When she started forward again, Tillery grabbed her. She fought him with sudden, hysterical desperation, kicking at him frantically and raking him with her long, silvery nails. He swore and let her go, clapping a hand to his face.

Then the big man with the sunglasses, the silent observer, stepped forward quickly and seized her by the arm, swung her around, and sent her reeling back against the wall with a full-armed slap. He moved in and kept slapping her, right hand and left, until her knees buckled and she sank to the floor, sobbing weakly. The big man regarded her for a moment, rubbing his hands together in an absent way.

"Tillery."

"Yes," said Tillery quickly, "yes, Mr. Sapio."

"This isn't getting us anywhere. Let's blow."

"Yes, Mr. Sapio. Come on Jake. Mr. Sapio thinks we'd better leave now."

As they started for the door, Roberta Prince looked up quickly, pushing the tangled pale hair out of her eyes. She had stopped crying.

"What about me?" she gasped. "Mr. Tillery, what about the protection you promised me? What about my money?"

Tillery turned. He looked down at the blood-stained handkerchief he'd been holding to his scratched face and he looked at the kneeling girl. He laughed sharply.

"You bitch!" he said in his high-pitched voice. "You nasty, vicious little tramp! I hope Frankie has lots of fun with you before he wrings your skinny neck! I just wish I could be there to watch."

As the door closed behind them, Roberta began to cry once more, softly and hopelessly.

## 15

Entering my room, I found another one on the bed. I mean, it had been a morning for beat-up females: first Beverly Blaine, then Roberta Prince—whom I'd left repairing her tear-damaged makeup—and now there was Charlotte Devlin sprawled face down on top of the bedspread with her shoes on. They were still, I noted, rimmed with dried mud. Her sheer, dark stockings were kind of loose and wrinkled about her legs, and her tailored gray suit was kind of bunched about her body. Her glasses lay on the bed beside her. She didn't stir as I closed and locked the door behind me.

I moved forward cautiously, expecting the worst, since a woman will almost invariably kick off her shoes before lying down on a bed unless she's in very bad shape indeed, drunk or dying. Exactly why anybody would want to kill the girl and dump her on me I didn't know, but then, there seemed to be a lot about the case I still didn't know, probably enough to motivate another murder or two. Frank Warfel could simply have decided she was making a nuisance of herself, and he was a man who seemed to take homicide quite lightly, particularly if he could get it committed by someone else.

Approaching the bed, I saw that one dangling hand retained a precarious grip on some white paper, perhaps a clue. I worked it free and found myself holding a genuine wad of damp Kleenex. I dropped it into the nearby wastebasket and studied the motionless figure before me more closely, realizing that it was breathing quite normally.

There was no blood or other sign of violence that I could see. I decided with relief that, not only wasn't she dead, she wasn't even wounded, bruised, poisoned, or drugged. Shoes or no shoes, she was merely sound asleep, looking only as disheveled as any woman is apt to, caught taking a daytime nap in her clothes. The brief skirt of her suit had worked up far enough behind, I noticed, to reveal an interesting sartorial detail: the currently somewhat untidy stockings weren't separate stockings at all, but integral parts of an all-in-one nylon garment, sheer below and only slightly more opaque above, apparently designed to render obsolete such old-fashioned undercover engineering items as garters and girdles.

"Mr. Helm!"

It was an embarrassed and rather indignant gasp as, waking, Charlie sat up to look at me reproachfully. After a moment, she made the standard sleeping-beauty gesture of tugging down her skirt—undoubtedly, the first conscious act of the legendary princess kissed awake by the legendary prince—then she sniffed and looked around helplessly. Guessing at what was required, I went into the bathroom, got a fresh bunch of tissues from the dispenser there, and returned to put it into her hand.

"Thanks," she said, applying it vigorously to her nose. Finished, she put on her glasses to see me more clearly, saying, "I'm sorry, Mr. Helm. I didn't mean to fall asleep—"

"Ladies occupying my bed generally call me Matt," I said. "How's the allergy?"

It was a casual, conversation-making question designed simply to put her at ease, but she took it seriously, hesitating over the answer as if it really mattered.

"Well," she said reluctantly, "well, if you must know, it's terrible. Or was. It seems to be considerably better now, but I had some kind of an asthma attack on the way down. I really thought for a while I wasn't going to make it here; I could hardly breathe. It was all I could do to keep the car on the road. That's why, when I got in here and found the room empty, I just couldn't help flopping down on the bed for a moment, but I had no intention of… My God, I look like something thrown out with the trash! If you want to be a gentleman, you can discreetly avert your eyes, just for a moment."

I said, "Cut it out, Charlie. A gentleman? A trigger-happy super-spook like me?"

She flushed slightly and, rather defiantly, rose and turned her back on me and went through the contortions necessary to take the slack out of her sagging hosepants.

Then, without deigning to look my way, she moved stiffly to the dresser. After making a wry face at her reflection in the mirror, she smoothed down her outer garments neatly, buttoned the collar of her blouse, and patted her short, crisp hair into place.

"Matt."

"Yes, Charlie."

"You don't like me very much, do you?"

"Now, what brought that on?" I asked.

"The way you keep throwing my words in my face. Heavens, I didn't think you'd be so sensitive, in your line of work. If you want me to apologize, well, all right, I will. I am very sorry I called you a trigger-happy super-spook, Mr. Helm."

It reminded me of Lionel McConnell, dying, apologizing for calling me a honkie bastard. The memory was not a happy one, particularly now that I knew he'd been shot down just to make me believe that Beverly Blaine was also in danger.

I said, "That's not the point. It's not what you call me, it's what you are while you're calling me that—and while you're talking about my 'line of work' as if it gave you a pain in your tummy."

She turned slowly to look at me, frowning. "That's a little complicated, Matt. You're going to have to explain it."

I said, "Hell, I'm just mildly allergic to cops, that's all. Particularly dedicated cops with high-moral, law-enforcement missions. And most particularly dedicated cops with high-moral, law-enforcement missions who look down their long blue noses at me and my job."

"I don't—"

"The hell you don't. I'm not supposed to kid you about what you do, but you're supposed to be quite free to sneer at what I do." I grinned. "I'm not complaining, understand. We're used to that attitude from you badge-toters. I'm merely pointing out that if you want my respect and affection you're picking a damn funny way to get it."

She didn't smile. She said sharply, "You're being rather stupid, aren't you? After all, you're kind of a cop yourself."

"Don't ever think it, Charlie," I said. "My job is defending the people and to hell with the laws. Your job is defending the laws and to hell with the people."

"That's not fair! I… we…" She checked herself and drew a long, ragged breath. "I don't know how we got into this, Matt, but I don't think we'd better pursue the argument any further, do you? Particularly since what I really wanted was… was to ask a favor of you."

"A favor?" I said. "Sure. In our detestable undercover line of work we hold no grudges. Anything your little heart desires. My house is yours, as they say down here."

She looked at me for a moment without speaking, then she asked gravely, "Why does it amuse you to needle me, Matt? Is it because… because I have no sense of humor? Would you tease me for being half-blind if I were missing an eye? Or for being crippled if I'd lost a leg?"

It was a hell of a thing for her to say. It made her, suddenly, a human being instead of a kind of stiff-necked female-type robot programmed to give interestingly pompous reactions to my excruciatingly clever stimuli. I regarded her for a moment, totally disarmed and disconcerted.

"All right, Charlie," I said at last. "All right. I'm sorry. Smack me if I get flip again. What's the favor?"

"You… you won't tell them at the Bureau, will you? Please?"

"Tell them what?"

"You know." She made a gesture towards the bed. "The way… the way you found me in here. I haven't had an attack like that since I was in high school. I thought I was all over them long ago, permanently cured. I don't know what brought it on, maybe strain; I've been working pretty hard on this Warfel thing. They say it's partly emotional, you know." She stopped. I waited, and she went on: "Don't you see, Matt? If… if the Bureau learns about it, and about the way I blanked out in here afterwards while I was supposed to be on duty… We're all supposed to be perfect physical specimens, you know."

I hesitated, not because it mattered to me, but because it seemed a little out of character for her—at least out of the character I'd built for her. I was surprised that she'd conspire with me to evade her own organization's health rules, dedicated as she was to upholding all laws and regulations.

I said, "Your secret is safe with me, Charlie. Sneeze and strangle all you want to. Your people won't hear a word about it from me."

"Thanks," she said. "Thank you very much. I mean it."

"Sure," I said. "Anytime."

"Matt."

"Yes?"

"It *wasn't* fair. What you said. We do care about people as well as laws. We do!"

I grinned. "Well, in that case you'll be interested to know that some people are going to break some narcotics laws—your specialty, I believe—in a village up the coast called Bernardo, apparently little more than an overgrown trailer court. The time is tonight. Your friend Warfel is expected to join the party briefly, at least long enough to pick up the first shipment of the laboratory's product, which will then be concealed in a toilet on his boat, the *Fleetwind*, ready to be pumped out the plumbing at the first sign of trouble. He will return innocently to his home port north of the border and await developments. If none develop within a few days, and the coast seems perfectly clear, he will bring his cargo ashore and, presumably, put it on the market."

She was looking at me, wide-eyed. "Matt! How did you learn all this?"

I grimaced. "That's the big catch, doll. The information was fed to me deliberately by some Cosa Nostra characters—well, they called it the corporation, talking among themselves—who thought they were being very ingenious. Maybe they were."

Her face registered disappointment. "Oh. You mean it's just a phony lead? Were they Warfel's men?"

"I didn't say it was necessarily a phony lead; and they weren't Warfel's men." I told her what had happened since I'd seen her last. She was a little shocked by the

Beverly Blaine part of the recital, particularly the end of it. She also made it clear that she didn't think much of the way I'd let a blonde trick me into a trap. I had a hunch she didn't really believe I'd done it intentionally, in spite of the information it had gained us. "So you see," I said, "the syndicate, whatever you want to call it, is trying to clean house. The questions are: Just what do they expect us to do with what they told me, and what are they planning to do that they didn't tell me about?"

"You mean," she said, "you think they're trying to trick us into helping—"

"Sure," I said. "Hell, in a way they want the same thing you do. They want this dope project stopped. The difference is, they want to keep Warfel's part in it quiet, and you want to make it as public as you can. So let's figure out why they'd go to a lot of trouble to hand me all this poop while pretending to have gotten me in there to question me about something altogether different—not that I don't think they'd have liked to get answers to their questions, but they were willing to settle without them. Anyway, I have a hunch that what they let me hear was the straight stuff, at least up to a point."

"But why would they want you to know it?"

"Because they know I'm working with you, and they know who you are," I said. "Because they figure I'll tell you, as I'm now doing, and you'll get the Mexican authorities to close down that Bernardo heroin-manufacturing installation, thereby saving the brotherhood, or whatever they call themselves—the corporation—a lot of trouble in a foreign country where their connections may not be quite as strong as back in the U.S. They don't care who hits the laboratory as long as it's hit. They just want it out of business, like you do. They know Warfel wouldn't be fool enough to have anything there that'll connect it with him."

"But what about Warfel himself. We know he took the boat out yesterday, but—"

"That," I said, "is the big problem. They certainly don't intend to let you get your hands on Frankie in U.S. waters with a big shipment of heroin on board; that's exactly what they're trying to prevent. They may have told me the truth about what Warfel is *planning* to do, or what they think he's planning to do, but you can be damn sure they intend to alter his plans in some fairly drastic way. But they have to get you thinking you know exactly where and how to arrest him, because obviously you won't raid the lab they want raided until you're sure of catching Mr. Warfel red-handed—maybe I should say white-handed—with a substantial sample of the goods."

"I see," she said slowly. "So you figure they hope I'll take care of the laboratory for them with Mexican help, and then—believing their information—hurry north and sit waiting for Frankie to appear with a boatload of heroin, only it won't happen."

"That's right," I said. "And it won't happen because Frankie will be taking a long, long dive with an anchor or a chunk of ballast tied around his neck—if they catch him before you do, and they must have some reason to think they can. And the *Fleetwind* will either sink, burn, blow up, or be found adrift and deserted, another mystery of the sea."

She hesitated, and looked at me uncertainly. "Matt, please don't think I'm ungrateful for your help, but actually you're just guessing, aren't you?"

I said, "An educated guess, sweetheart, by a guy with a criminal turn of mind. Don't quote me, but I've had the job of removing a too-greedy character or two, myself, in the interest of company public relations. I know what I'd do if I were in the shoes of Tillery, Jake, and Sapio."

"I see." Her eyes were steady on my face. "You're not really a very nice man, are you?"

I said dryly, "You can find yourself a very nice man later, to date and to marry, if you look hard enough, I'm quite sure. Right now, you need a nasty, experienced bastard like me to work with. I'm a pro, Charlie. I'm giving you the benefit of my professional judgment."

"I know. I'm sorry." She sighed. "So that's what you'd do if you were in the shoes of those Mafia characters. What would you do if you were in my shoes?"

"Hell, I'd clean the mud off them," I said. I grinned at her quick, downward glance; then I stopped grinning and said, "Obviously, you've got to take out those three and give friend Warfel a clear run home with the dope, much as it hurts to help that creep in any way."

"Take them out? You mean—"

"I mean take them out," I said. "Whether you use three separate bullets, a single hand grenade, or a Mexican jail, doesn't really matter. As a matter of fact—"

"What?"

I rubbed my sore diaphragm thoughtfully. "Well, it's strictly none of my business, and as I said, we hold no grudges in this racket, but I do have a kind of personal interest in those three gents. If you'll handle the Bernardo end, I'll see what I can do about the Tillery-Jake-Sapio axis. Just remember, if I give you a guy named Warfel, you owe me a guy named Nicholas."

Charlie frowned quickly. "Why, I thought you said that girl was Nicholas, the one who… who died."

"I said she *said* she was Nicholas. It's not quite the same thing."

"You mean you think she'd lie when she was about to kill herself?"

"How else could she strike back at me?" I shrugged. "Hell, one way or another she was through, finished, and she knew it, and it was my fault. The least she could do by way of retaliation was leave me with a misleading lie and hope it would louse me up badly, with her compliments. I'm not saying that's what happened; but I've damn well got to make sure it isn't."

The tall girl with the glasses was studying me warily. "I see. So you're not really helping me entirely out of the kindness of your heart, Matt. You've still got an ax of your own to grind."

I shrugged once more. "Does it matter?"

She hesitated. When she spoke again, her voice was cool: "Not unless… unless you mess up this job for me, doing your thing, whatever it is. I wouldn't advise your sacrificing my mission to yours, Matt. I think you'd regret it."

I looked at her for a moment. Her face was strangely cold, and there was a hard, bright, fanatic gleam in her eyes. I said, "Why, Charlie, that's a threat! Are you sure you mean it?"

"I mean it." Her voice didn't waver, and neither did her shiny eyes. "This job is extremely important, not only for me but for a lot of innocent people. Don't spoil it. If you do, you… you'll be sorry."

I don't react well to threats, not even from handsome young ladies in horn-rims who disarmingly admit to having no sense of humor.

"Now it's my turn," I said. "My speech on the subject goes like this, Charlie: don't get in my way, or put any people in my way, no matter what you think I may have done. For one thing, I probably won't have done it. I have no intention of turning Warfel or anybody else loose with a boatload of heroin; I'm going to do my best to see that you get him. Remember that, if anything goes wrong. But remember another thing, too. If you get mad at me, and send somebody after me, and he interferes with my assignment in any way, he won't come back, whoever he may be. Okay?"

She said softly, "You're really quite unbelievable, aren't you?"

"Hell, one good threat deserves another," I said. "But I'd better not be unbelievable, because if you don't believe me, somebody could die. Now let's stop making faces at each other. You were supposed to check on a guy named Sorenson."

"Are you still harping on that?" When I didn't answer, she said, "Oh, all right, I checked on him. He's had some chemical training, mostly stuff like gas analysis, but he might be able to master the necessary technique. But a more unlikely person for Warfel to pick to run his laboratory…" She paused. I didn't say anything. She said, "Well, so much for Sorenson. Now what about that syndicate man, Tillery, and his two friends? How do you intend to locate them and deal with them?"

I said, "I'll worry about the dealing after I've done the locating. And I think I have a pretty good lead, just a few doors down the hall."

"Do you think that blonde will tell you where to find them? Even if she knows, why should she tell?"

I said, "Never mind, Charlie. You have your little secrets and I have mine, and that's one of them."

She made a small gesture of distaste. "Well, do it your way. But remember, this is very important, to me and to—"

"I know," I said. "To thousands of innocent people. I'll remember. Well, I'll be on my way as soon as I've cleaned up a bit in the john. Help yourself to the phone if you need it… What's the matter?"

"Nothing. I just remembered, they had another smog alert on the Los Angeles radio as I was driving down. I hope it won't interfere with our plans. If Warfel should be delayed by weather…" She was silent, obviously considering that and other problems confronting her; then she looked up. "Matt."

"Yes."

"I didn't mean to be nasty."

"Neither did I," I said. I wasn't telling the exact truth, but then, I didn't think she was, either.

**16**

Approaching Roberta Prince's room, I made a little bet with myself as I had before, quite recently, under very similar circumstances. I mean, the girl had said she was merely going to fix her makeup while I went and cleaned up in my room, but once she got to thinking about the situation, I was fairly sure other ideas would occur to her, if they hadn't already. After all, this was Hollywood country or close to it, and once they get a good script out there, or even just a passable one, they'll all gang up on the poor, lonely little idea and beat it to death.

I knocked on the door and got no answer. Checking, I found it unlocked, as I had left it. I walked in, since I'd told her I'd be back shortly and she'd said that would be fine. The first thing I noticed was that the black and white pants outfit she'd been wearing was kind of scattered around the room along with everything that went with it, intimate and otherwise. The second thing I noted was that the bathroom door was closed and the shower was running. I made a mental check in my mental notebook to indicate that I'd won my own money once more.

I knocked on the bathroom door. "Roberta," I called. "Miss Prince. Bobbie. Are you all right?"

The shower stopped. After a little pause, the door opened, and as expected, she had on absolutely nothing except a towel wrapped around her head, turban-wise, to protect the long blond hair from the spray. Another towel was being used for drying purposes, but it was carefully deployed, at the moment, so as not to obstruct much of the view.

Her body was more feminine than I'd anticipated, despite its lean greyhound proportions. After all, even greyhounds come in two sexes, and there was absolutely no doubt which one she was. She was smoothly tanned all over. I reflected on the philosophic truth that the difference between being embarrassingly naked and interestingly nude can be just a nice coat of tan.

"Get my robe out of that closet, will you, darling?" she said calmly. "The blue terry cloth beach thing. You'll see it."

"Sure," I said, and grinned, not moving. "Just how long did you stand under that shower, Bobbie, waiting to make this spectacular appearance?"

She was slightly disconcerted; then she laughed. "Too damn long. I'm practically waterlogged. What the hell kept you, anyway?"

"I had a visitor. A lady dope-cop with the sniffles. We had to compare notes and strategy."

"The sniffles? What's she got to sniffle about?" Bobbie asked.

I couldn't see why she should be interested in Charlotte Devlin's respiratory symptoms, when there were other things in my statement designed to concern her more, but at the moment, feeling out the situation, I was happy just to follow any conversational lead she offered. As for my promise to Charlie, I'd only promised not to tell the people for whom she worked. The chances of this girl discussing with them the health of one of their agents was fairly small.

I said, "Apparently she had asthma as a kid and something brought on a recurrence this morning, but she's pretty well over it now."

"That's too bad," Bobbie said. "Cops! Wouldn't it be great if they'd all drown in their damn mucus? If you're quite through appraising the merchandise, you might get me the robe I asked for."

I still didn't move. "Merchandise," I said, regarding her boldly. "The word implies something for sale."

She looked at me for a moment. A kind of hardness came into her eyes. "Who said it wasn't? Are you making an offer, darling?"

"It depends," I said. "Are we dealing in cash or some other medium of exchange? I'm a government man, Bobbie. They don't pay us enough that we can afford to take on high-priced, Hollywood-type dames; at least not for money."

"You've got a gun, haven't you? You're supposed to know how to use it, aren't you? I need protection, don't I? From Frankie Warfel and... and maybe now from those other creeps as well. Why do you think I staged this nudie show, anyway?" There was a little silence. "Well, is it a deal?"

"Sure," I said. I licked my lips, as if they'd gone kind of dry, which they had. It was an automatic reaction that annoyed me. "Sure it's a deal," I said.

"Do you want to close it now?" Her voice was expressionless.

I shrugged. "Why not? No sense your putting on a lot of clothes just to take them all off again."

"Well, dump that junk off the bed while I lock the door," she said, very business-like, and turned away.

I walked over to the bed and yanked everything off it except the bottom sheet and the pillow. When I turned, she was coming towards me, pulling the towel-turban off her hair, which spilled over her slender brown shoulders, pale and gleaming.

She walked up to me deliberately, studied me for a moment, and reached out to unfasten the single button of my jacket that was fastened. She worked the jacket off my shoulders and arms and let it fall. She took the gun from my waistband, made a face at it, and laid it carefully on the bedside table. She pulled my shirt out of my pants all around, and unbuttoned it down the front. I stood quite still. She poked me lightly just below the ribs where some discoloration showed. I winced.

"You're a sadistic, naked bitch," I said.

"That's right," she murmured. "Isn't that what you want, a sadistic, masochistic, naked bitch? Do you have any preferences, darling? Any particular way you like to do it? What, no imagination, just sex, sex, sex?" She slipped her hands around my body under my loosened shirt, and pulled me hard against her, and kissed me on the mouth. "At least the man is tall enough for a change," she whispered. "You don't know how tired a girl can get, taking a couple of inches off her height just to feed the goddamn male ego! Well, can you take your pants off all by yourself or do you need some help?"

I cleared my throat, and said harshly, "Okay, Bobbie. That's enough. Cut, as they say in Hollywood."

It was a gamble, of course. I hadn't really made up my mind which way to go until the last moment. The safest course would have been to play along, I suppose, but quite apart from the moral aspects, which don't concern us greatly, there were practical disadvantages to that course of action. I will admit, however, that the thing that swayed me in the end, just a little, was that nice healthy tan and the funny kind of tomboy innocence her face had, close to mine, without all the dramatic movie star makeup.

She didn't move at all for a long moment. Then she released me and took one step backwards.

"What is this?" Her voice was hard. "What are you, a queer or something?"

"Now, now, Bobbie," I said. "Keep it clean. You know what I am: I'm a government man. And you know what you are: you're a girl who's been planted on a government man to find out exactly what he does with the information he's been carefully fed—to find out, and to pass the dope along to some guys, three at the last count, so they can act accordingly." I grimaced, dramatizing my indignation. "Jesus, don't you West Coast people have one original idea among you? It's been plant-a-dame-on-Helm week ever since I got out here!"

Bobbie Prince drew a long breath and started to say something, but changed her mind.

I said, with an anger that wasn't altogether faked: "Did you really think I'd buy that ancient routine, you pretending to be so concerned about the way those nasty big men were hitting poor little me, and getting yourself violently slapped around as a result? Did you think I'd buy it after just having had Beverly Blaine pretend to be violently kidnaped for my benefit—not to mention the last spectacular act she put on for me? My God, I'm in the business, Bobbie; I *work* here! Do you know how many times that turkey's been tried on me? Hell, even my own side, such as it is, has been parking stray females in my hip pocket! And that creaky old seduction bit: look-at-pretty-little-me-all-naked-and-desirable? What do you people think I am, a kid who's never seen a woman with her clothes off?" I sighed, like a man at the end of his patience. "For Christ's sake go cover it up before it freezes, Bobbie. Some day when I feel like it, and if you feel like it, I'll be very happy to go to bed with you—I've been looking for a tall girl to love and cherish and maybe you're the one—but I'm damned if I'm going to do it right before lunch just to oblige a precious little fat man named Tillery."

"Well, actually it was Mr. Sapio's idea. Tillery's mind doesn't work quite that way, if you know what I mean."

Bobbie's voice was low but steady. She started to say more, but changed her mind once again. She turned and walked to the closet and opened the door. Then she pressed her forehead against the jamb and stood there for several seconds without moving. "That's... that's quite a whip you carry, Mister. And you sure know how to lay it on."

"You had it coming. Put on a dress or something and I'll take you to lunch."

She didn't seem to hear. "I ought to be mad," she said. "A woman's supposed to be furious when her lily-white body's been cruelly rejected, isn't she?"

"Whose lily-white body?" I asked.

Still without turning her head, she said, "Either you're kind of a sweet guy who can't bear to take advantage of a girl, and then roars like hell to cover up his sentimentality, or you're a calculating sonofabitch who's trying to promote something by—"

I said, "I'm not a sweet guy. Take it from there."

"What do you want, then? What do you want that you couldn't have got by kidding me along, by letting me think you were a sucker for my charms, as the saying goes?"

She wasn't dumb. I hesitated briefly, because it was still a big gamble; then I said, "I want three things. They're called Sapio, Tillery, and Jake. If they've got friends here, I want those, too."

"Oh, Christ," she said softly. "How did I ever get into this?"

I said, "I don't see you getting into anything, not even a dress. Put something on and let's eat."

"Why should I double-cross them for you?"

I said, "Hell, I don't know. Because they didn't really ask whether or not you wanted to play in this game in the first place? Did they? Because you want out and maybe I can get you out? Maybe—that's not a promise. Or just because I'm a calculating sonofabitch who needs your help?"

"Help to do what?"

"Cut it out," I said. "Would it make any difference to you if I gave you a long patriotic spiel about the vital importance of my government mission, or lectured you on all the poor victims who'll become helpless slaves to the demon dope if Frank Warfel has his way? You don't look like a great patriotic humanitarian to me, sweetheart. Excuse me if I'm wrong."

I heard her laugh abruptly. Then she'd pulled a short, fuzzy robe from the closet and wrapped it around her; and she was coming back across the room to me. She stopped in front of me and, working deliberately, buttoned my shirt up and tucked it in all around while I stood without moving. Then she took the gun from the table and thrust it into my waistband. Finally, she picked my coat off the floor and put it into my hands.

"I don't promise anything," she said. "I don't promise a damn thing. Those guys scare the hell out of me. You know what happens when you double-cross them."

"I know," I said. "And I won't be able to protect you indefinitely. Right now, maybe, but in the long run, unless I can make a deal for you somehow, you'll just have to take your chances."

She frowned. "There you go again," she murmured. "Damn you, why don't you lie to me a little, and tell me how safe I'll be if I cooperate, with you and the government looking after me. Why be so damn honest?"

"It's all calculated, for effect," I said. "You refuse to make love to the girl under false pretenses, you tell her the truth all the way down the line, she falls for you like a ton of bricks and does what you want, see?"

"You bastard," she said; "you've got me all mixed up. Buy me a lunch and let me think, will you?"

# 17

The dining room was a big, light barn of a place with long glass doors, now closed, showing a deserted swimming pool patio. A little steam came off the water in the pool, indicating that the air was still pretty chilly out there, despite the sunshine. Inside, the rustic tables and chairs were arranged to leave a large open space in front of the glass doors, for dancing and entertainment in the evening, but now, at noon, the place was almost empty.

"Margaritas!" Bobbie said scornfully as I seated her at a table for two. "Darling, here I was beginning to think you might possibly be quite a guy. Don't go and spoil it by offering me *margaritas*!"

Partly, she was stalling, of course, while she tried to make up her mind, but partly she was putting on an act for Tillery and Co. If they should be watching, they'd see her making conversation vivaciously, entertaining the government boob she'd been ordered to work on, impressing him with her bright personality, making him think she was the girl for whom he'd been waiting all his life, a girl to whom he could confide his most secret hopes and fears—and his most secret information. Sitting down facing her, I played up by looking abashed at the way my suggestion had been received.

"Why, what's wrong with margaritas?" I asked humbly.

"Nothing," she said, "nothing, I suppose, if you *like* a tourist tipple made up of cactus juice and Cointreau—and they generally don't even use the genuine Cointreau down here, but a local product spelled, for God's sake, Controy!" She leaned forward and patted my hand across the table. "Don't be like all those other bigmouth big shots, darling. Don't try to impress me with your vast knowledge of Mexico and its products, alcoholic and otherwise. Hell, I was born in Yuma, Arizona, right on the border. I had my first slug of tequila—well, actually it was pulque, the stuff with the maguey worm in the bottom of the bottle—at the tender age of twelve. I can do the salt-and-lime bit for you like a native, and if I hadn't already known it, I'd have learned it from all the fat and greasy business types whose hobby is hauling blondes across the border and teaching them quaint bits of local lore while pouring cheap local liquor down them to get them into the mood. Margaritas were bad enough when they were a quaint local drink; now that they've become a national tourist industry, to hell with them. We don't have to play tourist, do we, darling? Let the quaint local bastards keep their quaint local salt-rimmed glasses. Just see if you can promote me a nice vodka martini, will you?"

It was quite a speech, and quite a vivacious performance went with it, but I didn't pay too much attention since I knew it wasn't really aimed at me. I didn't glance around the room to see if any likely targets were visible. I just sat there smiling and looking attentive, I hoped, maybe even fascinated, amorously enthralled, while I wondered what she could tell me if she decided to tell me anything, and what I'd do about it if she did.

"Yes," I said. "Yes, of course, sweetheart."

Since we didn't seem to be getting much action from the restaurant staff, I rose and walked over to the circular bar at the end of the room, returning with two vodka martinis, one of which I placed before my blond companion. She gave me a pretty smile of thanks.

"You're a darling, darling," she said fondly. "But tell me, honestly, why the hell should I stick my neck out for you?"

She was now wearing a sleeveless dress of yellow linen with a gaudy silk sash for a belt and hardly any skirt to speak of. I noted that she was another pant-stocking girl. Well, with that abbreviated dress, she pretty well had to wear tights, since practically everything showed when she sat down. I'm not usually so sharply conscious of these matters, although I seldom overlook them entirely. I guess I was feeling a few twinges of regret for a missed opportunity. It seemed that, like it or not, I was over my period of mourning for Annette O'Leary; I was no longer in a chaste and continent mood.

I sat down and tasted my cocktail, not bad, but actually I kind of enjoy a margarita once in a while. However, I wouldn't have spoiled Bobbie's act for the world.

"Honestly?" I said. "You put me on the spot, doll. Honestly, I can't think of a single damn reason why you should stick out your neck for me."

"Then why the hell didn't you take the ticket that was offered and go along for the ride? I mean, you haven't really got a conscience about tricking a girl into bed, have you? Particularly when she asks for it like I did. If you'd played along, you might have learned something, or overheard something."

"Learned what?" I asked. "As long as you thought I was just a sex-mad sucker, you'd have been damn careful not to let me learn or hear anything I shouldn't. I figured I'd try convincing you I was a reasonably smart guy you could trust, a guy with a few scruples, even, and see what happened. Maybe you'd see a way you could use a guy like that, for your own preservation."

"And *are* you a reasonably smart guy with a few scruples I can trust, darling?"

I grinned. "We buried the last guy with scruples who tried to break into this business a long time ago. I think he lasted about six weeks, and only because it took that long for somebody to decide to send him out on a job. And only a fool would trust anybody in my line of work, Bobbie."

She sighed. "There you go again, undermining your own buildup. What the hell are you trying to do to me, anyway, get me all confused? Don't you know I want to think of you as a knight in bright armor on a big white horse, riding to the rescue of poor little me?" When I didn't say anything, she made a face at me and took a big gulp of vodka slightly adulterated with vermouth. "I've got to really *know* why you did it... I mean, didn't do it. Hell, you wanted me all right, you wanted me badly. Why didn't you just take, me and do the talking afterwards? The average guy would have figured to give the little girl a great big treat first, and she'd be his sex-slave for life, ready to risk anything for more of the same."

I said, "Hell, maybe I'm just an insecure, inadequate type. Maybe I don't have quite that much faith in my virility." I hesitated. "Do you want to know the truth?"

"That's what I'm asking for, isn't it?"

I drew a long breath, and said, "Well, the truth is..." I stopped and cleared my throat and started over: "The truth is, you looked kind of nice, kind of pretty, with that thick movie crud washed off your face. I... I just couldn't do it to you, not like that." There was a little silence. I went on: "You can start the laugh track any time."

She was looking down at her glass, twirling it between her fingers, using the long blond hair to keep me from seeing her face.

"You're conning me, aren't you?" she whispered at last. "You know that's what I'd like to think, gullible me, so you're using it against me. Aren't you?"

"Sure," I said. "A little. Naturally. How can I help it? After years of practice, how do you stop? But that was part of it, I swear it." The funny thing was, as I've already indicated, I was telling the truth.

She sighed, and lifted her glass and drained it in one

motion. Setting it down gently, she said, "I can't tell you where they are right now, Matt, if that's what you need to know. They didn't say where they'd be staying. But I know they figure on taking some kind of drastic action tonight, and before they do they'll want to hear what I've found out about you—about what you and that female dope-agent are up to. So they're going to call my room late in the afternoon, Tillery is. Maybe… maybe he'll let something slip. I'll see what I can find out for you. That's the best I can do." She drew a ragged little breath. "Matt?"

"Yes?"

"Do you really want lunch?"

I said, "Frankly, for some reason, food isn't exactly what's foremost in my mind at the moment."

She laughed softly. "In mine either. Drink your damn drink and let's go finish what we started, before I climb the damn walls…"

Later, much later, I woke abruptly and started to take evasive action, aware of a hand on my shoulder that might be hostile. I didn't know, and I wasn't about to wait to find out. Those who wait, waking up in doubt, don't generally live very long. However, my instinctive movement just got me entangled in blinding masses of hair that had a faint, clean, pleasant smell to it and reminded me of everything.

I sank back onto the pillow. Bobbie, standing by the bed bending over me, straightened up and tossed back the long blond hair that had fallen into my face. She laughed a bit uncertainly.

"My God; darling, do you always wake up like that?

Next time I'll get a long fishpole and poke you from across the room."

She was fully dressed, exactly the way she'd left the dining room, so that for a moment I found myself wondering if anything had actually happened between us, although I knew it had. Then, as I looked at her, I saw a faint pink flush come to her suntanned face, telling me it damn well had. We'd merely managed to shed the clothes, intact and rewearable, before shedding the inhibitions.

I said, "I must have fallen asleep. What time is it?"

"Four-thirty."

I whistled. "I must really have been asleep. Sorry."

"What for? What do you think makes a girl feel more appreciated, a man who falls asleep in her arms, afterwards, or one who looks at his watch and reaches for his pants? I let you sleep as long as I dared."

"Dared?"

"Well," she said, "well, I don't think you'd better be here when Tillery calls, do you? For one thing, if they're watching, he may not call until he knows I'm alone." She hesitated. "Of course, if you don't trust me to talk to him alone…"

I grinned. "Never talk about trust to a man in my business. I told you, we don't *trust* anybody—and if we should make an exception, we certainly wouldn't want it advertised. People might think we were getting soft, or something. Where the hell are my shorts?"

She found them on the floor and kicked them to me. "Matt."

"Yes."

"You must be feeling pretty clever." Suddenly her voice was cold. "Kidding the girl into helping you at the risk of her life and… and getting a little bonus besides. Pretty smart! But then, you are a pretty smart operator, aren't you?"

I found my shirt and put it on. "What's the matter?" I asked. "Are you having second thoughts, Bobbie? Like buying a used car: it looks good, it sounds good, but you're not quite sure, as you drive it off the lot, that the slick salesman hasn't sold you a rebuilt wreck with a crankcase full of sawdust. Is that it?"

She made a face at me. "It's not nice to read a girl's mind, darling. That's exactly the way I feel. Can you blame me?"

I said seriously, "No, I don't blame you a bit. And you can still change your mind if you want to. And if you don't—" I rose to zip and belt my pants, and stood facing her. "If you don't change your mind, if you go through with this, I want one thing clearly understood: I've given out no guarantees. Have I?"

She licked her lips. "No," she said, "no, I'll hand you that for what it's worth. That's what makes me feel like such a sap. I'm supposed to be a pretty sharp character myself, but here I'm sticking my neck way out for you, and you haven't—"

The telephone cut her short. We both jumped and turned to look at it. It rang again. Bobbie drew a long breath and reached out to pick it up.

"Yes? Oh, yes, this is Bobbie." She caught my eye and

nodded; and lowered her voice to a conspiratorial level, speaking into the phone. "Yes, of course I recognize your voice, and I've got something for you, but... but I can't talk right now. Can I call you? Oh, I see. Okay, you call me. Yes, he's in the john, but I'm not sure he... Give me ten minutes to get rid of him and ring me again, okay?"

She put the phone down and looked at me. I grinned. "Okay, I can take a hint. Just let me get my shoes on, will you?"

Bobbie didn't smile. She said, "That was Tillery. I tried to get him to say where I could call him, but he wouldn't."

"Sure," I said. "I heard you. You did fine."

"Exactly what do I tell him when he calls back?"

"Mostly the truth," I said. "Tell him you wheedled it out of me that my lovely associate, the female heroin hound, is making arrangements to hit the laboratory in Bernardo, with Mexican help, as soon as Warfel has picked up his shipment and got clear out to sea again so he can't be warned. Then she'll head north across the border to be waiting for him when he brings the boat home. Just how she's planning to keep him from jettisoning the evidence when she marches on board to make the arrest, I don't know and therefore couldn't tell you, but apparently she has some plan in mind. As for me, since my official job finished with Beverly Blaine, I'm just hanging around to give the government girl a hand if needed, meanwhile making alcoholic passes at stray blondes and talking too much about things I shouldn't."

"Matt."

"Yes?"

Bobbie licked her lips. "I'm scared. I know those creeps. I... I think Tillery called while you were still here, deliberately, just to see how I'd react. If I'd been willing to talk in front of you, he'd have known I was tricking him."

"Maybe," I said. "And maybe he simply hasn't got enough men to keep an eye on us, and just called because he was ready to call." I picked up my jacket and took a step towards her.

She stepped back and said sharply, "No, don't kiss me, you damn Judas. Just get the hell out of here and let me crucify myself alone." When I reached the door, she spoke to my back: "I'll call you in your room, okay?"

"Okay," I said. "Bobbie—"

"Beat it," she said. "Just keep going and close the door behind you and hope I don't come to my senses when you're gone."

## 18

I noticed two things immediately upon entering my room. I saw that Charlie Devlin was reclining on one of the beds, in her shirt sleeves—well, blouse sleeves—with her shoes off, talking on the phone. I also spotted my suitcase, that I'd left in a Los Angeles motel, now resting on the luggage stand at the foot of the same bed. I was happy to see it. Not only could I use a clean shirt, but I also needed something hidden in that bag. That is, I would need it if everything worked out the way I hoped, and it wasn't something a conventional-minded lady policeman like Charlie would be apt to have handy.

"Yes, I said a skin diver," she was saying impatiently. "What's the matter, is the connection bad at your end? A man with fins and tanks and a wetsuit... That's right. A skin diver. And he should have some kind of big plastic bags, big enough to hold several gallons, and some kind of adhesive that'll work on painted wood under water... No, I don't know of any, but there must be something; nowadays they've got stuff that'll stick anything to anything anywhere. No, I'm not crazy. We've got plans of the boat, haven't we? They show where the plumbing comes out through the hull, don't they? Well, as soon as Warfel docks, your man will swim down and fasten a bag over each opening so when they pump out the evidence it just stays inside the plastic where we can recover... Oh, for heaven's sake, you can work out the details with your underwater expert, can't you? You don't really expect *me* to... Of course the plastic will rip off at high speed! I said to wait until he docks, didn't I? He won't be going anywhere at high speed after that, he won't be going anywhere at all if we do our part... All right, call me back if you have any real problems." She put the phone down and looked at me. "You heard, Matt. Do you think it will work?"

I shrugged. "It sounds a little Mickey-Mousey to me, but that underwater stuff is out of my line. Thanks for having my suitcase brought down."

"It's got to work," she said. "I can't think of any other way... The suitcase? Oh, you're welcome. How did you make out?"

"Make out?" I said. "Are you using the term literally or colloquially?"

She examined me and made a little grimace of distaste. "Now that I look at you, I can see how you made out, colloquially. You have that satisfied-stud look. If I thought all this meant to you was a chance to go to bed with a blond tart in broad daylight—"

I said, "Hush your dirty mouth, Devlin."

She looked surprised. "What's the matter, are you sensitive about your methods? Do you feel guilty about seducing the poor little girl, so to speak, in cold blood? Poor little girl, indeed! That six-foot phony-blond tramp knows how to take care of herself, I'm sure. I wouldn't waste a worry on her, if I were you."

I said, "Charlie, I don't mind that you talk too much, I just object to the way you say all the wrong things; and why the hell can't you fix your stockings so they don't bag at the knees? Other women seem to be able to keep up those nylon combination garments without any trouble at all."

She said stiffly, "If you could keep your eyes off my legs—off any woman's legs—my stockings wouldn't bother you. And I've been just a little too busy making diplomatic arrangements to worry about a few wrinkles in my hose. You still haven't answered my question. Did you find out—"

"I don't know yet," I said. "We should have the word shortly, so leave the phone clear for a few minutes."

"She's going to call you here with the news?"

"One way or the other," I said. "However it goes."

"And if she does give you the information you need, what's the next step?"

"I'll go after them, naturally," I said, rummaging in my suitcase. I threw some clean clothes onto the bed, and opened a trick compartment that yielded a small, flat leather case, the contents of which I began checking carefully. "I'll keep them from interfering with your pet dope smuggler, somehow."

"I've made arrangements with the Mexican authorities." Charlie got off the bed and pulled up her nylon tights, almost unembarrassed this time. Pretty soon she'd be adjusting her brassiere in my presence without a blush. I didn't really know whether or not I looked forward to such an intimate relationship with this girl. She smoothed down her skirt, put her feet into her shoes, and picked up her purse to check her reflection in the mirror, giving me a glimpse of a small revolver that reminded me who she was and who I was and why we were here. She said, "Any help you require, Matt—"

"Are you crazy? The last thing I need, from your viewpoint, is some eager Mexican cops. If they start arresting people, what's to keep them from throwing Warfel in jail along with everybody else? You don't want him in a Mexican jail, I gather; you want him in a U.S. jail."

"Yes, but what makes you think he'll be available for arrest?"

"Well, Sapio and Tillery and Co. must be planning to intercept him somewhere, before he makes the heroin pickup at Bernardo."

"They could be planning to move in on him on the high seas afterwards, while he's sailing north with the dope."

"That's not likely," I said. "They've tipped you off, through me, remember. They can assume that beyond Bernardo our boy is going to be under your surveillance all the way. Isn't he?"

"Well, we've got a plane watch arranged—"

"And Tillery's smart enough to anticipate it. No, he's got some reason to think he can catch Warfel and his boat somewhere else, earlier in the evening. It's the only answer that fits."

"But he wants the laboratory taken care of, you said. And he knows we won't move in on it until we know that Warfel's taken the stuff aboard his boat."

"Won't you? With the Mexican authorities breathing down your neck? They'll play along with you as long as your plan seems to be working, sure, but if you wait until daylight, say, without anything happening—no boat, no pickup—they'll take over the jurisdiction that's rightfully theirs, and clean out this source of infection on Mexican soil, and to hell with Frank Warfel and to hell with you, señorita. You do have the lab spotted by now, I suppose."

"Yes. It's a big, shabby-looking old house-trailer in a bunch of other ones on the shore, right out in the open behind a tiny village of adobe huts. One store, one gas pump. I must have looked right at that trailer half a dozen times, driving down the highway to Ensenada. They've got a boat; and fishing rods and stuff for camouflage, but the foundations gave it away, among other things. Usually they just prop those trailers up on a few cinder blocks, but this is really solid. Of course it's got to be. You don't want to spill any of the reagents employed in the process because your whole laboratory jiggles every time somebody moves. Several would-be heroin refiners have blown themselves sky-high when they got just a little careless." Charlie sighed. "I suppose you're right.

We really have no authority here; the local people are just being nice. If Warfel doesn't come; the lab goes out anyway, and with it goes our only chance to discredit—"

"Sure," I said. "So all I've got to do is sneak up on the Tillery contingent while it's sneaking up on the Warfel contingent, and put the former out of action without alerting the latter, letting Warfel proceed about his evening's business undisturbed."

"You make it sound very simple."

"Do I? I don't mean to," I said. "But it can be done, if I can find out where the intercept will take place. And if I'm not harassed by several squads of Mexican constabulary clanking badges and guns at my back. Just tell them to look the other way no matter what happens. That's all the help I'll need. I hope."

"What about communications? How will I know if you've been successful?"

"You'll see Warfel or one of his boys come for the dope at Bernardo, that's how. What's the matter?"

"Why," she said, looking over my shoulder at the small, fitted case I was about to close, "why, that's a *hypodermic*!"

She sounded as shocked as if she'd spotted a truly obscene object in my hands. I suppose, as a dope-cop, she associated a needle with only one purpose, although she must have had a few legitimate injections in her life.

I said, "They are used for other purposes than shooting happiness into the circulatory system, you know."

"And those little bottles?"

I sighed. "Inquisitive, aren't you? It's really none of

your damn business, Charlie, but if you must know, the one marked A kills instantly but is fairly easy to detect The one marked B is a little slower, but only a biochemical genius who knows what he's looking for and works fast can find it in the body after death. We've been waiting for years for them to develop a single agent to take the place of those two, but there have been bugs in every one they've come up with, so it's been back to the drawing board for the scientific lads... The one marked C puts the guy to sleep for four hours, more or less, depending upon the dosage. Any more questions?"

"I'm sorry I asked." She was staring at me in a funny, wide-eyed way. She licked her lips. "You really are a pretty horrible person, aren't you?"

I grinned. "That's what I like about you, Charlie, that and the way you've got no sense of humor and admit it, and the way you look so damn tailored and competent, but your nylons are always falling down... No, no, they're okay now. Nice and smooth. I was just speaking in general terms."

She licked her lips once more. "I can see that you're trying to be objectionable, but just what are you trying to say?"

"Why, that you're such a rewarding person to do things for, sweetheart. Here I'm setting out to tackle at least three violent, armed Mafia characters single-handed, just for you, and you stand there and insult me! Hell, a truly sensitive guy might get discouraged and say to hell with the whole lousy—"

The telephone rang. We looked at each other, silenced by the sudden, jangling noise; then I stepped over and picked it up as it rang again.

"Yes?"

"Matt?" It was Bobbie's voice. "How about buying me a dinner? I've earned it, darling."

"Swell," I said. "The top of the menu to you, with champagne. Just give me a couple of minutes to change my shirt."

"To hell with champagne," she said. "I need something stronger than champagne, and the Mexican bubble-stuff is terrible anyway. I need it right now. I'll meet you in the bar."

"That tough?" I said.

"It wasn't fun. But I don't think he suspected anything, and I think I got the location you wanted. You'd better try to scare up a good map, but don't be long. I... I'm kind of scared to be alone."

The line went dead. I put the phone down and looked at Charlie, who was watching me expectantly.

"Well, she got it, she says," I reported.

"Do you think you can really trust that bitch—"

"Devlin, shut up," I said. "Get me a detailed map of this coast, preferably topographic, while I take a quick shower. And if you can scrounge up a jeep or pickup truck or dune buggy or something, I'd appreciate it. We may hit some roads a little too rough for that rental Supermarket Special I'm driving."

"I don't have a good map, but there's a set of aerial

photos we've been working from, over on the bedside table. You can have them; we've got another set." She opened her purse and took out a key and laid it on the photographs. "As for a jeep, I thought you might be wanting one, so I checked. There don't seem to be any available at the moment, but you can take my station wagon—I'll be riding with the Mexican police when I leave. The wagon's got a little more road clearance than a sedan to start with, and the springs are beefed-up for hauling a trailer; it'll go practically anywhere."

"A trailer?" I said, curious. "What kind of a trailer do you pull, Charlie?"

"I keep a horse at a ranch outside L.A. Sometimes I haul it up into the mountains for a trail ride." She hesitated. "I didn't mean to sound catty about the girl— or maybe I did—but has it occurred to you that she could still be working for the syndicate and setting a trap for you? I grant your terrific masculine charm and all that, but isn't it odd she'd change sides so easily?"

I said, "You don't know how easy or hard it was. And whether she's trapping them for me or me for them doesn't really matter, does it? Just so she brings us together, the reasons aren't too important. This Baja California is pretty wild country, the kind of country I'm supposed to be good in, and if I can't handle anything a bunch of city boys dream up, I deserve to be trapped." I winked at her. "Now beat it, unless you want to stick around and scrub my back. And good luck at Bernardo."

She didn't move at once. "Matt," she said slowly,

"Matt, please be careful. I really appreciate what you're doing. Although I'm sure you're doing it partly for reasons of your own."

I grinned and watched her pick up her jacket and go out the door, a tall, neat, nice-looking girl with crisp, short hair and a complicated personality that would take some figuring out, if a man decided it was worth the trouble. At the moment, I had other problems considerably more urgent.

# 19

The Warfel rescue expedition almost came to grief before it got started, shortly after dark. Driving south along Ensenada's main street, barely a block from the hotel. I headed Charlie Devlin's big Ford station wagon down into a kind of dip and hit a foot of water—well, call it eight inches. It was careless driving, I suppose, but even an old southwesterner like me, used to the intermittent streams and flash floods of that country, doesn't expect to meet a running arroyo in the middle of town on a clear spring evening.

"Hell, you should see Tijuana," Bobbie said after I'd nursed the half-drowned engine back to life and made it through the wash. "Anytime it's rained within a week, they've got a temporary river cutting the city in half, and only a lousy little two-lane bridge to carry all the traffic from one side to the other. You probably didn't notice, if you came through in the dark before anybody was awake, like we did; but on a busy weekend it can be the world's biggest traffic jam."

"You came down with Sapio and Tillery? What kind of a car are they driving?"

"It's Tillery's car, a Chrysler, the fancy model with the fake spare-tire cover growing out of the trunk lid. Don't you hate air scoops that don't scoop anything, and tire covers that don't cover anything? I mean, how phony can you get?" She drew a long breath. "Darling, do you want to know something? I'm still scared. In fact, I'm more scared."

"You could have stayed behind," I said.

"Alone?"

"I offered you a bodyguard."

"A cop? Thanks, I'll take Mr. Tillery any day, him and all his nasty friends, male and female and in between."

I grinned in the darkness. "What's with you and cops, Bobbie?"

"What's with *you* and cops?" she retorted. "I don't get the impression you're particularly fond of them, either."

I shrugged. "In my business, we sometimes find the official badge bearers getting a little too official, even in home territory. Then we have to get on the phone to Washington, and strings have to be pulled, and everybody gets very unhappy with everybody, especially with us. And in a foreign country like this, of course, the constabulary can make things very awkward indeed."

"Well, it's the same in my business, darling," Bobbie said, "except that we girls can't get on the phone to Washington. You'd be surprised what a cop sometimes figures his badge entitles him to, and I don't mean just payoffs of one kind or another. Hell, look at all these student riots. If *I* walked down the street, and somebody called me a pig—and that's a pretty nasty thing to call a woman in some places—and I grabbed a club and busted his head open, you know what, would happen to me: when they finished trying me in court for assault and stuff, they'd make me pay damages till I was old and gray! A private citizen isn't allowed to hit anybody except in *real* self-defense; name-calling doesn't count. But if you call a cop a pig and he clubs you, he figures he's a hero and deserves a medal for saving the country—and most of the time he gets it, too. Don't wish any cops off on me, darling. I'll just stick with you and take my chances."

"Okay, it's your choice," I said. I switched on the dome light. "But since you're here you might as well do some navigating. Take another look at those aerial photos and see if you can figure out just how far we go before we turn off to this Bahia San Agustin place. You're sure that's what Tillery said? Bahia San Agustin?"

"You asked me that before," she said, a little annoyed. "Yes, I'm sure! And it's right here on the photo with a hand-lettered name on it, like on all the rest of the prominent natural features along the coast. And it looks like a good, sheltered spot to bring in a boat you don't want a lot of people to see, nice and deserted. There doesn't seem to be a house or road within miles, except the track leading in from the main highway."

"The question is, why would Warfel risk landing at all, except at Bernardo where his lab is?" I shook my head ruefully. "Well, maybe we'll find out when we get there. For now, let's just hope we can hit the right road in the dark."

"Well, we've got a long ways to go yet."

We rolled on southward through the outskirts of Ensenada. Charlie Devlin's big wagon, for all its bulk, was considerably more pleasant to drive than the rental sedan I'd left behind. The power brakes were less sudden, the power steering had some road feel to it, and the beefed-up suspension was taut and competent. The engine was smooth and incredibly strong. It gave the massive vehicle the performance, if not the handling of a sports car. Chalk up another point for the horse-loving, humorless Miss Devlin—but she was not the lady whose character concerned me now.

After studying the aerial photograph a little longer, Bobbie returned it to its envelope. She leaned back against the head rest, stretching her long legs as far as the car would permit. She was wearing sneakers and white jeans, a striped yellow-and-white boys' shirt with the tails out, and a fringed sarape—a coarse, gray-brown, patterned Indian blanket with a hole to stick the head through. Topping off the outfit was a brown hat with a broken-down brim, which she now tipped over her eyes. I cut the interior light and reflected on the various incarnations of Roberta Prince.

I mean, first there had been the sexy, Hollywood-type gangster-moll with the undulating walk, the heavy makeup, and the various glamor-pants getups; and then there had been the nice, tall, tomboy-kid-next-door-trying-to-be-ladylike—once she got some clothes on—in a pretty yellow dress, with just a touch of lipstick.

That was the attractive companion with whom I'd had dinner, during which she'd told me what Tillery had told her over the phone: essentially just that he'd be seeing her, and paying her for her services, later that evening when he got back from Bahia San Agustin down the coast. Afterwards we'd. taken a stroll along the waterfront hand in hand, watching the sun disappear into the Pacific and pausing now and then for some amorous by-play that was supposed to be just for show but didn't quite work out that way. We'd returned to the hotel slightly disheveled and reasonably sure that, whether or not the syndicate boys had had us under surveillance earlier, there was nobody watching us now.

I'd gassed up the car while Bobbie was changing into a more durable costume; and now I had this lanky, long-haired, female-hippie-type beside me, complete with sarape, floppy hat, and a hate for the pigs. You had to hand it to her. Any part she played, she threw herself into heart and soul; but it would be nice if I could ask the real Roberta to stand up and take a bow. I remembered Charlie's warning. Well, I hadn't really planned to turn my back on anybody tonight, anyway…

"You'd better stop, darling." Bobbie sat up and pushed back her hat. Her voice was calm. "It's the Mexican immigration guy. Let me handle him."

I'd already seen a man in a khaki uniform emerging from a roadside shack to flag us down. "What's he doing down here?" I asked, bringing the station wagon to a halt.

"Oh, Ensenada's treated as a border town, no red tape, but if you want to continue down Baja you're supposed to have a tourist permit and stuff." She patted her pockets. "Hell, I left my room key at the desk. Have you got yours?"

"Well, yes," I said, "but—"

"Never mind. Give it to me."

She took the key and cranked down the window. The immigration inspector, or whatever he was, came up to greet us politely. Bobbie broke into fluent, atrocious Spanish, waving the key and explaining, as far as I could follow her, that we were American tourists staying in Ensenada and just wanted to take a little moonlight drive down the beautiful peninsula since it was such a lovely night. The *señor* could understand how it was. *Si*, we'd be coming back shortly. An hour? Well, that was hard to say. It was *such* a lovely night. It might be just a little longer than an hour…

"You've got to appeal to their romantic natures," she said as we drove away with official permission. She tossed the key into my lap. "Well, actually they're not very strict. As long as they know you've got a room in Ensenada and are planning to come back soon, they'll generally let you through. Obviously Tillery and his bunch got through—at least I assume they're ahead of us, don't you? Of course, they may have thought to get themselves fixed up with the right papers, like you should have."

I said, "Hell, my dope-chasing associate could have got me honorary Mexican citizenship, judging by the way she talked, but nobody told me I was going to have to pass any check points. Thanks. Are there any other surprises lurking along this highway?"

"Not that I know of," she said. "Of course, I've been down only a little beyond the end of the pavement, some ninety miles south, but this bay we're going to isn't nearly that far. As a matter of fact, I think you'd better plan on slowing down as soon as we get through that black-looking range of hills ahead. There seem to be all kinds of lousy little goat-paths leading off into the boondocks, and we don't want to miss ours, do we?"

Actually, we had no trouble finding it. There was even a weathered sign, at just about the right mileage from Ensenada, reading *Bahia San Agustin 11 km.* As I'd expected, it wasn't much of a road, just a pair of ruts across the desert that was now vaguely illuminated by half a moon. I turned off the highway, stopped the big Ford, and got out to check the ruts by the glare of the headlights. After studying the tracks in the dust for several minutes, I got into the car once more, frowning thoughtfully.

"Well, can you track the varmints, Davy Crockett?" Bobbie asked. "Did the critters take this road, Dan'l Boone?"

"I think so," I said. "At least, a big car with new tires came through not very long ago. But there's been some other traffic before it. A truck of some kind—a husky, six-wheeled job, if I read the sign correctly—and a jeep."

"A jeep? That man called Willy was driving a jeep last night, wasn't he? Frank Warfel's driver and general handyman? I never met him while I was with Frankie, but I heard Jake telling Tillery about him."

I said, "Well, I don't know exactly whose driver and general handyman he is—when last heard from, he seemed to be working for Beverly Blaine—but that's our Willy, all right. Of course, jeeps aren't exactly scarce in this country, and a lot of them come with identical tires, but the tracks do look familiar. Maybe Warfel's putting into this San Agustin place simply to collect Willy, but it would seem even simpler if Willy just met him at Bernardo where he's got to land anyway. And who wants a big truck down by the shore tonight, and what's it carrying? Is Frankie's boat picking up another shipment we don't know about? If so, it can't very well be heroin. The world's yearly production would hardly take up that much room or be that heavy—hell, one kilo is a lot of H, I'm told, worth over a quarter million bucks; and that's only two and two tenths pounds."

Bobbie said, "Of course, it could just be coincidence. It could just be a Mexican rancher hauling feed to his cattle, or something."

"It could be, except that I don't see any cattle around or any ranches either, and there wasn't any sign of habitation in that aerial shot. Let me see the thing again."

She handed me the envelope, and I switched on the light once more and studied the photograph. It takes a little adjustment for a man brought up on topographical maps, as I was, to make sense of an aerial photo, but once you get used to the idea you can get a much better notion of the terrain from a print like that.

I said, "We'll be approaching from the northeast, but the road actually passes well inland and hooks back around to the south side of the bay where the land is fairly flat. On that side it looks like there are just some dunes running out into a long sandspit that more or less shelters the anchorage. But there seem to be some steep bluffs or rocky cliffs on the north side, terminating in a rocky headland and some reefs. If I were Tillery, I'd put myself somewhere on that northern cliff, where I could cover the whole beach. The only catch is, if I were Warfel, I'd put a couple of sentries up there first thing, just to keep guys like Tillery honest. Well, we'll see. Cross your fingers; here we go."

It was just as rough as I'd expected from my previous experiences with Mexican back-country roads, but the stiffly sprung station wagon took it better than I'd expected and only scraped bottom occasionally. My big concern was the people ahead who weren't supposed to know that there were people behind them.

I ran without lights as much as possible, a precaution that slowed us down considerably and annoyed Bobbie terribly. She'd started worrying that we'd be too late, and of course it was a possibility, but I was gambling that Warfel would have stayed well off shore, out of sight, as long as there was any light at all. The *Fleetwind* was no speedboat; it would take him some time to bring it in from beyond the horizon. Anyway, late or early, there was only one way for one man to handle three or more, and it didn't involve barging around carelessly with headlights glaring.

My precautions paid off after about five miles. Creeping over the top of a ridge in blackout status, we saw headlights in the basin below. They weren't going anywhere; and dark figures were moving around the dim shape of the stalled car that, in the weak moonlight, had something of the look of a stranded whale.

I said, "Well, there they are. I figured, if their transportation was an ordinary sedan, they'd stick it sooner or later. You can practically count on it. City folks just never do seem to master this kind of driving." I studied the dim, distant scene. "My God, how many of them are there, anyway?"

"I count five," Bobbie said.

I sighed. "Maybe I should have brought that regiment of Mexican policemen that was offered me." I let the Ford roll forward to get it off the skyline, stopped it by a clump of shadowy, wispy trees I didn't bother to identify, and cut the switch. "Wait here, doll," I said.

"Don't be silly. I'm coming with you."

I said, "Sweetheart, I'm sure you're a great dancer and entertainer, but how many deer and elk have you stalked in your life?"

She said, automatically indignant, "I wouldn't kill a poor defenseless animal—"

"Says the girl who had steak for dinner, rare. Only somebody else killed that poor defenseless steer for her, so it's all right. You should hear my chief expound on the subject of people who can't bear to inflict death but are perfectly willing to profit by it to the extent of a good meal." I grimaced. "All right, skip the defenseless animals. How many armed men have you sneaked up on and slit the throats of?"

"Ugh," she said with a shiver. "Well, none, but—"

"Then just what the hell do you figure qualifies you for this duty? Stay here. If they dig it out and drive off, wait and I'll be back. But if those headlights go out and come back on again after five seconds, hurry on down there on foot. I don't want to take the chance of getting this heap stuck in whatever they've found to bog down in, but I may need your help, so don't loiter. Okay?"

She hesitated, and drew a long breath. "Okay, Matt. Be careful."

"Sure," I said; "Hell there are only five of them. I'll be careful."

## 20

Actually, I had no intention of tackling five syndicate goons all in a bunch. We're not paid to be heroes—at least we're not paid to be stupid heroes. I was counting on their splitting up and making the odds a little easier; and when I got within range of their voices, I found that was exactly what they were doing.

It was their logical next move if the Chrysler was badly stuck, as it seemed to be. They'd got it buried to the bodywork in the sand of a dry watercourse. Well, it's happened to other pavement-type drivers on other desert roads, in Mexico and elsewhere. They never learn. All they can think of, when they start to slip and sink in the soft stuff, is to spin the wheels frantically and dig themselves in deeper.

Tillery was issuing last-minute instructions to the two men I didn't know, although I should have known there were some others around. Jake had intimated that he hadn't been alone when he'd watched me disposing of Beverly Blaine's body.

"You two strong men stay here and get the car out of this riverbed," Tillery was saying. "Jack it up, stuff brush under the wheels, and back it up on the bank. Get it headed back the way we came, ready to go. When you hear shooting—you'll hear it all right; we can't be more than a mile or two from the coast—start the engine and switch on the lights so we'll know where to find you even if we miss the road in the dark. Come out and cover us if it sounds like we need it... Okay, Jake, you take your rifle. I'll handle the chopper."

"*I'll* handle the chopper." That was Sapio's voice.

"Yes, Mr. Sapio."

"Well, let's put it on the goddamn road."

"Come on, Jake. Mr. Sapio thinks we'd better get moving."

I crouched under a bush—mesquite, judging by the thorns—and watched the three shadowy figures march off to the southwest. Jake was carrying a heavy rifle equipped with some kind of a bulky telescopic sight, or maybe an electronic night-fighting contraption, it was impossible to tell. Sapio packed the unmistakable, old-fashioned shape of a Thompson with a drum magazine. You couldn't miss it, even in the dark. Well, it's still a good, reliable weapon, even though superseded in most places by newer and sexier submachine-guns; and it has the sterling virtue that the big drum full of cartridges lets you stay in the homicide business, without interruption, several times as long as the clip-type magazines supplied with most later models.

I lay there and waited while the trio disappeared from sight; and then I waited some more while the two men left behind worked at jacking and brush-cutting—I mean, why should I do the work when I could let them do it for me? When it looked as if they had the big car almost ready to go, I moved in on them.

The edge of the wash, a perpendicular three-foot cut-bank, caused me a little trouble. I had to wiggle downstream a ways to find a low place where I could slither down it without making any noise. They weren't expecting trouble, however, and I caught them just the way I wanted them: bending over, one man with both hands on the jack handle, the other with an armload of brush he was just about to stuff under the rising wheel.

"Hold it, boys!" I said from the bushes behind them. "There's a .38 looking right up your rear elevations. If either of you would like an extra hole back there, I'll be happy to oblige."

"Who—"

"Never mind who," I said, rising. "Just call me a man with a gun. No, don't straighten up. Just stay bent over like that, turn around slowly, and stretch out flat on the ground, faces in the sand. Swell. Now, where the hell do you keep the light switch on this limousine…"

I'd hardly cut the lights for the required five seconds and switched them back on, when there was a muffled cry and a heavy thump behind me. I stepped aside quickly to where I could cover the new threat as well as the men on the ground, but it was merely Bobbie Prince picking herself out of the soft sand at the base of the bank off which she'd fallen. She got up, brushing off her jeans and straightening her floppy hat—the sarape had apparently been left behind as excess baggage. She came forward, limping a bit, a slim, pale, boyish shape in the night.

"Why didn't you warn me there was a precipice there?" she asked resentfully.

"You're supposed to be waiting back at the station wagon," I said.

"You and your deerstalking!" she said. "You didn't hear me, did you? And neither did they. I didn't make any noise at all, did I?"

I said, "Sure, you're great like Hiawatha and you damn near got yourself shot. Do you know how to work a hypodermic?"

"Naturally, but don't ask me how I learned. Why?"

"There's a kit in my left coat pocket. Use the vial marked Injection C. The other two are lethal, and I see no need to kill anybody, at the moment. The dose is a half cc, cubic centimeter to you. Put the boys to sleep for me while I keep them covered. Then we'll get this heap out of here and get after their friends."

It wasn't quite as easy as that, of course, mainly because, once our prisoners were safely unconscious, I made the mistake of putting Bobbie behind the wheel of the Chrysler. I told her to send it forward very cautiously while I stood by to lend a shoulder if required. Unfortunately, it turned out that he had the same lead-foot, sand-driving technique as the man who'd got it stuck in the first place.

It came off the piled-up brush nicely, moving well—I didn't even have to push to get it started—but the tires started to slip as she got eager and fed it more power. She felt them dig in and, instead of easing off, she gunned it hard. If I hadn't sworn at her in a loud, ungentlemanly way, she'd have sunk it out of sight once more.

"I'm sorry!" she said, cutting the switch. Her voice said she was actually more mad than sorry. "I couldn't help it! It's just too damn soft. You didn't have to get nasty about it!"

I said, "It was coming fine, sweetheart. I told you to take it *easy*, didn't I? What the hell do they teach you kids in Yuma, Arizona? A lot of crap about defensive driving, I bet, and not a damn thing useful like how to get a car out of a sandy arroyo. Well, come along if you're coming."

She started to open the door, but hesitated. "What are you going to do?"

"I'm going after them, naturally."

"But what about the car?"

"To hell with the car. We've got our own transportation all set to go. I thought we might ride this one down a ways and save some walking, but we can't waste any more time on the heap. If anybody wants to use the road, they'll just have to drag it out themselves, if they can't get around it somehow."

Bobbie said coldly, "I think the simple fact is that you can't get it out of here, either, in spite of all the expert noises you've been making. Isn't it?"

I regarded her for a moment. I'm not in the habit of

doing things just because pretty girls tell me I can't, but my instinct is always to tidy up as I go along—which was why I'd taken time to deal with the two men who might have threatened our retreat, later. Now I had the uneasy feeling that leaving the Chrysler stuck there was untidy and might just possibly cause us trouble eventually, although I couldn't see how. I sighed, studied the near rear wheel for a moment, and squatted down beside it. Bobbie got out and stood over me.

"What are you doing?"

"Letting some air out of the tires," I said. "It's an emergency measure, and I probably wouldn't have had to do it if certain people hadn't dug us such a deep hole to get out of."

"Lay off, Helm," she said. "We can't all be great boondocks drivers like you, if you are one. What's accomplished by letting the air out, anyway?"

"It's simple physics," I said. "With half the air pressure, it takes twice the tire surface to support the car, right? And with twice the amount of rubber on the sand, you're half as likely to sink in. Check the glove compartment, will you, and see if by a miracle these boys carry a tire gauge."

They didn't, of course, so I had to estimate the pressure by eye—if you get it too low, these newfangled tubeless tires will come away from the rim and let all the air out, leaving you in worse shape than before. When I'd lowered the pressures all around as far as seemed safe, I told Bobbie to stand by to push, if necessary. Then I got behind the wheel, started the engine, and tested it cautiously in reverse. The big sedan lifted slightly before the wheels began to slip, and I slapped it into drive and caught it as it rolled forward again, and kept it coming, very gently, out of the hole and on across the wash to solid ground. I cut the lights and waited for Bobbie to catch up and get in beside me.

"Well," she said, "well, *that* doesn't prove anything! Probably I could have done it, too, if I'd known about the soft-tire trick."

I grinned. "There's what we call a good loser! Crank down your window and use your eyes and ears. I don't want to overrun Tillery's bunch by mistake."

But they had close to a forty-five-minute start on us, and we never caught a glimpse of them ahead as we picked our way slowly along the rudimentary road, in the dark, until the ruts started to swing left to pass inland of some dark hills, presumably the high ground guarding the north end of San Agustin Bay. Here I turned the big car off the road to the right and took it several hundred yards across country into a bunch of scraggly trees with one dead giant spreading bare white limbs against the sky, a good landmark. I parked the Chrysler facing back along its own tracks.

"Now you wait here," I said. "And I mean *here*. If I jump somebody up there, I don't want to have to worry that it's you playing Indian again. I'd better take the drug kit, and where the hell did the handle of that jack get to…"

"Matt?"

"Yes?"

"Be careful, darling."

I looked at her for a moment. The long blonde hair shone dully in the darkness of the car, but her face and expression couldn't be seen beneath the wide brim of her hippie-hat.

"Sure," I said. "Hell, there are only three of them, aren't there? Sure, I'll be careful."

## 21

Half a mile from the car, I stopped to catch my breath and look and listen. From up here I could see the ocean shining faintly off to my right. I got the impression that over in that direction—westward—the ground dropped off steeply to the shore, or maybe straight to the water. Well, that's what the aerial shot had indicated.

Ahead of me, the top of the brushy, rocky ridge I was climbing was jagged against the sky, coming to a kind of peak to the left. If I remembered correctly, that rudimentary peak stood watch over the head of San Agustin Bay; and beyond it the ground sloped down to the dunes along the shore and the road curving in from the south.

Behind and below me, I could no longer make out the gaunt tree skeleton marking the Chrysler's hiding place. The curvature of the hillside blocked it from sight I drew a long breath and started to resume my cautious climb, but checked myself, smelling tobacco smoke. It annoyed me slightly. I mean, after all, I've got my professional pride.

Hunting three armed men in the dark was a challenge. Hunting any number of men, armed or unarmed, who were stupid enough to reveal where they were hiding by smoking on the job, was like stalking sheep in a pasture, hardly sporting.

There was a moderate breeze from the direction of the sea. I worked into it slowly until I'd spotted the guy, squatting in the shadow of a small tree. I couldn't tell much about him until, presently, he straightened up to stretch his cramped muscles. He tossed aside the glowing cigarette, his heedless gesture indicating that he'd grown up in fireproof surroundings of asphalt and concrete.

After a minute or two, he got a fresh smoke from his shirt pocket and lit it. He tried to shield the flame by turning towards the tree and cupping the match in his hands, but I got a glimpse of his face in the brief flare of light. He wasn't one of Sapio's bunch. That made him, presumably, one of Warfel's.

Well, I'd kind of expected Frankie to station some guards to cover his landing operation, whatever its purpose might be, but this man seemed like a pretty poor sentry in a pretty useless spot. However, I reflected, it was probably unreasonable of me to judge a bunch of Los Angeles hoods by strict military standards of strategy and discipline.

I considered putting the guy out of action—still cleaning up as I went along—but Warfel would probably miss him if he didn't return to the beach at some prearranged time; and we were supposed to be operating on the principle that Mr. Warfel was not to be warned or worried in any way. He was supposed to reach U.S. waters with his happy-dust in a peaceful and unsuspicious frame of mind, to meet Charlie Devlin and her skin diver and her arrest warrant.

I couldn't help thinking that I seemed to be spending more time, and taking bigger risks, solving Charlie's problems than my own, which was kind of ironic, since she'd originally been assigned to help me. However, I still had a hunch our problems were intimately related in some way, although I would have hated to try to explain the precise relationship to a critical audience, say a gentleman known as Mac...

I didn't like bypassing the sentry and leaving him behind me, but doing it was no trouble at all. He never looked up from his satisfying carcinogens. Fifteen minutes later I was on top of the ridge, discovering that whatever its actual geological origin might have been, it looked kind of like the remnant of a round volcanic crater, the south and west sides of which had crumbled and washed away over the centuries. Below me was Bahia San Agustin in the weak moonlight: a pretty little bay with a pretty little beach, on which were parked a small white Jeepster and a big, dark, covered, six-wheeled truck.

I'd apparently made it just in time: the guest of honor had already arrived at the party. A few hundred yards off the beach lay a white-painted ketch sixty or seventy feet long, quite a sizeable yacht—a ketch is the one with two masts, the shorter aft, but not so far aft as to make it a yawl. In case you're interested, if the shorter mast is forward, it's a schooner, and if there's only one mast, it's a sloop or cutter, but please don't ask me to explain the difference. It's a fairly delicate distinction, I gather, and seafaring men have been known to come to blows over the subject.

The *Fleetwind*, despite her racy name, was a rather chunky-looking, stubby-masted tub that looked as if she'd have to depend on her diesel in anything but a strong and favorable wind. I'd wondered from the start why Warfel had got himself a motorsailer, always a relatively slow type of craft, instead of picking up a jazzy twin-screw cruiser that would have had more glamor and could have made the Ensenada run in half the time. But obviously he'd had a reason, and now I was learning what it was. He had a cargo to handle that rested easily on the low flush deck of the big ketch, but would have been awkward or impossible to manage on the high, flimsy cabin top of a cruiser-type vessel. Besides, in this deserted anchorage, with no dockside crane available, the motorsailer's spars and rigging were needed to get the thing over the side.

It was a giant metal cylinder that fitted between the masts with only a little to spare. A missile came to mind—people are always mislaying the things nowadays, or letting them go astray—but this object didn't look as if it were intended to move under its own power. Slightly rounded at both ends, it looked just like a big cylindrical tank for water or liquefied gas, except that if it had been full of any kind of liquid, big as it was, it would probably have rolled the boat over. It just couldn't be that heavy or they couldn't have managed it.

On the other hand, it was heavy enough that the crew was making elaborate preparations for unloading it. The main boom, sail removed, had been angled high into the air for use as a cargo boom, and there seemed to be considerable shipboard activity with ropes and slings and tackles.

On shore, work was also being done. A couple of long cylindrical pontoons with pointed ends, and considerable lumber, had been unloaded from the six-wheeler, and men were assembling these ingredients into a raft of sorts, at the water's edge. Other men were laying planks behind the wheels of the truck to keep it from getting stuck in the sand. As I watched, the big vehicle backed cautiously closer to the water. Some planks were transferred from front to rear; and the truck moved another few feet down the beach and stopped, apparently located to everybody's satisfaction. Obviously; I'd been wrong about it. It hadn't come to Bahia San Agustin to deliver a mysterious load for Warfel's boat to pick up, quite the contrary.

Off to one side, by the jeep, stood two men watching critically. One, roughly dressed, seemed to be Willi Keim alias Willy Hansen, although I couldn't be absolutely certain at that distance. The other, taller and much stouter, in neat city clothes, didn't have the right shape to be Frank Warfel. I thought I could detect a mustache on a bland Oriental face, even in the poor light, but that could have been because I was kind of expecting to see a mustached Oriental. I was expecting the Chinese, Charlie Chan-type character with whom, I'd heard, Beverly Blaine had made contact in San Francisco—at the meeting that had been watched by Jake and his assistants, who'd lost the man afterwards in the streets of Chinatown.

I was expecting this particular man because I knew just such a man—although he had not been wearing a mustache when I'd seen him last—and because this was just the kind of secretive scientific monkey business in which he specialized. He was known to us only as Mr. Soo, and I'd encountered him twice before. The first time had been in Hawaii where I'd saved his life, more or less out of necessity, along with my own, and then turned him loose because he might have proved an embarrassing prisoner—we'd had some turncoat trouble with one of our agents that we didn't particularly want publicized. The second encounter, if you could call it that—I'd seen him but he hadn't seen me—had taken place in Alaska where I'd again let him go free, this time because we'd gone to considerable trouble to plant some false data on him, or, more accurately, on a handsome lady who had his confidence.

I'd wondered, from time to time, just what had happened to the attractive woman known as Libby, when our deceit was finally discovered, and to Mr. Soo. Apparently, I need not have worried about Mr. Soo. He'd overcome the professional setback somehow, and here he was—if it was he—doing business as usual, presumably for his old firm, the one with headquarters in Peking. The question was, what business?

I frowned at the dim scene for a moment longer, but I was wasting time. My curiosity would just have to wait.

Warfel might be coming ashore at any moment, and although the project didn't particularly appeal to me, it was my job to keep him safe. I crawled left towards the peak of the ridge until I was high enough that, looking back along it, I could see all of it. Tillery was easy to spot from up there. He was lying among some rocks industriously using night glasses. Beside him was Sapio, with the Thompson.

Well, it was nice to have them located, but the guy who really concerned me was Jake. He was undoubtedly the man who'd do the actual job, with his big rifle and its odd-looking sight. Tillery and Sapio were present only in an executive capacity, I figured, to give instructions and make sure they were carried out successfully, and perhaps to take a hand in discouraging pursuit, with the tommy gun, afterwards.

Anyway, Jake was the only one who worried me a little, as competition or opposition or whatever you choose to call it. He was a working pro in more or less my own line of endeavor. The other two might have been tough once, but they were desk slobs now or the syndicate equivalent. Well, in a dark alley or a vacant city lot they might still be formidable, but out here in the open—in the kind of terrain I'd grown up in—I didn't figure they'd give me much trouble once I'd managed to take care of Jake.

I caught a hint of movement farther down the curving rim of the old crater, if it was a crater. Moonlight glinted on a rifle barrel, and there he was. He'd picked a spot that was within easy rifle shot of the landing area, at least by daylight, but it was fairly low, one of the few places where the ridge looked easily climbable from the beach. I didn't get it at first, and then I realized that I'd underestimated Tillery's sense of strategy. The rifle would fire, Warfel would fall, and after a moment of shocked surprise, the gang on the beach, would rush the tempting low spot from which the shot had come. That would place them on the steep slope with hardly any cover, cold meat for the chopper on the crest. A couple of raking bursts from the flank, and the few who remained alive would become too interested in staying that way to think about further pursuit.

Well, there was my pigeon and it was time to get at plucking it. I headed down into the brush, working my way slowly and silently—well below the spot where Sapio and Tillery lay—and almost ran into a man leaning against the trunk of a tree with a carbine slung on his shoulder, presumably another of Warfel's lookouts, but what the hell was he doing way down here where he couldn't look out at anything?

It worried me, but I had no time to brood about it. I sneaked by him silently and kept going until I figured I was directly below Jake's position; then I moved upwards very carefully, to discover I'd gone a little too far. I was out in the rocks and brush to seaward of him. From here I could hear the beat of the surf on the promontory off to my right. I could hear another, less reassuring sound: the put-put racket of a small outboard motor in the bay. It could be driving a dinghy bringing Warfel ashore.

I could see Jake quite plainly. He lay between two

rocks, screened, from the bay side, by some of the coarse grass that grew in tufts here and there along the ridge. He had not yet put the rifle to his shoulder. If his target was approaching, it was, apparently, still out of range.

From my side, he had little protection. It would have been an easy shot if I'd been allowed to make the noise. I yearned for a silencer, dart gun, death ray, or bow and arrow; but wishing was getting me nowhere. There was no easy way of sneaking up on him where he lay; the ground was too open around him. I'd have to make him come to me.

I picked a suitable ambush site behind and below him. It took me some time to work my way to it, long enough for the outboard to cross the bay and fall silent, but Jake still did not lift the rifle. Either Warfel hadn't come ashore this trip, or he wasn't offering a good enough shot yet. I laid the jack handle from the Chrysler where I could grab it fast, and tossed a small rock down the hillside to land far below me.

I saw Jake stiffen slightly and lie there listening. I let a couple of minutes pass; then I tossed another stone, not quite so far, as if somebody down there were sneaking closer, very slowly and rather clumsily. Jake looked around uneasily. Seeing nothing, he glanced down at the beach in front of him, out of my range of vision.

Apparently he found nothing urgent down there; he backed away from the edge and rose, holding the rifle ready. He came towards me cautiously, scanning the brush for movement, pausing every other step to listen hard. I had a small stone, like a marble, between thumb and forefinger. When he paused five feet away, I flipped it after the others. He froze, looking that way. I came out of the bushes low and broke his leg with the jack handle.

## 22

I was taking a chance, of course. He might have yelled and alerted half of Baja California—including Sapio, nearby, with the submachine-gun—but I was counting on Jake and his tough professionalism and he didn't disappoint me. His mental computer was programmed for silence, and the sudden pain got only a sort of choked, moaning grunt out of him, as he came down on top of me.

Something hard struck me in the small of the back: the butt of the falling rifle. It hurt, but I didn't mind. If the weapon had hit the ground first, it would have made more noise; it might even have been discharged by the shock. But everything worked out well; and I threw the big man off me and came to my feet as he struggled to hands and knees and tried to rise. I had plenty of time to reach down and give him a judicious tap behind the ear with the short iron bar I held.

Then, standing above him, I had a fight with my conscience, but it wasn't much of a fight. I mean, the

question was which injection to use to keep, him quiet—
the temporary or one of the permanents—but the answer
came quite easily. To be sure, I'd promised myself the
pleasure of watching this man die in agony, back when
he was beating on me in Bobbie's hotel room, but that
had been merely a psychological crutch, to help me face
the ordeal with fortitude. Actually, I didn't have a great
deal against Jake. He'd knocked me around a bit, but I'd
walked into the situation with my eyes open, and it had all
been strictly in the line of business.

And in a sense, while he was undoubtedly a bad
citizen, tonight he seemed to be on the side of the angels.
Apparently he, and Tillery and Sapio, were trying to
prevent a man from smuggling dope, a worthy cause—
although the degree of virtue did depend somewhat on
their true motives.

The syndicate, Mafia, Cosa Nostra, corporation, or
whatever you want to call it, is not my bag, and I don't
know a hell of a lot about it. However, just because some
unpleasant people insist they're dropping an illegal activity
because it's become too hot to be profitable, or for any other
reason, doesn't mean I have to believe them. For all I knew,
Jake could have been assigned this job of marksmanship,
not because Warfel was disgracing his innocent Mafia
associates by dealing in dirty heroin, but simply because
he was stepping on the toes of some other mafioso—if
that's the correct term—somebody with better syndicate
connections than Frankie's, who'd been promised this
lucrative branch of the drug trade for himself.

Still, ostensibly, the project upon which Jake was embarked, homicide apart, seemed kind of praiseworthy even if it was interfering with Charlie Devlin's elaborate plans—and if somebody just had to be shot, I couldn't think of a more suitable candidate than Frankie-boy Warfel. Furthermore, Big Jake hadn't got any rougher than necessary, putting on his interrogation act for me back at the hotel—he'd added no personal frills to the beating—and I don't go around killing people merely because they hit me a little with their fists in the line of duty.

Finally, it kind of intrigued me to think of some ruthless syndicate rub-out men, bent on murder, napping peacefully on a Mexican hillside while their quarry sailed away unharmed. Killing one of them would have spoiled the joke.

As I slipped him the needle, Jake was trying to wake up, but the drug soon rendered him passive once more. I picked up the fallen rifle and studied it, frowning. Although it seemed to be a standard bolt-action sporting model—a fully loaded, short-barreled .308 Remington in their cheapest grade, if you must have the details—it had a Buck Rogers appearance due to the bulky, home-made-looking gadget that was solidly mounted on top.

What I'd taken to be a telescopic sight of sorts seemed to be a kind of fancy flashlight with a long black hood, or snoot, shielding the big front lens, presumably so that light wouldn't spill to the sides. Well that wasn't unheard of. Spotlights are frequently clamped on guns for nocturnal hunting use in some parts of the world, but generally the idea is merely to put some light on a leopard, or other beast, at close range—enough illumination to let you see the sights to aim and shoot. Apparently that was not the principle involved here. Jake had been planning a shot of better than a hundred yards, too far for ordinary spotlighting techniques, and his rifle had no sights other than this odd contraption...

My research was interrupted by the sound of the outboard motor, that had been silent for a while, starting up once more. I sneaked up to the rim and saw that the *Fleetwind*'s dinghy had taken the completed pontoon raft in tow and was heading out towards the ketch, which now had a decided list to port due to the great metal cylinder suspended from the boom swung out over the side. The two men I'd tentatively identified as Willy and Mr. Soo still stood together by the jeep at the far side of the beach. There was no sign of Frank Warfel, although one of the dim, small, distant figures on the deck of the motorsailer could have been him, and probably was.

I eased away from the edge, and squirmed back to Jake, checked that he was sleeping soundly, and made my way into a gully well below where, I hoped, I could experiment a bit with the trick rifle without attracting attention. I aimed it at a rock some twenty yards away—as close as I could line it up in the dark without sights—and pressed the switch on the side of the Flash Gordon gizmo, bracing myself for all kinds of spectacular fireworks, although it didn't seem likely that a gadget intended for night operations would be too bright or too noisy.

Actually, nothing much happened. A small, sharp, intense cross of light just appeared silently on the rock at just about the point where, I estimated, the gun was aimed. Very neat. All you had to do, apparently, was put the X on a guy, and he was dead when you pulled the trigger.

Well, it still wasn't a totally new idea. Back when I was making my living with a press camera, in another and more peaceful incarnation, they'd rigged a light to shine through the range finder optical system, projecting two bright spots as far as you'd be likely to take an ordinary flash picture. Working at night, in light too dim for ordinary focusing, you merely brought the two spots together on the celebrity you wished to photograph, and fired your flashgun.

The only really impressive thing here was the remarkable sharpness and intensity of the illuminated cross, good enough to make feasible shots of over a hundred yards—at least Jake had obviously thought so. I wondered if laser technology might not be involved in some way. I also wondered if Jake had cooked up the thing himself, swiped it from some top secret Army project, or whether perhaps the syndicate also had inventors and armorers hard at work dreaming up interesting new toys for the boys.

I switched off the beam and crouched there, considering the next step; but a rustling sound brought my thinking to an abrupt halt. I flattened out and lay absolutely still, waiting. Presently a shadowy figure appeared by the rock I'd used for a target: a thin little man with a sawed-off shotgun like the one that had been used on Lionel McConnell. He stood by the rock for several seconds, first studying it, and then looking warily around. Obviously, wherever he'd been hiding, he'd caught a glimpse of something bright and had come over to investigate—another of Warfel's sentries, who probably, judging by his uneasy attitude, was wishing he were back in good old smoggy L.A.

That made three, all stationed well down from the rim. I could no longer kid myself that this was simple gangster stupidity. On the contrary, somebody was obviously being very clever, and it was high time, I told myself, that I got the hell out of there. It was bug-out time at Bahia San Agustin.

After all, I told myself, the job for which I'd come here was done, more or less. I'd pretty much kept my promise to Charlie Devlin: Warfel was fairly safe. The syndicate's expert rifleman was out of action and I had his dressed-up rifle. That left the rub-out squad with a tommy gun as its principal weapon—great for cleaning up streets and alleys, for putting the fear of God into hostile characters at close range, but hardly the preferred choice for selective long-range homicide. Without Jake and his specialized weapon, Tillery's project had turned from a near certainty to a risky gamble, even if Warfel came ashore, which he showed no signs of doing.

If I took off in high gear now, or as soon as the man with the carbine decided to move away, I could probably get clear undetected. If not, well, I had the Buck Rogers gun and my knife and revolver to fight with, and all of Baja California to hide in. That's what I told myself, but I didn't move.

The trouble was, there were too many things I wanted to know that I couldn't learn by running. I didn't know what was being brought ashore or why; I still didn't even know for sure who was bringing it ashore. And while I was leading Warfel's boys a merry chase through the mesquite and cactus, the big truck and its mysterious load would be disappearing into the wilds of Baja along with Mr. Soo, if it was Mr. Soo.

Strictly speaking, it was none of my business, but I couldn't help wanting to know what this was all about— and even if I made it out of here safely and reached a phone, there was no guarantee that we'd be able to locate the vehicle again, and if we did find it, it would probably be empty. The big metal tank or cylinder that was being landed with such care and secrecy—obviously somebody considered it very important—would be missing and so would Mr. Soo, if it was Mr. Soo. And eventually, I had a hunch that was a little more than just a hunch, they would both turn up north of the border for some purpose, undoubtedly nefarious, that I still couldn't even guess at…

The man below me was retreating cautiously the way he had come, with his shotgun in his hands. He kept turning, and swinging the muzzle around in a jittery fashion, as if his ears were playing him scary tricks. I gave him plenty of time; then I started moving along the hillside, slowly and silently, towards a point that, I figured, would put me directly below Tillery and Sapio. I mean, we don't get paid to be stupid heroes, but we do get paid; and occasionally we've got to do something to earn our bread, like sticking our necks out just a little.

Down in the bay, beyond the ridge, the outboard dinghy was still wrestling noisily with its unwieldy tow, but the hillside was very quiet except for the murmur of the sea breeze in the low brush and the scattered, lonely, small trees. I froze as something dark moved by one of those trees ahead: another man, shifting position uncomfortably, as if tired of waiting.

Something gleamed in the hand that was raised to push irritably at the wide-brimmed hat... I realized that the figure was not really dark, nor was it a man. It was my ubiquitous female companion in her light jeans and shirt. Well, I hadn't really expected her to stay where she was told.

"Quiet!" I whispered, coming up behind her. "Don't move. Lay that pistol down, sweetheart."

"Matt! Oh, you scared...!"

"The pistol, doll-baby," I breathed. "No, don't drop it, stupid. It's only in the movies you toss firearms around like beanbags. In real life they have a nasty habit of going off... That's right. On the ground with the safety on. Now straighten up and step away from it."

"Matt, what in the world...?"

"You don't follow orders very good," I said harshly. "I told you to stay in the car."

"I got scared. I saw some men moving this way, and I was afraid you'd be trapped up here..."

I picked up the automatic she'd deposited on the ground, and glanced at it. "A Walther, eh? Not a bad little gun. Where'd you get it?"

"It was in the glove compartment of the car. I stuck it in my pocket when I was looking for that tire gauge you wanted." She hesitated. "May I have it back, please?"

"No," I said. "If there's anything that scares me worse than plague, smallpox, rabies, and Montezuma's Revenge, it's an amateur with a gun. Particularly an amateur who won't obey orders."

"I told you," she said angrily, "I came to find you and warn you..."

"How many men did you see?"

"Just two, but..."

"We'll worry about them later," I said. "I've taken care of Jake, but his two Cosa Nostra friends are somewhere up above us if they haven't moved. They've got a Thompson with a hundred-round drum if my firearms identification is correct. If I can get hold of that, a couple of goons more or less won't matter a bit. There's also a pair of night glasses I'd like to have the use of for about thirty seconds... I don't suppose there's the slightest chance of your following instructions a third time, after ignoring them twice."

"Damn you, I was trying to *help*..."

"Shh, keep your voice down. Do you think you can make a tremendous, gigantic, supreme effort and stay right here, just for a few minutes? Please? Ten minutes by the watch? Have you got a watch?"

"Yes."

"Well, look at it. If you don't know what the time is now, how are you going to tell when it's ten minutes from now?"

"Darling," she said stiffly, "darling, you're being very objectionable…"

"Here's the drug kit," I said, ignoring her protest. "In ten minutes, I hope, you can come up and do your stuff just like before."

The final stalk was no great problem. Big-town characters, accustomed to tuning out the roar of traffic and the bleat of canned music, have generally forgotten how to listen, and the two men on the crest were no exception. I got within twenty-five yards of them without eliciting the smallest sign of uneasiness. Then I aimed the Flash Gordon contraption at Sapio, since he was the man with the chopper, and switched on the beam.

## 23

The fierce little ray of concentrated light caught Sapio's attention, all right, even from behind. I saw him start to turn his head and stop, and reach for the submachine-gun instead. I stopped that by pressing the safety of the Remington forward more sharply than necessary, making a tiny but unmistakable click.

The hooded, sharply focused light had not disturbed Tillery, off to one side, but the sound brought his head around quickly.

"Jake, what the hell…?"

"Jake's taking a nap," I said. "So are your other two boys, Tillery."

"Helm? What are you doing here? What do you want?"

"I want your hand to stop moving, *amigo*. I think Mr. Sapio does, too. I don't think he really yearns for a thirty-caliber slug through his liver."

"Cut it out, Tillery."

"Yes, Mr. Sapio."

There was a faint clatter of dislodged pebbles nearby.

I stepped back into the gloom of a low evergreen, keeping the beam steady, but it was only the girl in her light clothes and big dark hat, rather breathless.

"Matt?"

"Right here," I said. "No, don't look at this light, it's pretty bright. Don't get between us. Walk around, real careful, and take care of them… Oh, just a minute. Sapio, you seem to be the man with the final authority here. What's your full name?"

"Manuel Sapio. Why?"

The Spanish first name didn't really belong in the company he kept—the Mafia originated in a different part of southern Europe—but his national heritage was his problem, not mine.

"I want you to listen hard, Manuel Sapio," I said. "I know you're a big, dangerous man, and I know you're already thinking what you're going to do to us by way of retaliation. I also know that when you get over your mad, you'll be too smart to try for me—"

"You hope!"

"I don't just hope," I said. "I know. Your superiors in the corporation would amputate your manhood with a dull knife if you started a private feud with the U.S. Government. But it may occur to you to take it out on Miss Prince. I've got some advice for you: don't do it. And don't have Tillery or anybody else do it for you. I'm holding you personally responsible for Miss Prince's health and safety, Sapio. Anything that happens to her, no matter who does it, happens to you. If she gets hit by a car, you'll have a bad accident. If she catches pneumonia and dies, you may as well start coughing, because you'll go next. Even if she dies in childbirth, I'll figure out some way to make it happen to you. Do you read me?" I waited briefly. He didn't speak. I said, "Okay, Bobbie. Fix them up."

Five minutes later I was lying on the crest with the big, seven-power binoculars at my eyes and the Thompson under my elbow—I'd set aside the rifle as less suited to the immediate situation, and also less impressive, than the chopper. There were other reasons for making the trade, but I didn't let myself think about them. Not that I believe in telepathy, really; but I've found it best, when being tricky, to put entirely out of my mind just how tricky I'm being. Why take a chance of tipping off the opposition, telepathically or otherwise?

There's no optical viewing instrument that, by itself, will put light where there isn't any—there are some electronic see-in-the-dark systems, but that's another story. Where there's some illumination, however, a good pair of night glasses will brighten things up remarkably; and here I had a bit of moonlight to work with. I could see down there quite well.

I checked first on the men by the jeep, except that now there was only one man standing at the far side of the beach. The other man was gone, and so was the vehicle. I listened for a moment trying to locate it by sound, but I could hear only the murmur of the wind and the angry buzzing of the outboard motor in the bay. I focused on the lone, remaining man and saw that, as I had guessed, he was indubitably Mr. Soo, not much changed from the first time I'd seen him, or the last, except for the unfamiliar mustache. Well, I hadn't really known him long enough for him to age perceptibly, although I'd done my best to hasten the process.

Having identified him, I swung the glasses to the bulky cylindrical object that was now being floated ashore on the pontoon raft behind the straining, racketing little outboard dinghy. Here, however, the binoculars were no help to me. The thing just looked like a big metal tank seven times closer, that was all. The way the seams ran hinted that the slightly rounded caps at the ends might be removable, but what would be revealed when they were removed, I still had no idea.

Bobbie Prince stirred beside me. "Matt?" she whispered.

"What?"

"Will you really go after Sapio if… if he has me killed?"

"Hell, no," I said. "Why waste time, and effort on something that won't bring you back to life? Anyway, my boss doesn't like private vendettas, either; we're supposed to operate strictly and solely in the national interest. If the bluff doesn't work, I'll come put some flowers on your grave, that's all. But I did the best I could for you, didn't I?"

"You were very menacing and convincing. Even if it doesn't work, thanks for a good try." After a moment, she asked, "Can you make out anything down there?"

"A little," I said. "I recognize the gent standing across the way looking administrative. He's a fairly high-powered Chinese agent specializing in scientific espionage and sabotage. There was another guy with him earlier I'm fairly sure was Willy Hansen, but he's gone off somewhere in his jeep. I wish I knew where. I don't like having him running loose; and I've got an idea about Willy I'd like to check out. And I wish I knew what Mr. Soo was doing, tied up with a bunch of dope peddlers."

"Well, they produce a lot of drugs in China, Matt. It's practically the home of opium, isn't it?"

I glanced at her. "That's a thought," I said. "Maybe we've got this smuggling operation figured out all wrong, or my friend Charlie has. But if Mr. Soo is transporting any drugs from that far away—presumably with the consent and assistance of his government—it would be the concentrated heroin, wouldn't it? He'd hardly go to the trouble of shipping a lot of inert waste material halfway around the world when he's undoubtedly got access to refining facilities back home. But in that case, if Warfel's arranging to obtain the pure stuff from the Chinese, I can't see why he'd bother to set up a refining laboratory of his own here in Mexico. Unless—"

"Unless what, darling?"

"Unless that Bernardo trailer-lab is just a decoy to make our drug people *think* they're dealing with Mexican heroin—to keep them from guessing where it's really coming from." I grimaced. "My badge-bearing girlfriend is going to be very unhappy with me if I've steered her onto a phony setup. But what about that crazy thing they're towing ashore? I don't know a great deal about dope, although I'm learning fast, but if that's a load of horse in the large economy carton, I'll eat it raft and all. Again, like the truck, it's just too damn big. There aren't that many poppies in all of China."

Bobbie didn't speak; instead she reached out her hand for the binoculars, and I gave them to her. We lay there and watched them beach the raft. Then they lowered a ramp from the rear of the van and ran out a cable from a winch somewhere inside. When they had the cylinder hooked up properly, they started winching it up the ramp with several men steadying it on either side.

"I wish to hell somebody'd tell me what that thing is!" I said irritably at last.

"Are you trying to kid me, darling? Don't you *really* know?"

I glanced sharply at my blond companion. She'd lowered the glasses and turned her head to smile at me in an odd, speculative way. Something moved behind me, but I pretended not to hear it.

I said, "I haven't any idea, Bobbie. Have you?"

She said calmly, "Of course. That is, I don't know how it works, exactly, but I know it's a Sorenson Catalytic Generator, the only one in existence at present. We've been running some tests on it... Please don't move darling!" Her voice sharpened slightly. "The man behind you will shoot if you move at all. Don't even think of using that machine-gun. Please!"

I was aware of the Buck Rogers beam that was suddenly focused right between my shoulder blades. Well, as I'd already learned, it was a tempting weapon if you needed to get the drop on a man at night: he'd certainly know when he was covered.

I said sadly, "Roberta, I am shocked and surprised. You seemed like such a nice girl!"

She ignored that, and went on: "We thought you *must* know about the generator. After all, we know you've had your girlfriend, as you call her, checking on Dr. Sorenson for you. What led you to him?"

"A piece in the newspaper and an itch at the back of my neck," I said. "We secret-agent types are intuitive as hell."

"I'm not sure I believe that answer, but I won't worry about it now. Mr. Soo, as you call him, will question you later. Now, if you'd just roll up your sleeve..." I saw the gleam of my own hypodermic in her hand.

I didn't move at once. There were still things I wanted to find out while she was in a talkative mood.

"Is that Willy behind me?" I asked.

"No, but he's coming. You can hear his jeep climbing the hill. I'd rather have you asleep when he arrives, Matt. He's a rather violent man, Willy is, and I don't want to give him any excuse for killing you."

"A rather violent man called Nicholas," I said.

"So you know."

"I guessed. He's been playing the humble, stupid chauffeur and errand boy for years, and he's got the face for it, but he's the real Nicholas, isn't he? He just carefully sets up somebody else, male or female, as the current big shot—somebody like Beverly Blaine. If anything goes wrong, the figurehead takes the rap and swallows the cyanide, and Willy's just the dumb assistant who was lucky enough to get away."

"You've got it all figured out, haven't you, Helm?"

That was not Bobbie talking. It was a man's voice from the darkness beyond the intense light source: the harsh voice of Willi Keim, alias Willy Hansen, alias Nicholas— Santa Claus to us. I didn't answer him because he didn't wait for an answer. He went on, now speaking to the girl beside me:

"Did he do a good job for us, *Liebchen*?"

"I'm not your *Liebchen*," Bobbie said, "and he did a very good job. There are two of them back where the road crosses that dry riverbed, and two more under those bushes to your left. The last one, Jake, the trigger-man, is down the ridge a little ways. All sound asleep, you don't have to worry about—"

Without turning my head to look, I was kind of aware that Willy had turned away. There was a sudden spurt of flame at the edge of my vision, and a painfully loud crash of sound: obviously Willy-Nicholas was still hooked on his heavy Magnum hardware. Only a .44 could make that much noise. A moment later the fireworks were repeated. Bobbie kind of flinched beside me. She started to speak angrily, but checked herself, as Willy turned back to us.

"*Now*, I don't have to worry about those two," he said. "I've already settled the two in the wash. I'll take care of the last one in a minute. I never did like Jake; he was always throwing his weight around when we were working together. I had to take it then; I don't have to take it now. I'm just sorry he's doped so he can't see it coming… But first I want a word with Mr. Helm, here."

"Not with that oversized revolver!" There was a snap to Bobbie's voice. "The Chinaman wants him alive and talking."

"I won't hurt his singing voice a bit." A heavy boot caught me in the hip. "I've just been wanting to meet Mr. Helm very badly, ever since the last time he stuck his long nose into my business."

He kicked me in the ribs. There was nothing to do but lie there; I knew he was hoping for a sudden move on my part that would give him an excuse to blow my brains out. Then Bobbie snatched the Thompson and aimed it upwards.

"Get out of here!" she snapped. "Go shoot somebody, or something!"

"All right, but he's mine when the Chinaman gets through with him!"

I heard Willy turn and stamp away down the ridge. Bobbie drew a long breath and lowered the submachine-gun.

"How do you work this thing, anyway?" she asked of nobody in particular. "Are you all right, Matt?"

"Sure, I'm great," I said. "What's eating him?"

"Don't you know? You spoiled a big assignment for him—something right here in Mexico, I understand—and he didn't dare go home and neither did the girl you knew as Beverly. They weren't exactly going to be made heroes of the Soviet Union on their return to Moscow, if you know what I mean. So they took employment elsewhere, but our friend has a low opinion of Orientals and feels humiliated, working for one. He can't forget that he was a big shot called Nicholas until you came along."

I said, "You don't seem to share his opinion of Orientals."

She laughed. "Darling, I was born over there. I understand the Chinese a lot better than I understand you. Now, please roll up your sleeve…"

I rolled it up, and felt the sting of the needle. It was the first time I'd had the stuff used on me. It wasn't bad. As I started drifting off, I heard the big revolver crash once more, farther down the rim. It seemed as if Willy had gone and spoiled my funny joke about five tough syndicate soldiers peacefully sleeping on the job. Well, maybe it hadn't been so funny, after all.

# 24

I awoke in a noisy, unsteady place that, after a little, I
identified as the rear of a big van going down a paved
highway at a good clip. There was a kind of erratic
booming sound, the source of which I couldn't determine
until I opened my eyes.

Then I saw that the tanklike mystery object I'd seen
brought ashore was now looming above me, almost
filling the cavernous space that was dimly lighted by a
weak yellow bulb up forward. The jolting of the truck was
causing the great metal cylinder to reverberate hollowly. I
hoped they had it properly lashed and wedged into place
so it wouldn't shift my way. It didn't leave too much
room as it was.

I tried to sit up and discovered that my hands and feet
were tied. My gun and knife were missing, of course; in
fact, my pockets seemed to be quite empty. My hip
was sore; and breathing now hurt me, not only in front
where I'd been socked earlier in the day, but also at the

side where I'd been kicked more recently, but I didn't feel too badly about that. I mean, I had my orders. Mac had indicated that we'd lost too many good men and women to Nicholas, and that something permanent ought to be done about him, by me. That being the case, it would have been awkward if he'd turned out to be a sweet, gentle, lovable sort of guy I couldn't bear to harm.

"How are you feeling, darling?"

I turned my head and there she was, my blonde betrayer, looking even more like a lady hippie with her long hair mussed and her white jeans smudged by the night's adventures. Not that it mattered. If I'd wanted an immaculate vision of radiant loveliness I could have turned on the TV, if I'd had a TV. At the moment, I much preferred a tousle-headed human being in grubby pants. As a matter of fact, a great deal—including my life— might depend at least in part on just how human this girl would turn out to be.

"Are you all right?" Bobbie helped me to a sitting position. "That's a potent injection you carry. You've been asleep for six hours."

"It works better, I guess, when the victim hasn't been to bed for a couple of days."

She made a face at me. "That wasn't a very nice thing to say! Whose bed haven't you been in for a couple of days? I seem to remember your indulging in a nice little nap in mine, quite recently, after… after some preliminary exercise. Well, if you're going to be so rude and forgetful, I'll just put you right back to sleep." She took my little case from her shirt pocket and opened it. "I'm supposed to keep you under. The Chinaman seems to have a lot of respect for you. He doesn't trust you awake, even tied and guarded."

I said, "The Chinaman. They don't call him that back in China, surely."

"No, and they don't call him Mr. Soo, either, and it's none of your business, anyway."

"Where is he? Where is everybody? He had a small army working for him at Bahia San Agustin."

"If what you're trying to find out is whether or not we're alone in here," Bobbie said dryly, "the answer is that we aren't. There are three men over on the other side of the generator; and three more up in the cab, so even if you overpower me, you've got your work cut out for you. The rest are riding in the jeep and your station wagon. They left Tillery's Chrysler behind because the tires were too soft—anyway, it was too closely associated with a lot of dead bodies that might be found, prematurely, by the Mexican authorities."

"And where are we?"

Bobbie hesitated, and shrugged. "I don't suppose it matters if I tell you. I think we crossed the border back into the U.S. a little while ago, using some kind of a cross-country smuggling route known to Warfel's men. At least the going was slow and rough for a couple of hours. You were lucky to be asleep. Now that's enough questions. Just lie down again like a good boy and let me squirt you with some more of this nice sleepy-stuff."

"Just one more question," I said. "What the hell is this

overgrown stovepipe that's threatening to squash us?"

Bobbie frowned at me. "Don't you really know?"

"I said I didn't. You said it was the Sorenson Catalytic Generator. What does it generate?"

She said, "Don't be silly. It generates catalysts, naturally."

"Oh, naturally!" I said. "Excuse me for asking! What kind of catalysts… Wait a minute!" I stared up at the metallic flank of the cylindrical object that bulged out over us as we sat with our backs against the side of the truck. I noted that, while the convex cap at the rear was clean, the cylinder itself had a smoked, scorched look at that end, kind of like a jet engine exhaust. Apparently it had been subjected to fairly high temperatures. I said thoughtfully, "Sorenson was interested in air pollution, wasn't he? That's how he came to be an anti-auto nut. Do you mean to tell me he discovered something…?" I stopped. Bobbie didn't speak. I said irritably, "No. That's too damn science-fiction screwy."

"What is?"

"If you're trying to tell me that's a smog machine…"

"Not exactly, darling," Bobbie said. "It doesn't produce smog, not directly. It just generates a finely-dispersed catalyst that will cause smog to form if the necessary pollutants are present in the atmosphere. Dr. Sorenson's theory was that both elements—catalyst and pollutants—have to be present for active, visible, dangerous smog to form. He isolated and identified the catalyst, some kind of trace element that's present in just about anything anybody's likely to burn. Then, of course, for his experiments, he had to learn how to produce it in reasonable quantities. He discovered that we really don't know how lucky we are."

"What do you mean?"

"His experiments," she said, "indicate that the reason a lot of cities haven't been affected by smog problems yet, and those that have are still inhabitable, is that there just isn't enough of the catalyst to go around. Without it, the air can absorb quite a bit of pollution without significant effect. But if you were to supply all the catalyst needed, so that *all* the garbage we pump into the atmosphere would react or precipitate or whatever it does…" She stopped. There was a little silence, except for the rattling of the truck, and the drumlike reverberation of the cylinder.

I said, "And that's what Mr. Soo is doing with this gadget?"

"Yes. Of course, Sorenson checked out his theory on a laboratory scale, but that's considerably different from testing it under practical conditions."

"Practical conditions," I mimicked sourly. "You mean you're going to start that thing up somewhere, windward of a suitable metropolis, and let the stuff drift in and see if the sky turns brown and people start coughing and strangling…"

My voice kind of trailed off. I looked at her quickly, and she nodded.

"Yes, Matt. We *have* run it. On a ship off the California coast. And, darling, in Los Angeles the sky did turn brown in places—you were there; you saw it and smelled it! And in places people did start coughing and strangling. You told me that your dope-fighting girlfriend had a recurrence of an asthma condition that hadn't bothered her for years, remember?"

"I remember," I said. "But—"

"I don't know the exact figures," Bobbie said. "Maybe the Chinaman does, by this time. But I do know, from early radio reports that, although curiously spotty and erratic, it was, on the whole, one of the worst smog attacks recorded in Los Angeles. The ambulance services were swamped with patients suffering from serious respiratory ailments and the hospitals were overloaded. Of course, we didn't run it long enough to cause a real catastrophe. It's just a pilot model. We just wanted to see if it would work, and it did."

I frowned. "I see. And having used it successfully on Los Angeles, where conditions are generally pretty favorable for a test like that, I suppose the Chinaman is now going to try his gadget on a tougher subject somewhere inland. But where?"

"I can't tell you that. As a matter of fact, I don't know. I didn't have anything to do with the preparations for the second test."

I said, "No, I guess that was Beverly Blame's job, and Willy's. The two of them were supposed to have made several trips east together recently, according to our late friend Jake. The question is, how far east?" Bobbie made no comment, and I changed the subject: "This ship, now.

It must have met Warfel's boat well out at sea and turned over the generator—also, I suppose, a nice big batch of Chinese heroin."

"Yes. Ten kilos," Bobby said. "That was his payment for helping with his boat and truck and men. Of course, he also had to promise to arrange things so that nobody'd suspect where the drug actually came from. Besides—" She stopped abruptly.

"Besides what?"

She didn't look my way. "Besides, that phony Bernardo installation he set up as camouflage also made a good cover for getting rid of Dr. Sorenson, poor man. I suppose it was necessary, but I wish they hadn't had to do it."

I glanced at her, and shrugged. "Oh, you'll get used to it, sweetheart," I said callously. "First Tillery and his friends, then Sorenson, then me. After a while, you'll find being accessory to murder coming quite naturally to you, no sweat at all."

Bobbie spoke without looking at me. "The Chinaman promised me you wouldn't be hurt. He said… he said he owed you a small favor."

"Sure, like his life. But Willy owes me something, too, or thinks he does. And Mr. Soo needs Willy and doesn't need me, so I'm not counting too strongly on his sense of gratitude." I waited, but Bobbie didn't speak. I went on: "So they ditched the good doctor after pumping him dry. Well, that figures."

"Yes. He was saving the world, of course."

"They all are. What was his angle?"

"Isn't it obvious? He wanted his generator used—by anybody he could persuade to use it, regardless of political affiliations—in order to make people realize just how much junk was in the air already. He wanted to make the situation look so bad right now that immediate, drastic steps would be taken…"

I grinned. "And of course the Chinaman pretended to be burning with enthusiasm for the same great cause, and in a sense he was. I mean, what could be nicer for the communists than having us obligingly wreck one of our own biggest industries, and throw our own transportation system into complete chaos."

She gave me a reproving glance. "You sound as if you actually approve of the automobile!"

I said, "Approve, disapprove, nuts! Actually, I get a kick out of driving a good car, but that's beside the point. But I don't see anybody building a lot of new railroads and streetcar lines, with smogless power. Until they do, we're damn well stuck with the automobile, and probably with some form of the internal combustion engine, enthusiasts like Sorenson to the contrary notwithstanding. All we can do is detoxify it a bit and pray." I grimaced. "So they got his machine going, and then they didn't need him any more, and they certainly didn't want him talking, so they killed him. How?"

"I don't know." Bobbie's voice was dull. "He was really kind of a sweet little man. I don't want to know. All I know is that he was found dead last night in the flaming wreckage of the trailer laboratory—and of course, nobody's going to be very concerned about the death of a scientist, already considered something of a radical crackpot, who blows himself up refining heroin for the Mafia. Anyway, that was the plan, and I gather it worked very well. Your lady agent and her Mexican allies were just moving in to seize the laboratory when it went up. Fortunately nobody was hurt, nobody outside the trailer, that is."

"I see," I said. "And Warfel and his ten kilos of horse? Ten kilos! My God, that's about twenty-two pounds, worth a couple of million dollars!"

"More than that, on the current market," Bobbie said. "If you're asking whether Frankie-boy was caught with the drugs when he brought the *Fleetwind* into its Long Beach marina, the answer is that he hasn't landed yet. That boat isn't very fast and he had quite a ways to go. But he knows the fuzz will be waiting for him, and I think it's very unlikely they'll find a single crystal of junk anywhere on board."

I sighed. "That's going to make my girlfriend very mad; she took this pinch very seriously." I hesitated, and went on: "So it was strictly a one-time operation? Frankie wasn't really setting up to make a career of smuggling drugs like the syndicate boys feared; he just wanted to get this one big batch into the country without tipping anybody off that he'd had unpatriotic dealings with the Chinese communists?"

"That's right. With so much heroin involved, he

could afford to make elaborate preparations for a one-shot deal. And from the Chinaman's point of view, well, American dollars are hard to come by on the other side of the Pacific, but poppies grow very well over there. His government probably confiscated the stuff in the first place, so it didn't cost them anything. He could afford to offer a fancy price in drugs for Warfel's assistance, much higher than he could have bid in real money."

I asked, "Where's the heroin now, if Warfel hasn't got it on his boat? Could it be somewhere in this truck, perhaps?"

Bobbie laughed scornfully. "You've met Frank Warfel, darling. Can you imagine him trusting us with two million dollars belonging to him? Can you imagine him trusting anybody? No, he's taking care of it all by himself. But he knows that if his men don't get us safely across the border, the U.S. authorities will get an anonymous phone call that'll make it impossible for him ever to cash in on that shipment he hopes will make him rich; he'll be watched too closely."

"Sure," I said. "Well, according to you, we're safely across the border now, so Frankie's fortune is made." I glanced at her slyly, and went on: "Figuring our elapsed time, and guessing at our probable speed and direction, I estimate we should be somewhere near your dear old home town of Yuma, Arizona. Maybe you should stop and visit some of your friends and relations."

Bobbie grinned. "I told you I was born in China, darling. I don't know anybody in Yuma. I've seen pictures of the town and memorized a lot of maps and information, but I've never been there in my life."

I said, deliberately, "Well, that figures. A real Yuma girl, brought up that close to the border, would know that it was mescal, not pulque like you said, that's got the maguey worm in the bottom of the bottle." Bobbie looked at me sharply. I went on: "And a real Yuma girl, brought up in that dry, dry country, would know a little about desert driving. I mean, doll, when you try to blast your way through deep sand like you thought you could lick it with sheer horsepower, even a dumb guy like me starts to wonder where the hell you spent your formative years, since it certainly wasn't Arizona. And you were so insistent on getting that Chrysler unstuck; you didn't want it there, blocking the road for Willy and Mr. Soo. And, finally, no reasonably bright girl, dressing for dangerous adventures in the dark, would pick white pants and a light-yellow shirt—not unless she was making sure her hidden friends didn't open up on her by mistake."

Again there was silence except for the rattling of the truck and the rumbling of the metal cylinder above us. Bobbie was staring at me with something close to horror.

"You knew?" she whispered. "You *knew*? And still you let me… You let yourself be…" She stopped.

I said, "I took out a little insurance. There wasn't any cartridge in the chamber of that trick rifle of Jake's your man was holding on me, and I had the chopper right under my hand. If things had looked bad, I could have sprayed both you and the guy behind me before he realized he was trying to shoot back with an empty gun. And then, with

Mr. Thompson's hundred-round squirter to help me, I'd have had a pretty good chance of shooting my way clear in the dark."

"But you didn't." She licked her lips. "Why, Matt?"

"Because there were things I wanted to know—if there seemed to be a reasonable chance of learning them without getting killed. And because you came to my defense like a little heroine when Willy started kicking me around."

She said, shocked: "Matt, you're crazy if you think I'm going to help you further just because I—"

"I figured there were some other things working for me," I said when she paused. "I figured Mr. Soo might feel a slight sense of gratitude; and in any case I knew he wouldn't have me killed at once because he's got some reason to think I know something dangerous to him. He'll want to find out if I really do, and if so, if I've told anybody else about it. That'll keep me alive for a little. But mostly," I said, "I'm counting on you."

"*No!*" she gasped. "No, you're crazy! You've got no right to expect—"

I shrugged. "Okay, I've got no right. So don't help. Just watch Willy kill me, slowly, when the Chinaman is through with me. Willy will make it worth watching, I'm sure. He'll milk it for all the entertainment value possible."

She licked her lips. "What makes you think I care what happens to you, damn you?"

"You cared what happened to Sorenson. Aren't I a sweet little man, too?" I put the playful note out of my voice and demanded harshly: "How many people have to die before you've had enough, sweetheart?"

"Damn you!" she breathed "Just because I kept him from kicking you to death… I had my orders. The Chinaman wanted you alive. That's absolutely the only reason I interfered!"

"Sure," I said. "Sure."

"You… you egotistical jerk! If you think yon can blackmail me just because I went to bed with you in the line of business… These people have been good to me! They took me out of… out of conditions you can't even imagine. They educated and trained me—"

"Sure," I said. "The Chinese are in a bad spot when it comes to agents. There are lots of Russian girls and boys, for instance, who with a little training can be planted over here to blend with the U.S. background until needed, but a Chinese boy or girl is always a bit conspicuous in our society. Sure, they could make good use of a pretty blond kid of European or American parents, who'd got lost or left behind during one of China's numerous upheavals."

Her expression told me I'd come close enough to guessing her story. She said quickly, "Their reasons don't matter! The fact is, they saved my life and… and my sanity!"

"By running you through the brainwash machinery, and then training you to serve them as an agent in place? Well, I guess that's one kind of salvation. But I don't hear you holding forth about the great god Marx and our decadent capitalist society. Apparently the indoctrination didn't take—or has it worn off during the pleasant years you've spent over here playing American and waiting for orders?"

"I wasn't playing American, I *am* American!" When I didn't say anything, she went on less fiercely: "Well, my parents were. I think. Anyway, what makes you think my years over here have been so damn pleasant?"

I said, "I've been studying you pretty closely, doll, and I think what you most want to be in this world is a typical U.S. miss with love beads and long stringy hair throwing rocks at the pigs. You tried out a lot of roles on me, but that was the one that really carried conviction. Well, I don't know about the rocks and the pigs, but the rest can probably be arranged, if your services warrant my going to the trouble. At least I can probably clean the slate for you somehow, if I'm alive to do it. Think about it."

She said bitterly, "Now it's a bribe!"

"Call it a deal. It sounds better."

She had the hypodermic in her hand once more. "You'd better lie down, Matt. Otherwise you'll fall over when this takes effect, and I won't raise a finger to stop you!"

## 25

The next time I woke up, I was outdoors. Even before opening my eyes, I knew I was lying on the ground in broad daylight, breathing warm fresh air that was untainted with truck exhaust fumes but carried instead, strangely, a smell of fresh paint or lacquer. Somebody was hammering on metal not far away.

A shadow passed over my face. I opened my eyes and saw Mr. Soo leaning over me, whatever his real name might be. I probably couldn't have spelled it, or pronounced it correctly, even if I'd known it. Behind him stood Bobbie Prince, whatever *her* real name might be.

"You wake up now, Mr. Helm," said Mr. Soo, straightening up. As Jake had suggested, the unfamiliar mustache did make him look like Charlie Chan, or more accurately, like the movie actor—a non-Asiatic name as I recall—who used to play Charlie Chan. He said, "Very good. Now we talk."

My hands and feet were still tied. Nobody'd given me

back my knife and gun. I managed to sit up awkwardly, feeling kind of doped and vague, which was no way to feel if I was going to match wits with the Chinaman. Looking around, I saw that we were in a narrow canyon with sheer walls, the kind of abruptly eroded cleft that's fairly common in the dry southwest.

If I'd been a geologist, I could probably have made a fairly good guess at my location, using the exposed, colorful strata as a guide. If I'd been a botanist, I could have figured the approximate area by the cacti and stuff growing around us. As it was, I just had a feeling that I was somewhere in southern Arizona or New Mexico. My watch said that it was still early in the day; we hadn't had time enough to get to Texas. In any case, I was reasonably certain we weren't heading there, or back to California, either.

Willy's white Jeepster was parked nearby, along with Charlotte Devlin's big blue station wagon. The vehicle, and its trailer hitch, reminded me of the tall, tailored girl with the clipped chestnut hair who'd said she liked horses and riding. She'd also warned me not to louse up her operation for her, but apparently it had got loused up anyway, if Bobbie's information was correct Well, we were sorry about that.

There was no sign of the six-wheeled van that had brought me here—me, and the science-fiction gadget dreamed up by Dr. Osbert Sorenson, deceased. I wondered what had happened to the crazy catalytic generator. Then, glancing in the direction from which the hammering noise was coming, I realized that I was looking straight at it.

It was another truck, a gleaming white job. A couple of men were working under it. Another man was waiting for them to stop pounding so he could continue lettering a name on the door. He'd already got it on the cylindrical, white-painted, horizontal tank that formed the afterbody of the vehicle: ARDOX BUTANE. Somehow the cylinder looked smaller like that, in daylight, than it had looked being wrestled ashore in the dark.

"Clever," I said.

Mr. Soo followed the direction of my glance. "You approve, Mr. Helm?"

I said, "Very slick. Anywhere it goes, out in the boondocks, it'll just be another gas truck chasing out to fill some rancher's tank. It'll be practically invisible. Nobody'll look at it twice."

"That is my hope," the Chinaman said. "I am glad you agree. Mobility is essential, you understand."

"Sure," I said. "Because of the wind. A ship was ideal, you could move it anywhere there was water, but on land you've got to have wheels, and hope there's a lonely road somewhere upwind of the place you want to cover with your poison."

"Catalyst, please, Mr. Helm. You supply your own poison, we merely activate it. You'll be happy to know that the Los Angeles experiment was a great success, considering that this is merely a small pilot model of the generator."

"Sure," I said. "But just like a gas attack, you're at the mercy of the weather."

"That is true, of course. Even though we know generally prevailing wind direction, the most favorable location changes from day to day, so permanent installation is impossible. Of course, this also makes it less easy for your people to find us, even when they realize what they are looking for. But we do have permanent headquarters in general area to store necessary chemicals and fuels— but you know that, Mr. Helm."

"Do I?"

Mr. Soo shook his head impatiently. "To pretend ignorance is stupid. Refuse to speak, if you wish, but do not pretend, please! That is an insult to my intelligence."

I looked at him for a moment, and then I glanced at Bobbie Prince, now sitting on a nearby rock with her sneakered feet dangling. She'd combed the snarls out of her hair, but she still looked like a tall skinny blond kid after a dusty game of sandlot football. Well, it had been a rough night for everybody, and I fell somewhat short of sartorial perfection myself.

I said to Soo, "Just what makes your damn intelligence think I know anything about your headquarters?"

He laughed. "Please, Mr. Helm, give us credit. When you made sudden appearance in Los Angeles… Well, sir, you have given trouble in the past. I have respect for your capabilities; once they saved my life. Naturally, I made investigation to learn what activities had preceded your visit to the Coast. It seemed at first as if your presence was coincidental, caused merely by stupid and unnecessary killing of one of your people…"

"What was stupid and unnecessary about it?" That was Willy's voice; the man seemed to make a habit of barging in on conversations. I heard his footsteps behind me. "That redheaded agent of his had us pegged, Beverly and me. She had to be silenced, didn't she?"

He came forward into, my field of vision and stopped beside Bobbie. He was wearing the same gray work-shirt-and-pants outfit in which I'd first seen him; at least it was creased and grimy enough to be the same one. Except for Mr. Soo, who seemed to shed dust and wrinkles, we were not a prepossessing outfit. Willy needed a shave, and his small blue eyes were bloodshot in his lumpy, coarse-skinned face. He didn't look like a man who was a top agent, but then top agents aren't supposed to.

"Didn't she?" he repeated angrily. "What were we supposed to do with her, keep her for a pet?"

"Something could have been worked out, with a little thought," the Chinaman said smoothly. "When hunting the antelope, does one throw rocks at the tiger? We had simple scientific test to perform. Unfortunately, Mr. Warfel's connections involved us in syndicate displeasure, and Mr. Warfel was essential to the operation, so that could not be helped. But it was not essential to attract attention of government bureau specializing in violence by shooting personnel thereof. That could have been avoided."

"Tell me how. Anyway, I didn't shoot the girl; Beverly did."

"So you say, Mr. Hansen." Apparently the Chinaman was willing to use the cover name under which Nicholas had established himself locally; but I had not heard him refer to the code name assigned to the man by an agency of another country. I had a hunch that we'd have no more trouble with Santa Claus, which didn't mean that Willy wouldn't be a menace under other aliases, with Mr. Soo to guide him. "So you say," the Chinaman repeated, "But does Mr. Helm believe you?"

I said, "Oh, I believe him, all right. It took somebody two shots to put down Annette O'Leary—two shots at pointblank range with a .44 Magnum, for God's sake! Even then our girl almost survived. Obviously, neither bullet went where it should have. I give Willy credit for being a better marksman than that. That's the kind of nervous, flinchy shooting you'd expect of a little girl using a big pistol that scares hell out of her although she'd never admit it; a pistol she's carrying only because it's part of her cover as Nicholas. That's why Beverly took poison, because she *had* committed the murder; and that's why I let her. But I'm still under orders to find the man who set her up to take the rap, the man who gave her the murder orders so he could keep his own hands clean, technically speaking."

"Well, you've found him," Willy said harshly. "What are you going to do about it?"

Usually, there's nothing sillier than, when you're a prisoner, provoking your captors by telling them all the terrible things you're going to do to them, by way of retaliation, at some future date. That's the sort of gaudy rhetoric in which movie stars are made to indulge in order to show the audience what brave Hollywood heroes they are. In real life you generally try not to make your jailers any madder at you than they already are.

In this case, however, I had a reason for drawing Willy's ire down upon me, and I said bombastically, "Why, you murdering bastard, I'm going to kill you according to instructions, sooner or later."

Willy laughed and, stepping forward, swung an oversized hand at my face, knocking me flat. Then he kicked me hard in the hip and laughed again.

"Well, you'd better make it sooner, Helm, because you won't be around much later!"

"That's enough, Willy." Mr. Soo stepped forward.

"All right, all right. I can wait. Just don't make me wait too long."

"You will wait as long as I say." The Chinaman's voice was quite soft. "You will wait forever if I say so."

"Maybe." Willy's voice was harsh. "And then again, maybe not. I'm doing a job for you, Soo. You need me. Okay, so throw the dog a bone for being a good doggie. That's the bone I want, right there. I want that interfering, lucky, creep who—"

"We'll talk about it later, Mr. Hansen. If we are to take advantage of this favorable weather system, we must hurry. You had better see what progress is being made with the truck." There was a brief pause. The Chinaman was looking steadily at Willy, who made a sudden, growling sound in his throat and turned away. When he had gone out of earshot, Mr. Soo gave a short laugh. "He is not really very good dog. But even bad dogs have their uses, if they are vicious enough. It is merely matter of establishing proper control, somewhat difficult when subject has been accustomed to independence. We are still somewhat lacking in discipline, as you see, but training is proceeding well. I am pleased to have acquired Mr. Hansen; I foresee much employment for him. I thank you for the present, Mr. Helm."

"*De nada*," I said. "Be my guest."

He studied me narrowly for a moment, and said, "Well, sir, will you be brave and stupid or will you tell me what I need to know without, shall we say, further persuasion?"

I looked back at him, making no attempt to check the blood that trickled down my chin from a split lip—not that there was much I could have done about it with my hands tied in back. I forced myself not even to glance at the blond girl sitting on a rock in the sunshine.

She was not a pro, not in my sense of the word. At least I sincerely hoped she wasn't. Of course she'd been trained to a certain extent: she'd been taught how to behave more or less like the kind of pretty, mildly talented, young American girl who might have been drawn to Hollywood from Yuma, Arizona. Maybe she'd also been taught a little about codes and ciphers, and instructed in the various data-transmitting techniques she might have to employ; but I was betting that she'd had no instruction or experience in the arts of violence. An agent in place seldom has. As Charlotte Devlin had once put it in a different connection: Bobbie was information people, not action people.

Anyway, I hoped this was the first time she'd seen a helplessly bound man slapped and kicked around—not to mention seeing him killed. Of course, she'd intimated that she'd been through some fairly unpleasant times as a kid, before the Chinese communists selected her for this work. Maybe she was tougher and more callous than I thought. If so, I was in real trouble.

But in my favor was the fact that the man who was being knocked around—the man scheduled to die before her eyes, if Willy had his way: me—was a man who'd made love to her and bought her a pleasant dinner; a man with whom she'd walked hand-in-hand along the shore to watch the sun set into the Pacific. Certainly no gentleman would trade on such a tender relationship; but if Mac ever caught me being gentlemanly, he'd be justified in firing me on the spot. You play the cards you're dealt, all of them, and those were mine.

So, having already planted, in her mind the treasonous— from her point of view—idea I wanted her to consider, I now refrained from looking at her, lest she suspect what a calculating louse I really was. I just let the stuff drip messily on my shirt while I endured my bruises bravely…

"Well, Mr. Helm?" the Chinaman said again.

"What was the subject under discussion?" I asked. "I kind of lost track."

Mr. Soo spoke deliberately: "When first notified of your presence in Los Angeles, I assumed it was coincidental, as I have said. However, investigation soon proved this assumption untenable, Mr. Helm."

"Untenable?" I said. "Why?"

"It was determined that you had spent several weeks in New Mexico before appearing on the coast," the Chinaman said. "You had rented a car there and driven several thousand miles. To be sure, you had carried along fishing tackle and even employed it upon occasion, but I do not really think you were after trouts or basses. You were seeking larger fish, were you not, Mr. Helm?"

The trouble with being a pro is that sometimes you get too smart and suspicious for your own good. No professional ever permits himself to believe in coincidence; it's against his principles.

Yet coincidences do occur, even in our business, and it was becoming fairly obvious that Mr. Soo had accidentally picked, for his second test with the Sorenson generator, the one state of the fifty in which I'd once made my home, to which I occasionally returned for rest and relaxation. However, I knew I'd never be able to convince him that this was wholly coincidental, particularly since I had a hunch that at least one of my casual fishing expeditions must have taken me into the actual area in which he was operating.

This was why he'd tried to have Beverly Blaine attach herself to me a second time, hoping that she could wheedle out of me just how much I'd learned about the New Mexico end of his project. The late Mr. Tillery had been quite right in thinking that I was suspected of knowing something dangerous to the opposition; his only mistake had been in thinking that I knew what it was.

Mr. Soo was still talking. "…so you see, sir, it is

essential for me to determine how much you discovered, and how much you reported to superiors. At present, generator is almost completely discharged from previous test. It will require additional catalyst and fuel before we can proceed…"

"What's this fuel bit?" I asked. "That's the second time you've mentioned it."

"You are stalling," the Chinaman said. "However, I will answer question. To call it generator is, perhaps, misleading. Actually, it does not generate catalyst; that has already been produced and purified elsewhere. What so-called generator does is to project this rare metallic substance into atmosphere in finely divided form so it can be carried by air currents high above earth. To provide power for dispersion, fuel is required; kerosene-type liquid such as is employed by jet engines. Catalyst is mixed with fuel, and mixture is burned under controlled conditions. I hope that is satisfactory explanation."

"Sure," I said. "So what you want to know is whether it's safe for you to visit your secret hideaway for refueling, or whether I've arranged a nice little trap for you there."

"Precisely, Mr. Helm."

I said, "I suppose it's no use insisting that I was just relaxing with a fishing rod after a hard winter's work."

"None whatever," said Mr. Soo. He held out his hand to the side, and Bobbie put into it a hypodermic syringe, not mine. The girl, and the case, seemed to be just bristling with needles. Mr. Soo said to me, "You can guess what this is."

"The old babble-juice, otherwise known as truth serum?"

"That is correct. Quite effective, but not too pleasant for the subject."

I said, "I know. And I'm already feeling like a human pincushion. I don't really need any more shots of anything, thanks." I drew a long breath, and went on: "Okay. You win. Why waste time trying to fight your damn drug? There *is* a trap waiting for you, Mr. Soo, so you're going to have to get your kerosene and chemicals elsewhere."

The Chinaman returned the hypo to Bobbie without taking his eyes from me. His mental processes didn't resemble mine very closely, so I didn't even try to guess what he was thinking. I just hoped my quick surrender had made him very suspicious indeed. To sell somebody a bill of goods, you should start behind a cloud of suspicion, and dispel it convincingly as you go along, making them feel guilty and apologetic for misjudging you.

"Mr. Helm," said Mr. Soo gently, "Mr. Helm, you would not be bluffing, would you? You would not be trying to keep me away from my supplies to prevent me from causing disaster to one of your cities?"

This was, of course, exactly what I was trying to do. I grinned and said, "Sure. That's exactly what I'm doing. So drive along to your hidden base and replenish your goddamn catalyst. Don't mind me, Mr. Soo. Like you say, I'm just bluffing."

He stared at me coldly, unconvinced. It was time to pull one out of the magic hat, long ears, fuzzy tail, twitching nose, and all. I said, "Not that I give a damn what happens to Albuquerque, you understand. I never did like that city much; all they do is take in tourists. Now, if it was my little old home town of Santa Fe, that would be something else."

The Chinaman's bland poker face showed just the tiniest crack, the faintest hint of an expression, to tell me I'd guessed right. So far, so good.

"Of course," Mr. Soo murmured, "there are not many cities in New Mexico suitable for experiment. In fact, there is only one that has sufficient population, sufficient pollution, and is located in a suitable, smog-retaining valley... I think you are very good guesser, Mr. Helm."

I said, "Sure. So let me guess a little more. It was a tough job at first, since I wasn't told what I was looking for. You know how they are, in Washington as well as—I suppose—in Peking. They never tell you anything you need to know. They just gave me some snapshots and descriptions and said these characters are up to something nasty, unspecified, in California, Arizona, New Mexico, and/or Texas. We've got the other states covered, they said; you know New Mexico, start looking. Those were my instructions."

"A big order. But you filled it successfully?"

"Not at first," I said. "All I could do at first was move around at random, pretending to fish and keeping my eyes open, looking for a familiar face from the photographs, or some off-color activities. It wasn't until I got a little more information, like a description of your smog machine and its purpose, that I realized I was wasting my time in the northern half of New Mexico. As you say, Albuquerque is the only really likely target in the state, and it's just about in the middle. The prevailing winds are from the southwest. That means you'd probably want to work your gadget somewhere down south in the Rio Grande valley, to have your stuff blow the right way." Mr. Soo's face gave me no help now. I gambled on the fact that there was only one place down the river that I'd done any fishing during those weeks; only one place south of Albuquerque where I could have been recognized by somebody alert for snoopers. I said, "Well, that narrowed it down some, but it still took a lot of scurrying around before I managed to spot one of your people and tail him out into the Jornada del Muerte country."

"What country?" The Chinaman laughed. He looked relieved. "Oh, Mr. Helm, you are very good, very good indeed, you almost had me convinced, but you are still guessing and guessing wrong. I do not know what this Hornada is, but I can assure you it is not the place—"

"Spelled with a J, *amigo*," I said calmly. "You may not have heard the area called that. It's not a name strangers generally know, unless they've studied some history or examined the fine print on the map. It's the old trail east of the Rio Grande past what is now Elephant Butte Reservoir and a town with the silly name of Truth or Consequences—they took the name of a radio show for some reason—formerly Hot Springs, New Mexico."

Something changed in Mr. Soo's eyes. He said softly,

"Truth or Consequences. That is indeed an odd name for a town. Go on, Mr. Helm."

"The present highway runs west of the river and is easy driving," I said, "but the old trail through the desert to the east was a real hot and thirsty man-killer, which is why they called it the Journey of Death. As for your boy, the one I tailed—"

I paused. This was where I really had to stick my neck out with some wild guesses, but the Chinaman gave me no help.

"Yes, Mr. Helm?"

I said confidently, I hoped: "I tailed him from T or C, as we New Mexicans call the town, across the dam, and east to a village called Engle where the pavement ends. There are some dirt roads going back into the boondocks where the old trail used to be. Otherwise there's nothing much on that side of the river except a government installation of some kind and a lot of empty, arid real estate. And there's no good way out of there except the one paved road through Engle. I figured I'd learned enough. I didn't want to be spotted snooping around those empty back roads. With that much to go on, the search planes and helicopters could pinpoint the location cautiously—and when I reached Los Angeles, later, I got word that they had."

It was, as I've said, a gamble, based on my knowledge of the area and the fact that somebody must have seen me hanging around the town or fishing the reservoir—else why would Mr. Soo suspect me, erroneously, of knowing so much? Well, if a man had seen me there, I could presumably have seen him, and followed him.

Of course, my logic wasn't airtight by any means. Maybe they'd avoided using the obvious route into the area; maybe they'd gone in across country by jeep. And maybe I'd even picked the wrong side of the river. There was plenty of rough, uninhabited country to the west in which you could also hide a few men and supplies. But if you really wanted privacy, you'd be apt to choose the spectacularly desolate region I'd described, even though it might not always be directly upwind of the chosen target area...

"Engle, New Mexico," Mr. Soo murmured.

"That's the place. Just a couple of shacks and some railroad cars. Am I getting warm?"

"Warm?"

"Sorry. It's a kid's game we play in this country."

"Ah, yes, I remember now." He sighed. "Yes, you are very warm, Mr. Helm. It is unfortunate. It will involve a drastic change of plan—"

"He's lying!" It was Bobbie Prince. She was on her feet glaring at me. "He's just guessing. He is bluffing, Mr. Soo!"

"What makes you think so?"

Bobbie licked her lips. "He says he figured out where to look after he learned about the Sorenson generator. He claims he was told about it several days ago, in plenty of time for him to snoop around this T or C place, but he's lying! *He didn't know anything about the generator until last night!*"

Mr. Soo was frowning. "Are you sure of that, Miss Prince?"

"Of course I'm sure! I was lying right beside him when they brought it ashore. He had no idea what it was until I told him. Even then he didn't know what it did, not until I explained it to him hours later. He'd never heard of such a thing before. In fact, he laughed at the idea at first. He wasn't acting, I know he wasn't!"

Well, it had been a good try; and after all, while I'll make a stab at it if I have the chance, keeping the atmosphere of our cities pure isn't really my job. At least I'd learned where I stood with respect to Miss Roberta Prince.

At the moment, needing her help as badly as I did, I couldn't feel it was a very healthy place to be standing—particularly since Willy was coming back this way briskly, presumably to report that the truck was ready to roll.

# 26

I was loaded into the rear seat of the station wagon with my hands re-tied in front of me so that I could sit naturally and in reasonable comfort. I appreciated this; but actually I was happy just to reach the vehicle alive. Willy was becoming very impatient. Since there was apparently no useful, or truthful, information to be obtained from me, he couldn't see why he couldn't have me. Objectively speaking, I couldn't see why, either.

While Mr. Soo came from a country with different traditions and customs than mine, he was in more or less the same line of work; and I couldn't really believe that he'd be greatly influenced by an obligation that was several years old by this time. After all, he undoubtedly knew that I hadn't saved his life to be nice; it had just worked out more conveniently for me that way.

Nevertheless, he told Willy sharply that he could perpetrate private vengeance on his own time, please. Right now, said the Chinaman, since Willy was the man who had laid out the route from here, he'd better get into his Jeepster and lead the way. Speed should be lawful, so as not to attract attention, said Mr. Soo; spacing between vehicles should be generous, so they would not seem like a caravan, but merely like a jeep, a butane truck, and an out-of-state station wagon that just happened to be using the same road.

Bobbie Prince got in beside me. A lean, dark-faced individual in jeans and a gaudy cowboy shirt took the wheel, after pausing to strip off the paint-smeared coveralls he was wearing, which he tossed into the rear of the wagon. Mr. Soo took the seat beside him, and watched Willy, alone in the jeep, drive off. When he was well down the road, the Chinaman signaled to the white truck, which had two men aboard. When they had gone almost out of sight, he spoke to our driver, and we set off in pursuit.

Well, the odds were diminishing, I reflected. I now had only five men and one woman to deal with, instead of the young army of the night before. Apparently the reinforcements supplied by Frank Warfel, having completed their part of the operation, had pulled out while I was asleep.

Mr. Soo turned to look back at us, and frowned at my appearance. "I suggest you clean up prisoner, Miss Prince," he said. "We do not wish to be conspicuous when we reach more traveled roads. Mr. Helm seems to be foresighted man with water jug in car. Here."

He passed a gallon thermos jug over the back of the

seat. He seemed to be under the impression that the station wagon was mine. I could see no particular benefit to be gained from this, but I didn't take the trouble to set him straight.

The blond girl beside me leaned over to wash my face with a handkerchief that looked familiar; she must have acquired it when she cleaned out my pockets. A hint of a bulge in her loosely worn shirt at the waist and a ridge in the pocket area of her snug jeans, indicated that she was also the custodian of my gun and knife. Having made my face presentable, except for the swollen lip she could do nothing about, she attacked the spots on my shirt—doing it all without any more visible emotion than if she'd been cleaning-the upholstery of the car. Finally, she dropped the handkerchief to the floor and settled back beside me, looking straight ahead.

It was a long, hot, dusty ride. On the coast, we'd found a rather chilly spring; but here, inland, it was summer, or what would pass for summer in most regions of the country. The real summer, down there along the border, is strictly for lizards and Gila monsters and rattlesnakes; even the jackrabbits lie panting in the shade, if they can find some shade.

I didn't recognize the road or the countryside, but then, most of those desert roads look alike. I did spot a lonely highway marker indicating that we were definitely in Arizona. At last, heading eastwards along one small road after another, mostly unpaved, we reached some scenery that looked more familiar to me. It was the kind of endless, wide-open, yellowish landscape, interrupted here and there by small, dark mountain ranges that I associate with southwestern New Mexico.

Sure enough, the next road marker indicated that we'd crossed the state line, making me feel pretty clever until I remembered that I was still tied hand and foot, regardless of what state of the Union I was in. Well, there were things that could be done about that—we're issued a few tricks to help us cope with such situations—but they'd have to wait until I wasn't under quite such close surveillance. The girl beside me might not condescend to look at me directly, or talk with me, but I didn't think she'd continue to remain motionless and silent if she saw me trying to cut my bonds with, say, a gimmicked belt buckle.

The opportunity was slow in coming. We continued to drive eastwards interminably, bouncing over washboards and breathing dust that found its way into the car even after Mr. Soo ordered the windows closed and the air-conditioning turned on. At last we turned onto a paved road heading north which, eventually, dumped us into civilization in the form of a four-lane freeway crowded with high-speed traffic. The change from the lonely silence of the desert was kind of shocking; and you couldn't see where, in that empty country, all the trucks and cars were coming from, or going to.

A police car went by as we pulled off the ramp. It was cruising quite slowly; and after a mile or so we repassed it. I was aware of the Chinaman glancing my way warningly and of Bobbie slipping her hand inside her shirt to grasp my gun, but I made no move. Frankly, even if I could catch his attention, I didn't really know what I could do with a cop except get him killed.

Of course, a policeman might help me break up Mr. Soo's scientific experiment, to the benefit of Albuquerque and any other cities whose skies the Chinaman might decide to seed with catalyst if the first two tests turned out successfully. It seemed unlikely, however, that a single cop, unaware of what he was getting into, could handle the job; and anyway, Mr. Soo and his project was not really my responsibility. Nobody'd ordered me to do anything about him, or it. Perhaps somebody might have if the facts had been known; but for a field man like me to try to guess what instructions an individual in Washington might have issued if he'd known something he didn't is almost always unprofitable, and often dangerous.

I'd made my gesture towards public service when I tried to bluff the Chinaman away from his supplies. We're not employed to wander around doing good, knight-errant fashion. We're hired to follow orders, and my orders actually concerned one man only. Nicholas might no longer exist, officially speaking, but the man who'd built up a sizeable dossier under that code name was still around and still keeping busy at the same trade. *I foresee much employment for him*, Mr. Soo had said.

Although somebody else had pulled the trigger, Willy was the man really responsible for the murder I'd been ordered to investigate and avenge. He was also on the high-priority list, and his change of employer wouldn't change that. You know the standing orders, Mac had said, and I did. And those orders didn't include turning Willy over to any cops, at least not alive…

"Mr. Helm!"

I looked up to see a small automatic pistol aimed at me over the back of the front seat. Bobbie also had her gun out—I mean, my gun. I looked at Mr. Soo, bewildered.

"What's the matter?"

"Just what signal did you make to police cruiser, sir? No, do not look back… Jason, take first turn you see. We must lead this policeman away from others, if he will follow. Shine your headlights briefly as you turn to signal vehicles ahead. Mr. Helm, sit perfectly still, please. I will not hesitate to shoot."

I said, "I didn't signal anybody. Why should I? I'm perfectly happy right here with all you nice people."

The man at the wheel, whom the Chinaman had addressed as Jason, said: "The cop's gaining. He's after us, all right."

"Us, or truck up ahead?"

"Well, I can't tell that, sir," said Jason. "Here's an exit coming up. If I remember rightly, it's a long way to the next one. Do I turn?"

"Yes, turn." Mr. Soo sounded quite calm. He was studying the overpass ahead. "Let us see if he follows us, or goes on. Be ready to return to highway very quickly if he does not come after—"

"He's switching on his turn signal. He's coming after us, all right," Jason said tightly as we hit the off-ramp leading up to the crossroad and the bridge. "Which way do I turn?"

"Left, towards those mountains. Accelerate over highway and maintain high speed until we are beyond the first rise of ground, that will hide us from highway. As for you, Mr. Helm—"

The Chinaman frowned at me thoughtfully. I knew what was on his mind. He had a decision to make. On the one hand, if we were stopped by the policeman following us, a tightly bound prisoner would be hard to explain. On the other hand, if he cut me loose, I might cause trouble.

"As for you, Mr. Helm, you will remain tied," he said. I should have been flattered. It showed that he thought highly of me. He went on, "If you place any value upon human life, you will do nothing further to arouse suspicion. You understand. If we cannot satisfy this policeman somehow, we will be forced to kill him."

Bobbie Prince gasped. "But you can't... I mean, if you shoot a cop, you'll have them all—"

She stopped, jolted into silence as Jason made his left turn onto the overpass, accelerating hard. The sound of the engine and the exhaust hammered back at us from the concrete railings. A quick descent followed; and we had the highway behind us and were heading up the gentle slope away from it, still picking up speed. Jason was having his hands full keeping the wagon headed straight in the soft gravel of the little ranch road.

"The fuzz is off the bridge, sir. He's coming right after us."

"Get us over the hill; then slow down and let him overtake us."

"Yes, sir."

Mr. Soo looked at the girl beside me. When he spoke again, his voice was dangerously gentle: "Your concern for the life of a bourgeois constable speaks well for your humanitarianism, Miss Prince, but not so well for your training and loyalty."

"No, you don't understand!" Bobbie licked her lips. "I just meant that for practical reasons… I mean, we can't very well finish our job if every pig in the state is hunting for us."

"I promise to consider all practical aspects carefully, Miss Prince." The Chinaman's voice was still soft. "You will concern yourself with prisoner. He is your responsibility. Do you understand?"

"Yes, sir."

Jason spoke without turning his head. "Do I slow down as soon as we're out of sight?"

"Yes."

The station wagon was almost airborne as it topped the rise, the road dropping away unexpectedly beyond. For a moment I thought Jason was going to lose it in a wild skid; then he had it under control once more, coasting, letting the speed drop without touching the brake.

"Here comes Fuzzy. He's turned on his flasher," Jason said. "Do we stop?"

"Of course we stop. Would we resist officer of the law in performance of duty? Jason."

"Yes, sir."

"I will speak with him. If I make signal, you know what to do."

"Yes, sir."

We rolled to a halt at the side of the gravel road. At once, Mr. Soo got out and walked back towards the patrol car as it parked behind us. When I started to turn my head to watch, Bobbie gestured with my gun.

"Don't move!" she breathed. "Sit perfectly still, darling!"

Jason had got out more slowly than the Chinaman. He walked back there deliberately, leaving the station wagon door open. Now I could hear them talking back there.

"...stolen car?" Mr. Soo was saying. "My dear officer, you must be mistaken."

"No, sir. This station wagon was reported stolen just a few hours ago. The word came from California. They said for us to watch for you, you might be heading east I'm afraid I'll have to ask you to—"

"*No!*"

That was Bobbie Prince, beside me. Her small sound of protest was drowned by the reverberating noise of a single shot. I heard something fall to the ground behind me. Bobbie was staring out the back window. Slowly she turned to look at me. Her face was white and her blue eyes were wide and shocked.

"Hell, it's just a pig," I said.

"Damn you!" she hissed. "Damn you, be quiet!"

"You'd better get out there and take a look," I said. "You don't want to miss the chance of seeing a freshly dead pig, do you? Anyway, you might as well start getting used to stiffs. Practice up. You'll see a lot more of them shortly, including mine—"

She made a funny little sound in her throat; then she was scrambling into the front seat, hampered by her long legs and the headrests. Finally she got all of herself over and behind the wheel. The jerk, as she sent the car forward, slammed the open door and set me back against the vinyl-upholstered cushions. I looked back to see the lean man called Jason aiming a big revolver at us, but before he could shoot, Mr. Soo had pulled his arm down.

The last I saw, as we dipped into an arroyo, was the two of them dragging the uniformed body towards the police car parked at the side of the road, its red light still flashing steadily.

## 27

For a girl born in the land of the rickshaw, if her story was correct, she had internal combustion ambitions. She took the gravel road at a pace that had me bouncing around the rear seat while I tried to peel away the decorative foil that covered my sharp-edged belt buckle. Succeeding in this, I got to work on my bonds. They were tough, braided clothesline, which is difficult stuff to cut under the best conditions; and in spite of the jolting of the car, it seemed desirable to do the job without severing any essential veins or arteries…

Abruptly, Bobbie swerved the big wagon to the side of the road, skidded it to a halt, cut the engine, and began to cry, burying her face in her arms, folded on the steering wheel. We were now quite high in the foothills of the mountain range towards which the road seemed to lead. Looking out the rear window, I could see the geometrically correct line the distant freeway made across the empty landscape. A little closer, I could see the police car where we'd left it. Somebody had turned off the flasher. It had company; a jeep and a truck mounting a big white cylinder. Mr. Soo was undoubtedly holding a council of war.

If I could see them, they could see me, and I renewed my efforts with the trick buckle, but it was slow going.

"Oh, stop *wiggling!*" Bobbie said abruptly, lifting her head. She ran her sleeve across her eyes, and did some wiggling of her own, digging into the pocket of her jeans, not designed for quick-draw work. There was a metallic click. "Here... Well, stick out your wrists, stupid!"

She was holding my knife over the back of the seat, open, edge up. I held out my hands. A moment later I was free. She turned the knife around and presented it to me handle first. I reached down to cut the ropes about my ankles, and straightened up, closing and pocketing the knife.

"Thanks," I said. "What about my gun?"

She shook her head quickly. "No. I can't give you that. I'm helping you get away, isn't that enough?"

"Not really," I said. "It's not my job to get away."

"Well, I don't want to be involved in any more killing!"

I said deliberately, "What are you so uptight about, sweetheart? Like I said before, it was just a lousy cop. I thought you hated the pigs."

"You're not very funny. You're not funny at all!" She drew a ragged breath. "I don't want anybody else to be killed, not even you! Don't you understand? I certainly can't help you kill *them*... Ouch, what are you *doing*?"

I'd seized her left hand, which had been resting on the

top of the seat as she sat twisted around to look at me. There are several ways of exerting pressure on a hand so that the owner thereof can't move without tearing a few ligaments in the fingers or wrist and causing himself— or herself—excruciating pain in the process. I picked the one that seemed most appropriate.

When, having tested my grip and found it agonizingly effective, she was quiet once more, I looked over the seat. My revolver was lying where she'd dropped it when she started driving, on the seat beside her. I picked it up.

"What about the Walther you had?" I asked.

"Mr. Soo took that back. It was his. Didn't you recognize it just now?"

"All right," I said, releasing her. "Sorry if it hurt."

She rubbed her fingers and spoke without looking at me. "You're a lousy, treacherous bastard, aren't you? I saved you, and instead of being grateful—"

I said wearily, "Bobbie, cut out the corn. Didn't they teach you *anything* about this business except how to imitate a movie-mad kid from Arizona?" She didn't speak, and I went on: "We're not playing kid games with grateful and ungrateful. I have a job to do. Mr. Soo has a job to do. The two assignments are, let us say, incompatible. Therefore you'd damn well better forget about converting the whole world to non-violence, at least for the moment, and make up your mind whose side you're on."

She was silent for several seconds. "I don't know!" she breathed at last. "Can't you understand, Matt, I don't *know* any longer. Everything's changed. It all looks so different from when I came over here. Oh, God, I wish I were still the same stuffy, dedicated, brainwashed little creep who came over here so cocksure she knew exactly what was right and noble and Marxist—and what was wrong and decadent and capitalist!" She made a face. "I really don't know what's the matter with me, darling! It isn't as if this country of yours had been particularly good to me. You'd think I'd had a wonderful time over here and everybody'd treated me swell, the way I'm talking, but I haven't and they didn't. It's been a hell of a grind, even apart from knowing that sooner or later I'd get the word from somebody and have to start earning my keep…" She stopped, and drew a long breath. "I don't want to be a goddamn spy!" she said. "Not for them or for you. I just want to… All I want is to be left alone to live my own life, don't you understand?"

I said callously, "Sure, so did that cop. So, undoubtedly, did Dr. Osbert Sorenson, not to mention our girl O'Leary, and a colored pugilist type named McConnell, and five Cosa Nostra characters who were shot to death in their drugged sleep. They all wanted to be left alone to live their own lives, such as they were."

She said, "I know, darling, I know! That's why I… Oh, I'm just so damned mixed up! I don't know what—" She was silent again, briefly; then she sighed. "I suppose I've got to go back there."

"Why would you want to do a silly thing like that?"

"I didn't say I *want* to. I said I've got to." Bobbie hesitated. "I've got to, because they spent a lot of time and money on me, and I'd be dead now if they hadn't... No, don't bother to tell me again that they did it strictly for their own sinister purposes. I know that. The fact is, they did it, and I benefited from it. There's got to be a little... a little loyalty, even a little gratitude although you make fun of it. There are just too damn many people making up too damn many beautiful reasons for switching sides these days. I'm not going to be one of them."

There was nothing I could say to that. The fact that the people to whom she was returning, dutifully and gratefully, might very well shoot her for setting me free would, I knew, make no difference to her, so I didn't bother to point it out. Nor did I trouble to warn her that if she rejoined them I might have to shoot her myself. She knew all that, and considered it irrelevant. When their consciences get into the act, no logic has any effect on them.

I suppose I could have overpowered her and tied her up to prevent her from making a serious mistake. There are people who make careers of saving other people from themselves—Charlie Devlin, for instance—but it's not my line of work. Anyway, I didn't know how much of a mistake she was actually making, practically speaking. She might just as easily get killed if I kept her with me.

So I said only, "I have to have the station wagon. Sorry."

"Of course." There was a hint of scorn in her voice. "I wouldn't dream of depriving you of it." She opened the door and stepped out into the road. "Good-bye, Matt."

"Good-bye, Bobbie."

She looked at me for a moment longer. Neither of us found anything more to say. She turned abruptly and marched away towards the tiny group of vehicles in the distance. Her back was very straight and she never glanced around. I remembered the slinky satin Hollywood-blonde she'd been impersonating when I first met her. I remembered the nice girl-next-door type in crisp linen to whom I'd made love. I remembered the reckless tomboy-in-jeans who'd been so eager to help me take care of five armed and dangerous Mafia hoodlums... She wasn't any of those girls now. I guess I'd found the real Roberta Prince at last.

I should, of course, have been feeling greatly relieved by the turn of events, and diabolically clever to boot. After all, my hands and feet were free. I had my gun and knife. I even had a car. I was back in business. I'd gambled that, whoever she was, the kid would come through for me, and she had. There was no reason for me not to savor my moment of triumph, except that I just didn't feel particularly triumphant...

I got behind the wheel of the big Ford wagon, started the engine, and drove ahead slowly towards the piñon-studded mountains ahead. Somebody would come after me, I was sure. Mr. Soo couldn't afford to let me reach a telephone. I hoped he'd send the right man ahead to take care of me. He did.

From a vantage point on the shoulder of the mountain, with the station wagon parked out of sight down the road, I saw the white jeep heading my way, dragging a plume of dust behind it. I watched it approach, disappearing here and there in the dips and folds of the terrain, but always reappearing a little closer. Once it remained invisible for several minutes. When it showed again, there were two figures behind the windshield instead of one. Obviously, Willy had met the girl trudging down the road and stopped to question her. He'd brought her along. Well, I couldn't let that make any difference to me. I'd pointed out to her the choice she had to make, and she'd made it.

I checked the loads in the revolver I'd retrieved from her, but it was not at the moment my primary weapon. Trying to shoot somebody out of the seat of a fast-moving vehicle with a snub-nosed .38 Special is not recommended as sure-fire homicide. Even if you solve the problems of lead and timing correctly, there's always something to deflect the bullet. I had to get him out of his car... I got back into the station wagon and sent it slowly up the road, watching the rearview mirror.

It was the usual twisty, unpaved mountain road carved into the side of the slope; not exactly the ideal spot for a two-ton family vehicle almost six feet wide, even though it did have all the power anybody could want who didn't have drag racing ambitions. I cruised along deliberately, waiting for my man to catch up with me. When he burst into sight behind me in the bouncing and swaying jeep, I hit the gas pedal as if I hadn't really expected pursuit; as if I'd been panicked by his sudden appearance.

It was quite a race for a while, up into the pass and down the other side. In sports cars, it might have been fun, but neither of our vehicles had been designed for competitive mountain driving. I could see him, behind me, sweating over the wheel of the sturdy four-wheel-drive job that wanted to plow right off the road in the curves. I had the opposite problem. The heavy rear end of the wagon had a tendency to whip around whenever I got gay with the power.

He was a good driver. I remembered being told that he'd been a motorcycle racer once. He may have been better than I was, although I'd done a bit of sports car racing in my time, but it didn't really matter. The road was too narrow and my car was too wide and had too much power for him to get up alongside, and a little ahead, where he'd have to be to nudge me over the edge. At last, desperate at being blocked every time he tried it, he stuck his big revolver out the jeep's window, left-handed, and fired a couple of shots. However, there are very few men who can shoot well from a moving car, particularly if they have to steer the car, and neither of the bullets hit the station wagon.

Finally, as we roared down the curves and switchbacks, he was reduced to trying to ram my rear bumper to send me, he hoped, out of control and off the road. Just how a straight push down the road was supposed to accomplish this desirable purpose wasn't readily apparent, but it's something they're always doing in the movies, and I guess he figured he'd better try it and see if they knew something he didn't.

It was, of course, what I'd been waiting for. It was why

I'd held my speed down in the straights where the big Ford engine could easily have given me a good lead. Now I let him nudge me once, lightly, and did some frantic jockeying through the next set of curves to make him think I'd been terrified by the contact.

Another straightaway showed ahead. I jacked up the speed to tease him along. In the rearview mirror I saw him coming in beautifully, straight as any bullfighter could wish, to ram me again. I slammed my brakes on hard and slid down in the seat to support my head and neck since the headrests provided didn't look as if they'd take a lot of strain.

Under the influence of the brakes, the nose of the station wagon went down, of course, and the rear went up. I heard him skidding in the gravel behind me as, too late, his brakes locked up; that would put his nose down, the way I wanted it, to run his bumper under mine. Then he hit. It was quite a crash. Metal bent and tore; but I'd already determined that my gas tank was located in one of the fenders; there wasn't much except bodywork that he could hurt back there.

We slid to a stop, locked together. Before he could do any shooting, while he was still standing on his brakes, I hit the gas pedal hard, praying that he hadn't wedged me so high in the air that my rear wheels had lost traction. They did spin a bit; then they grabbed hold, and the station wagon tore free with more tortured-metal sounds. Looking into the mirror as I pulled away, I saw that Charlotte Devlin's big trailer hitch had done a fine job. It had driven through Willy's grill, fan, and radiator like a spear. A lot of steaming brown water was pouring out onto the road.

The jeep was still running, however. Willy came after me recklessly, knowing that he had only a little driving time left, but I stayed ahead of him without too much trouble. Behind me, the four-wheel-drive job began to steam like a tea kettle; finally something got too hot and seized, and it slid to an abrupt halt in the middle of the road. I stopped the station wagon a hundred yards farther on, out of easy pistol range, and took out my little Smith & Wesson. I had him on foot. It was time to complete the assignment.

"Helm!" That was Willy, shouting. "Helm, drop your gun and walk this way with your hands up!"

I looked that way and sighed. It was too bad. His dossier said he'd been a good agent once, and maybe he still was, except where I was concerned. You can't afford to hate—any more than you can afford to love—in this business. It clouds the judgement.

He'd dragged Bobbie Prince out of the Jeepster, and had pushed her down the road ahead of him until they were clear of the clouds of steam and other fumes billowing from the crippled vehicle. Now he was standing there with a gun—presumably his big .44 Magnum although I couldn't see it—thrust into her back. Well, from that position he'd find it rather difficult to shoot me. I started walking. I figured it would be best to get within twenty-five yards, and twenty would be better.

"Drop it, Helm! Drop it or I'll shoot her!"

It was the same old tired routine. They will keep on trying it. One day I'll have to sit down and count how many times it's been tried on me.

I suppose he knew we'd been to bed together. He knew she had thought enough of me to turn me loose; he presumably figured I'd feel myself under a certain obligation, even if I wasn't passionately in love with her. In any case, I came from a nation noted for slushy sentimentality about children, dogs, and women.

It was too bad. Of course, he was hampered by the fact that he didn't just want me dead; he wanted me dead on his terms. He hated me too much to simply kill me painlessly; he wanted to have his fun first. And, like so many of his kind, he was under the delusion that he had a monopoly on cold-blooded ruthlessness. He was banking on the fond belief that nobody could possibly be as mean as he was…

"Stop right there, or I'll blow her spine right out through her belly!"

I lifted my gun and shot him in the right eye.

## 28

When I awoke in the hospital, that was what I remembered immediately: the narrow mountain road, the steaming jeep with the smashed grill, and the stocky man hiding behind the tall, slim, blond girl who watched me steadily. She knew what I was about to do—what I had to do— and what it might do to her. I hoped she realized I had no choice. If I was fool enough to throw down my gun as ordered, Willy would simply kill both of us after he'd amused himself sufficiently. This way there was a good chance for me and a small chance for her, depending somewhat on my marksmanship.

I remembered the shot. I remembered the good, pistol-man's feeling of knowing it was right, even before the bullet hit. I'd done the best I could. The rest was up to luck or fate or God. There was a moment when it looked as if I might be allowed to get away with it. Then a dying nerve sent a final message to the dying muscles of Willy's hand, and I heard the muffled roar of the big revolver still pressed against Bobbie's back…

After a little, I walked up to the two bodies in the road. I checked first on the man. Willy was quite dead. I kicked the .44 Magnum into the roadside ditch nevertheless, before kneeling beside the girl. She was still alive, just barely. Her blue eyes looked up at me, wide with shock and pain. I started to say something stupid about being sorry for the way things had worked out, but it was no time for such foolishness. Being sorry has never yet put a bullet back into the gun that fired it.

"I wish…" Bobbie whispered. "I wish…"

They always wish for something. They never tell me what it is. Her voice just kind of stopped. I remembered kneeling there in the road with my gun still in my hand containing one empty cartridge and four loaded ones, but there was nobody left to shoot… Now I was lying in a hospital bed with a bandaged head and a pounding headache, trying to remember where I was and why I'd been brought there.

Somebody knocked on the door. Mac came in before I could clear my throat and issue the invitation. I watched him approach, vaguely flattered that he'd come to see me on my bed of pain, wherever it might be. He doesn't get out of Washington much, and I didn't really think I'd been transported that far while unconscious from causes I still couldn't recall.

Mac was, as always, conservatively dressed in a gray suit, like a banker, but his eyes were not a banker's eyes beneath the black eyebrows that contrasted strikingly with the steely gray of his hair. They were the eyes of a man who dealt, not in money, but in human lives.

"How are you, Eric?" he asked.

"It's too early to tell from this end," I said. My voice came-out kind of creaking and rusty. "What's the medical opinion? My head hurts like hell. Where am I?"

He raised his eyebrows slightly, but said, "I believe this is the Hidalgo County General Hospital, twenty-five beds, at 13th and Animas Streets, Lordsburg, New Mexico. You don't remember?"

"I remember dealing with Willy," I said. "The film ends there. Incidentally, you can get out your red pencil and scratch one Nicholas. He was Nicholas."

"You're sure?"

"Yes, sir."

"Very good, Eric," Mac said. "In that case, I commend you for a satisfactory job."

"Thank you, sir."

"However," he went on deliberately, "I would like to point out that your assignment ended with Nicholas. We do not encourage suicide missions beyond the call of duty, Eric. Trained men are hard to replace."

"Yes, sir," I said. "What suicide mission?"

He did not answer directly. Instead he said, "Furthermore, certain people in Washington feel that the total destruction of the Sorenson Generator was not necessary. They would have liked to examine the machine more or less intact."

I grinned. "No matter what we do, or how we do it, they

never like it, do they, sir? There's always something much better we could have done, by much more satisfactory means. Just how did I destroy the damn thing, anyway?"

"You rammed the truck carrying it, as it was coming down the mountain. The rig went off into the canyon, caught fire, and exploded. Apparently you jumped from your station wagon before the collision, but hit your head on a rock and knocked yourself out. I think a visit to the ranch is indicated, Eric. An operative should be able to unload from a moving car without sustaining even a mild concussion of the brain. You'd better do a little practicing under controlled conditions."

The ranch is the grim and business-like place in Arizona where he sends us for rest and rehabilitation between jobs if we can't manage to talk him out of it, but this didn't seem like the right moment to try. Nor did it seem diplomatic to point out that he could logically chide me for embarking on a suicide mission, or for being clumsy in surviving it, but not both.

"What about Mr. Soo?" I asked.

Mac's eyes narrowed slightly. "So it was Soo. Not having heard from you, we had no way of knowing, although certain evidence indicated the Chinaman might be involved."

"I gather he wasn't caught."

"No. When the police arrived at the scene, they found the truck burning down in the canyon. They also found that your station wagon—"

"I don't suppose it matters, but the heap wasn't exactly mine," I interrupted.

He said, "The station wagon you were driving, having been knocked crosswise to block the road, had then been struck by a patrol car for which the police were searching, which had apparently been following the truck too closely to avoid becoming involved. The officer assigned to the car was found in the rear, dead from a bullet wound. You were lying unconscious at the side of the road. Later, the half-consumed bodies of two men were removed from the cab of the burned-out truck. However, the man who was driving the police car at the time of impact, and his passengers if any, have not been found."

"Well, Mr. Soo was probably the passenger," I said. "The driver was most likely a lean gent who looked as if he might know this country: a tanned, outdoors type called Jason, who seems to be a sign painter by vocation or avocation. Mr. Soo isn't really built for hiking, but Jason could have led him to safety somehow."

"There are indications that the Chinaman either reached a telephone or was in position to give some orders in person," Mac said. "A mysterious explosion, thought by one of our associated agencies to be connected with the case, has been reported back in the wild country of the Jornada del Muerte, if I've got my pronunciation correct—"

"Actually, it's pronounced Hornada, sir."

"To be sure. Perhaps you can throw some light on this subject. Our associates are highly interested in any information you can supply."

I said, "Well, Mr. Soo had a cache of the catalyst and fuel for his generator—"

"Oh, don't tell *me* about it, Eric." Mac's voice was dry. "This demolition project upon which you embarked without orders is no concern of mine. There will be some people in to question you about it, doubtless, at great length. Save your strength for them." He frowned. "Eric?"

"Yes, sir."

"One thing puzzles me. This is the third time you have encountered the Chinaman, is it not?"

"Yes, sir."

"Each time you've got the best of him, if I remember correctly. Yet, finding you unconscious and helpless by the roadside—according to the police, he couldn't possibly have missed you—he walked off and left you alive, the man responsible, once more, for wrecking all his elaborate plans. Doesn't that seem a trifle odd to you?"

I said, without conviction, "Well, I did save his life after a fashion, the first time we met."

"Soo is a professional. I do not think gratitude figures largely among his motives."

"I know," I said. As usual, Mac had put his finger on the sour spot in the performance; the thing that had been bothering me, also. "It's puzzled me, too," I admitted. "Willy wanted to kill me for old times' sake—he still carried a grudge about that Mexican operation I loused up for him a year, or so back—but the Chinaman fought him off me like a she-bear defending her cub. I wonder—"

"What, Eric?"

I hesitated. It was a wild idea, but I had to ask the question, anyway. "Just how effective was the damn generator?" I asked. "Just how much damage did it actually do in Los Angeles?"

"I don't have the exact figures, but apparently it was quite a serious smog attack, serious enough to warrant a second alert."

"Second out of how many?"

"The third is the one that calls for full emergency measures."

"Then the second wouldn't indicate a major catastrophe?"

"I would say not."

I drew a long breath. "Suppose the generator didn't work nearly as well as Sorenson had claimed it would, sir. You know these scientists, they always oversell their discoveries. Suppose the damn thing was actually a great disappointment to Mr. Soo."

Mac frowned thoughtfully. "Go on, Eric."

"Suppose Mr. Soo and his people originally thought they'd got their hands on a hell of a murderous weapon, sure death on heavily populated targets; and then suppose they learned that all it could really produce for them was a few additional cases of asthma and a lousy second alert. Suppose Mr. Soo decided, after analyzing his Los Angeles figures, that the Albuquerque show just wasn't worth putting on; that as a matter of fact it should definitely be aborted, because it might tip us off that the Sorenson generator wasn't nearly as dangerous as had been thought."

"It is an interesting idea, Eric. Continue."

"He left me alive. He went to a lot of trouble to keep me alive, when it would have been much simpler to let Willy have me. Why? Could it be that he planned to turn me loose eventually, to beat the drum for this terrible weapon I'd seen the Chinese testing? *Testing!* Who tips off the enemy by *testing* a weapon like that—a pilot model, he claimed—in the enemy's own territory? I don't think it was a pilot model. I think it was the real thing, and I think Mr. Soo was trying to stage a real, deadly, double attack, meant to throw us into a real panic. Only it fizzled. And then the Chinaman had to figure out some way of salvaging something from his investment, so he decided to fill me full of misleading and terrifying information. That would explain why everybody kept telling me stuff about that generator, making it sound like a real doomsday device, when there was no need to tell me anything at all."

"Go on," Mac said, when I paused to catch up with my thoughts.

I said, "I'm beginning to think, sir, that having misfired, the machine was slated for destruction anyway. I just obliged Mr. Soo by shoving it off the road for him, giving him a plausible excuse for calling off the Albuquerque 'test' and destroying his supplies. I'd also, previously, obliged him by escaping, with… with the help of Bobbie Prince, but he gave me some help, too. He kept Jason from shooting when we were making our getaway. I thought I was being smart, or lucky, but if I hadn't managed to make my own escape arrangements, I bet he'd have made them for me. He *wanted* me loose, repeating all the scary information I'd been fed about the dreadful smog machine the Chinese had got hold of, that had run into a little bad luck on this test run, but would be back to threaten us as soon as they could slap together a real working unit. His hope was, I suppose, that to counter the threat, our country would institute a crash cleanup program that would totally disrupt our transportation system and our economy… Naturally, he couldn't allow Willy to kill me. I was his only hope of salvaging something from this expensive fiasco."

There was a little silence after I'd finished. Mac was looking, for him, oddly indecisive. At last he said, "It is a temptation, is it not, Eric? Perhaps we should not be too clever. Perhaps, if we let it be believed that the threat is real, it would stimulate…" He stopped.

I said, "It might stimulate a lot of nice anti-pollution activity, yes, sir. That's presumably what Sorenson himself had in mind when he invented the gadget and turned it over to the Chinese. He must have figured it didn't really matter who scared us into taking action before we strangled in our own stinking by-products." I paused, and asked deliberately, "Well, sir, do I spread the word that the Chinese have got hold of a real humdinger of a doomsday weapon, just like Mr. Soo wants me to?"

I won't say Mac disappointed me. A man who's spent most of his adult life in the bureaucratic maze reacts in certain predictable ways when it comes to making major decisions outside his particular province; and that goes even when his province is as vague and peculiar as Mac's.

"No," he said slowly, "no, I don't think so, Eric. It is not our decision, is it?"

"No, sir," I said, and that buck was passed.

Having passed it, Mac said briskly, "We are not qualified to play God, although sometimes it might be tempting to try. Officially, I am concerned here only with the murder of one of my agents and the successful elimination of the enemy operative responsible for her death. Nicholas *was* responsible, was he not?"

I nodded. "He didn't pull the trigger, but he was responsible. And the girl who did pull the trigger took poison and died."

"Yes, I was told about that," Mac said. "And my official interest extends no further. There will be a team of scientists arriving from Washington very shortly. You will report your facts and theories concerning this aspect of the case to them. *All* your theories. They will make whatever decision needs making."

"Yes, sir," I said, but we both knew that a committee of scientists would only take the buck we passed them and send it along in an upward direction, where it would eventually get lost in the dim stratospheric regions of official policy-making without anybody ever having had to make any awkward decisions about it.

Mac said, after a pause, "Of course, I don't have to emphasize the need for discretion in matters that don't concern these scientific gentlemen."

After a moment, I started to grin, but thought better of it. Things were normal, after all. It wasn't tender concern for my health that had brought him two thirds of the way across the continent; it was my amnesia. He'd come to assure himself that, concussion or no, I remembered enough to know what to say when I was interviewed, and what not to say.

In particular, he was making certain that I understood that, while I was free to talk about the Sorenson generator and related subjects to my heart's content, I'd have to make up an innocuous story to explain how I'd got involved in the case in the first place. I mean, it wouldn't do to tell a bunch of tame officials from a science-oriented Washington bureau that I'd got mixed up in their complicated affairs while engaged in the relatively simple task of tracking down a guy called Santa Claus for purposes of homicide. Our duties and methods are not supposed to be discussed out of school.

"No, sir," I said. "I'll be discreet as hell."

He hesitated. "Is there anything else you should tell me now, Eric? Of course, I expect a full report eventually, but in the meantime, what about, for instance, a young lady attached to the West Coast branch of a certain special narcotics agency who seems to have taken a violent dislike to you?"

"Charlie?" I said. "When did you see Charlie Devlin?"

"This morning, in Los Angeles. I wanted to get the background before I came here. The girl is almost pathological on the subject of one Matthew Helm. She seems to think that you are responsible for blighting her promising career. Apparently certain plans of hers went badly wrong, bringing embarrassment to her department and an official reprimand to her—men like Frank Warfel are very quick to scream about false arrest and illegal search when no evidence is produced against them."

I sighed. "Sir, how the hell did we get mixed up with that bunch of do-gooders, anyway?"

He said without expression, "Narcotics are a serious threat to the public welfare. I am certain the agents fighting this insidious menace are all fine people and dedicated public servants."

"They may be," I said, "but they don't hesitate to use their official positions for private revenge. At least Miss Devlin doesn't. When she decided I'd double-crossed her, she used her cop connections to spread the word that I'd stolen her damn station wagon, just to make trouble for me."

"You're certain of this?"

"She'd threatened me with dire retribution if I loused up her play. And the officer who stopped us said they'd got a report the car had been stolen in California and was probably heading east; who else would have made a report like that? As it happened, it worked out very well for me, but it was kind of tough on the officer. Charlie probably figures I killed him myself—I also made a few threats, I'm afraid. Undoubtedly that's one reason behind her anti-Helm feeling. She can't bear to let me get away with it, but she doesn't dare try to pin it on me lest her part in the business should come out. Anyway, this is the same little girl who's hell on other people following all the laws and rules, but who swore me to secrecy about a violent attack of asthma that, according to the health regulations of her agency, might have affected her career adversely."

Mac said, "Well, the personnel problems of other departments are really none of our business, are they, Eric?"

"No, sir," I said. "But ten kilos of heroin are everybody's business, wouldn't you say, sir?"

He looked at me sharply. "Do you know where the shipment is?"

I said, "My information is that such an amount of Chinese heroin was given to Frank Warfel as payment for his services in connection with the Sorenson generator. He had the stuff on his yacht down at Bahia San Agustin. From what you say, it wasn't on board when he was searched by Miss Devlin north of the border. As far as we know, he only put ashore at one other place: Bernardo. Charlie was assuming that he'd come ashore there empty-handed and leave with a cargo worth a couple of million bucks, produced by his camouflaged trailer-lab. But the lab was a fake, set up merely to hide the Chinese origin of the dope. Warfel already had his twenty-two pounds of high-priced happiness when he reached Bernardo. Suppose he did exactly the opposite from what Charlie was expecting. Suppose he went ashore loaded, cached his white treasure right under the noses of Charlie and her Mexican allies, and sailed away carrying with him nothing but a sly smile, knowing he'd be searched as soon as he hit U.S. territory."

Mac drew a long breath. "It's another interesting theory. A blow on the head seems to stimulate your imagination, Eric. I'll notify the head of the agency…"

"No," I said. "Let's heap some coals on the fire, sir. Let's notify Charlie herself, to stand by for Warfel's *next* trip; he's not going to leave two million bucks lying by the seashore any longer than he has to." I grinned. "Whether or not she meant to be, she was a big help, sir. We can afford to give her a hand, the vicious little idealist."

"Very well, Eric." Mac studied me thoughtfully. "You do seem to get considerable assistance from the ladies, one way or another. What about the girl who was shot? The circumstances, as reported by the police, seem to indicate that her position was rather ambiguous, too. If the organization owes her a debt of any kind, you'd better tell me now, so I can take the proper steps to repay—" He stopped. "What's the matter?"

I was staring at him. I cleared my throat and said, "Bobbie Prince? She isn't dead?"

"Why, no," Mac said calmly. "Apparently it was close and she is still on the critical list, but barring complications she should be all right." He was watching me rather narrowly. After a moment, he said, "I see. You thought you had sacrificed Miss Prince's life to our duty. That's why you set off on that quixotic charge back up the mountainside, which you have now conveniently forgotten."

I said politely, "Be so good as to go to hell, sir." It was all coming back, and of course he was perfectly right, damn him.

He ignored my remark. "You haven't said whether or not we owe the girl anything."

"Yes, sir, we do," I said, "like my life. And I promised her a clean slate in return."

"Whatever her record may be, within limits of course, it shall be officially cleansed." He frowned. "Would you consider her a potential prospect, Eric? There is a vacancy, as you may recall."

It took me a moment to catch his meaning; then I said quickly, "No, damn it! You're not going to recruit this one, at least not through me. Anyway, she wouldn't work for us. She's the non-violent type. That's what got her a .44 bullet in the back." After a little silence, I asked, "Where is she? Not that it matters. I'm probably the last person she wants to see."

"She is two doors down the hall. You will be informed when she can have visitors. And judging by the few words she spoke on the operating table, before the anesthesia took effect, I would not worry about my welcome." He was looking out the window as he spoke. Then he sighed. "Well, I see a delegation of intellectuals approaching with briefcases and tape recorders. I will leave you to them and trust to your discretion. Oh, and Eric—"

"Yes, sir."

"I will not insist on your attending the ranch when you are well again," he said, walking towards the door. "Not if you should happen to find a more relaxing way of spending a month's convalescent leave, in more pleasant company."

I did.

## ABOUT THE AUTHOR

Donald Hamilton was the creator of secret agent Matt Helm, star of 27 novels that have sold more than 20 million copies worldwide.

Born in Sweden, he emigrated to the United States and studied at the University of Chicago. During the Second World War he served in the United States Naval Reserve, and in 1941 he married Kathleen Stick, with whom he had four children.

The first Matt Helm book, *Death of a Citizen*, was published in 1960 to great acclaim, and four of the subsequent novels were made into motion pictures. Hamilton was also the author of several outstanding stand-alone thrillers and westerns, including two novels adapted for the big screen as *The Big Country* and *The Violent Men*.

Donald Hamilton died in 2006.